HER CAPTAIN
and commander

PEARL BERRI

MS APHRODITE PUBLISHING

In loving memory of John.
An extraordinary husband and best friend.

For the amazing, overworked women and men who make our lives on their cruise ships so wonderful. Thank you for your hard work caring for all the millions of passengers – even the difficult ones.

CHAPTER ONE
CRUISE DAY 1

$\mathcal{K}$ imberlee Tuckmann stood at the railing of the deck overlooking the pool. Hugging herself, she gazed out over the side of the ship into the night as they cruised through the Caribbean Sea. She wanted to remain hidden in the darkness until her stupid vacation miraculously dissolved into nothingness.

Which of course, wouldn't happen.

Her parents made her middle name Hope because they believed in her future. And so did Kimberlee, but she'd lost any optimism. She wanted a career where she could be financially successful and help her parents as they aged. Now, that was dead.

She took a deep yoga breath, freeing the tension locked in her body. Slowly, the knots in her shoulders eased, allowing her body to unfurl as she moved her hands to rest lightly on the high-gloss handrail. She let the breeze from the moving ship and the silky warmth of the humidity work their healing magic.

This time of night, she remained the only person on the upper deck—now embraced in blissful silence after the champagne-filled, boisterous sail-away party. Others were at dinner or socializing on their embarkation night aboard a seven-day Western Caribbean cruise.

Even if this wasn't the right ship for her, she still appreciated the design of the small, 200-cabin, elegant vessel, as well as her first tropical holiday.

She enjoyed watching the lights from the ship reflecting on the wake as the white hull glided through the ocean. Even the air smelled unique, with its salty tang.

This was her introduction to the joys of cruising. Not surprisingly, she loved the peace and beauty that came from sailing these alluring and tranquil waters.

Letting go of her self-pity, she repeatedly told herself she'd find a way to put her life back together. She built a life once; she could do it again. She was only thirty-five. She had her whole life ahead of her.

As her body softened in the gentleness of the night's embrace, a drunken voice boomed out from behind her. "Well, well, little lady, I see you're all alone, just waiting for the right man, and that's me." His loud and invasive Texas-sounding drawl startled her, shattering the fragile peacefulness.

She whipped her head around finding herself facing a flamboyant Hawaiian shirt barely covering a fat, protruding belly. Dismissing him with her hard New York glare, she turned back to the sea saying, "I'm waiting for my husband, so please leave me alone."

"No, sirree, I'll just wait for him—this so-called husband of yours."

Kimberlee would have walked away, but the bulk of her inebriated tormentor blocked escape. Deciding what to do next, she heard a new male voice. "The lady said she isn't interested," he said. "On my ship, we respect people's wishes.

I want people to feel safe, especially on a sex-themed ship. We have single women who would appreciate your company. In fact, we have the singles sail-away cocktail party in the Dolphin Club on deck five. They've got free drinks."

Not that he needed any more alcohol.

"Got it, Captain. I don't have to waste my time here," the Hawaiian-shirt said, sauntering away toward the aft of the ship.

Releasing her breath, Kimberlee turned around to thank the Captain. She gazed into concerned, smoky-blue eyes in a weather-worn face. "Thank you, Captain. I didn't need him bothering me. Men like that I can do without."

He held out his right hand in a cool, professional manner as he introduced himself. "I'm Captain Johan. I'm sorry that man harassed you. As I told him, we work hard to make this ship a safe and fun place for people. How may I help you?"

Shaking his hand, she said, "I'm Kimberlee Tuckmann. Thank you for rescuing me. To be honest, this isn't the right ship for me. I came with three friends. They thought a sex-themed cruise would perk me up. Instead, I feel out of place and just want to jump ship."

"Please don't do that. In all my years at sea, I haven't had a person fall overboard. I'd rather not have you be the first one and need to turn around looking for you. It would make me late docking in Key West. If I might ask, Ms. Tuckmann…"

"Please, call me Kimberlee."

"Kimberlee, what brings you on a cruise you'd rather not be on?"

Stalling for time to gather her thoughts, she turned back to face the endless expanse of sea, keeping her rigid back to him. After a few calming breaths, she said, "You see, Captain, my life has been focused on making partner in one of the Big Four accounting firms in New York City. With a CPA and a JD/MBA, that's a law degree with an MBA, I should be on the partner track. But I was told three months ago that I'm not, and never will be, partner material. Even though my mergers and acquisition clients love me, I don't have the 'partner look.' Which in accounting speak means that I'm not slender, busty, or do a good job drinking, socializing, and flirting with clients."

Gathering her courage, she turned back to face him. "I come from German Midwestern farming stock. You wouldn't find me on the cover of *Vogue* or on the bachelor shows. Even some shops in NYC don't carry clothes my size."

Oh, fuck. Too much information. He doesn't want your chunky-body history. Just stop talking and get your ass back to the cabin.

During her emotional dump, the Captain stood quietly watching, as if he were evaluating her. Almost like looking at a bug under a microscope.

Finally, when she stopped rambling, his voice filled the void, as if her monologue never happened. "In the special forces, life-and-death world I come from, your success would be based on job performance and the quality of your work, not your physical looks and party skills."

She shook her head. "That should be true, but it's not. In my world, technical expertise competes with a woman's looks and social skills. I don't have the physical looks, figure, or personality to bring in the clients and their big bucks. So, I make a great senior manager, but I'm not equity partner material."

"That's a stupid business practice...and it's counterproductive."

"But that's the way my world works."

"I put my personal life on hold for that partnership.

Working twelve to fifteen hours a day, I gave up dating. I was OK with that because the end goal was worth the price—both the partnership and a growing nest egg for my parents' retirement. Now, I have neither and no social life."

But then she never had much of a social life to begin with. More a loner than the prom queen.

Clearly a man of few words, he finally asked, "What accounting firm did you say you worked for?"

Something in his voice, a sudden harshness, rang a warning bell in her head. Instead of proudly telling him the name, she said, "It doesn't matter. They're in New York and I'm here. I took this cruise to get away, not bring work with me."

As if wanting to break the awkward quietness gathering between them, the Captain continued, "You aren't the typical MS *Aphrodite* passenger. What made you decide to join your friends on a ship designed for sex and BDSM games?"

"Excuse me, did you say BDSM?" she squeaked, with eyes widening. She knew it was a sex-themed cruise, but not to this extreme.

He answered, "Yes. While this ship provides sexual opportunities for consenting adults, we do offer BDSM spaces and events. Of course, this is up to each individual and couple."

She took a few moments to process this unexpected information. Trying to portray big-city sophistication, she plowed ahead with what she was going to say before he upended her mental balance. "Bonnie, Paulette, and Lori have been my closest friends for eight years and we only want what's best for each other. When the firm eliminated my partner track, my friends wanted to cheer me up. I didn't know this was a… a…a sex ship. They just told me it was a themed cruise. I figured that meant something like a wine and food cruise or a

70s party. I didn't find out the truth until I stepped on board. Of course, I could have gotten off, but then what I've been doing with my life hasn't been successful, so I decided to try something new."

She began twiddling with her rose gold loop earring—a nervous habit she'd picked up from her mother. *Stop fidgeting, Kimberlee. You've faced a room full of bulldog, nasty attorneys from big Wall Street law firms…and beat them.*

Slowing her breathing, she brought her hand back to her side as she continued, "I'm the woman men pass over at parties—nothing special, nothing exciting, nothing memorable, nothing to show off to your friends as a trophy. So I was hoping this cruise would help make a new me. And maybe that new me might be able to become partner material." It was worth a try, at least.

She wasn't naive enough to believe after a week on board, she'd step off a size six with bigger bra cups. She was who she was. Men weren't going to find her sexy. But maybe this trip would help her repackage herself with more sexual pizazz, to go along with the brains.

Out of the night, his voice reached her saying, "Passengers don't join this cruise to make themselves over. People sail with us to explore their desires in a safe, nonjudgmental environment. They're basically comfortable in their own skin.

"Vacations are a good way for people to reevaluate their lives and careers. It seems this is what you're doing. For the next week, the MS *Aphrodite* is your home. We have a lot to offer you that isn't sex and BDSM. Let's find a way for you to have a good time. Have you explored the ship?"

Once again, her hand reached up to fiddle with her earring. "No. I was afraid of running into drunk men who wouldn't respect my wishes."

"There are plenty of them around, as well as women who

find it difficult to take no for an answer. That's why we have crew and officers throughout the ship making sure passengers remain safe. Come on, let me give you a quick tour. We'll start at the top, on deck ten—the Aphrodite Lounge—and work our way down."

WHY IN THE HELL DID HE MAKE THAT OFFER? WHAT WAS HE thinking? He wasn't thinking, that's what. He should walk away. She was trouble waiting to happen. Might as well get this over with. Besides, with the hostile takeover he was facing, he needed to find which accounting firm she worked for. Maybe she wasn't as innocent as she appeared. She could be a spy.

Showing Kimberlee around the ship, Captain Johan pondered what to do with her. In his two years captaining this ship, he'd only had a few passengers who weren't comfortable being on a sex-themed ship. Most people knew what they signed up for. He was going to have to ask one of his female crew members to watch out for her.

He had a ship to command, a crew to take care of, and passengers he had to make sure were getting their money's worth—as well as spending it. He wasn't a babysitter. He was also in the middle of a hostile acquisition.

His ship had come under attack from a mega cruise line that had launched a takeover. When he accepted this position on the MS *Aphrodite*, he figured a small, themed ship would be off a corporate raider's radar. But he should have known better—a painful past experience with his father's fishing business had taught him gluttony always gorged on the innocent.

Throughout the ship's tour, he surreptitiously studied her as they walked side by side. He'd been on enough cruise ships to identify rich people. She had that stylishly dressed, sophisticated look. But what surprised him was she didn't have the slender, angular appearance he expected in someone from the Big Apple. Rather, he appreciated her attractively rounded body. Instead of the standard bottle-blond, flowing mane, she wore her warm, golden brown, chin-length hair simply styled with blunt-cut bangs. Even with the girl-next-door appearance, her sophisticated simplicity spoke of big paychecks and even bigger bonuses.

She was one of those greedy, blood-sucking leeches from New York City. Even if she wasn't the one actually attacking his ship in the takeover fight, she would have if she'd had the chance for more money.

Walking through the ship, he'd occasionally give her an evaluating glance. She came up to his chin. Because he was five feet eleven inches, that would make her about five feet six inches.

But she wasn't for him. A fling wasn't worth losing his job over.

As the tour of the ship ended on deck four, he debated if he should show her deck three—the specialty grottos. If she saw how those cabins weren't torture chambers, she might relax. So he walked her down one flight of stairs to the grotto deck.

Speaking in an impersonal, academic voice so she wouldn't freak out, he said, "Here's deck three. These are our playrooms we call grottos. They're furnished with basic sex furniture. Passengers rent the grottos by the hour, half day, or full day. Some people reserve them for their entire cruise. Housekeeping scrupulously cleans each room after they're used. With 400 passengers on board, the grottos remain rented most of the time."

She didn't appear spooked, so he continued extolling the

wonders of the cabins. "We have waterproof mattress protectors under our high-quality, Egyptian cotton sheets. People do have to bring their own sex toys, whether from home or bought from the ship's store. They also can request special furniture items that we provide given enough notice. We also offer room service for those passengers who want to spend hours in their grotto and need nourishment.

"Sorry. Sometimes I get too detailed about the ship telling people more than they want to know."

KIMBERLEE REMAINED QUIET DURING HIS EXPLANATION. SHE wasn't sure she wanted to investigate the cabin after the Captain's marketing pitch, but she forced herself to walk in as he politely held the door open.

It wasn't that large of a room but contained a double bed with a metal frame and strange rounded eyelets—for what, she wasn't sure. In the corner was a black upholstered V-shaped chair, which she figured was for kinky stuff. For "normal" furniture, the cabin had an extra-deep love seat, small table with two chairs, and an armchair with overly padded arms. Well, maybe it wasn't quite normal, but definitely not as unusual as the other strangely shaped chair. The tiny closet had shelves and a place to hang clothes. Not as freaky as she expected.

She stared wordlessly at him, shocked at how matter-of-factly he discussed kinky sex. Where she grew up in central Iowa, as a Methodist, sex stayed hidden in the marital bedroom and nobody talked about it—not a peep. Even her parents, with their wonderful marriage, only discussed the basic birds and the bees with their two kids. And here was this charming Viking god, with his delightful Norwegian-accented English, talking about cleaning a sex-permeated cabin and needing food during all-day sex marathons.

Looking around, she noticed a subtle antiseptic smell, telling her the cabin had definitely been cleaned and disinfected. This gave her some confidence she wouldn't pick up a disease while standing here. Thankfully, the ship did emphasize cleanliness.

During their visit, her focus bounced between the sound of his captivating voice and his neutral words about socially disapproved sex with the need for waterproof mattress protectors. *Yucky. Yucky.*

Throughout the Captain's talk, Kimberlee remained too embarrassed to say anything. Even when he paused to give her an opportunity to comment or ask questions, she kept her lips tightly clamped, afraid she'd make a fool of herself by showing her ignorance.

When he stopped talking, she breathed a sigh of relief at being free from listening to a gorgeous stranger discussing sex. She could finally escape from this bizarre situation to the sanity of her cabin.

Like the officer and gentleman he was, he held the door open for her again. Once back in the hall, the Captain asked, "Would you like me to walk you back to your cabin?"

"I can find my way back after your excellent tour. Thank you for taking the time to show me around. Good night, Captain." Off Kimberlee fled, trying not to appear as if she was running away from him and his waterproof mattress protectors.

Speeding back to her room, she felt an unexpected and unwanted tingling in her lower abdomen, causing her sensitive nipples to tighten and an urgent yearning to ignite in her. She knew that feeling too well. In the past, she tried masturbating, but nothing happened, which left her even more frustrated and discouraged. She had thought of getting a vibrator from Amazon, but never found the opportunity.

What a terrible time for this. The only person I find the least bit attractive is the Captain and he's off-limits. Just my luck to want the unattainable. Couldn't I find a drunk man in his gaping Hawaiian shirt appealing? Oh God no, he was awful. I'm better off with nobody, which is what I have in my life already. So, no loss there.

Maybe she was one of those women who couldn't climax. An "ice queen" one date called her. But then, maybe the few men she'd been with were not of the highest quality in bed, so the issue may not be with her. It took two, she reminded herself.

She could use this cruise to determine what exactly her problem was: either she was designed wrong sexually or she selected sexual losers.

She'd apply her skills for turning lemons into lemonade. For the next week, she'd find a way to have fun with her friends and maybe learn something new about herself in the process.

When she got back to her cabin, her friends were still out. They must have been having a great time in one of the public rooms. Hopefully, they found attractive and skilled men to spend the evening with. Paulette, Lori, and Bonnie really were beautiful and caring women, who always had men in their lives. She was thrilled for them, but also wanted a taste of that life too. It was time for her to step out of her safety zone.

She'd get ready for bed and see what happened tomorrow. A new day for a new life.

Putting on her pajamas, she considered how many of her personal problems would be resolved when she made partner. She expected the promotion would provide the necessary sexy factor, giving her social life a gigantic boost. Deep down, she'd hoped professional success would deliver the man of her dreams. In New York, without the fashion model look, she had a nonexistent love life, but with a partnership everything was possible.

Lying in bed, she tossed and turned, agitated by an unexplained restlessness, a humming tension throughout her body, and feeling irritable with her life. She kicked off the covers when she became too hot, then pulled them up to her chin when the ever-blowing air conditioner made her cold. Twenty minutes into trying to sleep, she gave up in frustration. Even her yoga breathing didn't help. She hated when she felt this way—like she wanted to jump out of her skin.

She had brief flashes of the Captain—the sound of his caressing voice, his irresistible smile, his laughing eyes with their deep creases in the corners, and his gentle, embracing warmth. Oh great. She had the hots for the captain. That was a line she didn't want to cross. Plus, as a passenger, he'd have nothing to do with her. How could she be so smart and so dumb at the same time?

As she lay in bed feeling stupid for wanting what she couldn't or shouldn't have, a thought popped into her head. *I used to take risks. What's the worst that could happen? He could politely tell me he's not available. He wasn't wearing a wedding ring, so he might not be married. But then maybe he's got girlfriends in every port. Someone like him should have women falling all over him. Do I want to be one of those women? No... Yes!*

She decided she might as well get up to wait for her friends. Putting on jeans and a top, she tried kicking the Captain out of her thoughts to no avail. He wouldn't exit.

As she sat on the side of her bed all dressed with nowhere to go, a younger version of Kimberlee popped into her thoughts. This woman used to be spunky and fearless. When did she lose this courageous younger version of herself? When did she become afraid of adventure? She let her need for making partner take over her life. Yes, she wanted money for her security and her family, but she also required something non-monetary for herself. It was time she took her life back—even one little step was better than feeling the hopelessness of seeing the world pass her by.

She couldn't give herself a new body, but she could open new doors. Experience new worlds she never realized existed. And explore new parts of herself kept locked away.

This one time she wasn't going to overthink her actions and make sure everything was ticked and tied. She had no clients to worry about letting down and no stick-up-their-ass partners to please who cared only about billable hours. This was her window of opportunity to discover something new.

And so she would.

She was just going to do it, whatever *it* was. Kimberlee grabbed her room keycard and headed out the door before she could tell herself all the reasons she should stay in her cabin and wait for her friends. Before she could list all the negative consequences of her rash, irrational, and impulsive behavior —behavior that she stopped allowing herself when she became focused on a big career.

If the Captain didn't want her, so be it. She'd rather fail than not try. With that last thought, she softly closed the cabin door behind her.

CHAPTER TWO

*A*fter he closed the grotto door behind them, the Captain narrowed his eyes in silent speculation as Kimberlee fled…from him. Now that was a new experience —scaring off women.

It's really for the best. He wasn't a nursemaid or a sex educator. Her friends could instruct her about this cruise. It wasn't his job. He had enough to worry about—the ship's safety, keeping to his inflexible docking and undocking schedules, staying within a tight budget and making sure that all 600 souls on board—passengers and crew—were well taken care of.

Then, he had the ever-present hostile takeover, with now the possibility of a spy on board. When he got back to his cabin, he'd Google Ms. Tuckmann to see what accounting firm she worked for. Even though the corporate fight wasn't part of his responsibilities, the stress and uncertainty hovered in the background, grating like a grain of sand in a shoe.

He definitely had enough on his plate without Ms. Innocent Corporate Jock sucking up his energy.

Having some precious free time, he decided to walk

around his vessel, observing how this first night was going. He checked out the public rooms, making sure passengers were enjoying a good evening and nobody turned into a disorderly drunk. Plus, he needed to ensure everything was going smoothly for his hardworking and often underappreciated crew.

The Captain valued talking with his crew and passengers. He enjoyed learning how their night was going, finding out what people needed and using this time getting to know his passengers. In between conversations, his mind pondered what made him give Kimberlee a tour and, especially, his reasons for showing her the grottos. He had no answers. She was innocent—too innocent to be on this ship. He could see by her clenched lips, crossed arms, and astonished facial expressions that she was both uncomfortable with and curious about the grotto.

In his eight years as an officer on cruise ships, he'd never been in a relationship with a crew member or passenger. This was both a company policy and his own ethics. He lived his life by this law…and he wasn't breaking it now. For him, this value remained an integral part of his identity as a ship's captain.

After watching other officers sabotage their careers, he knew how a shipboard romance could destroy a captain's authority and future. Plus, he wasn't in the market for a relationship or even a short fling. His first loves were now his ship and the sea—and that worked perfectly for him. He was never happier than when sailing.

Shaking his head in bemusement, he couldn't understand what motivated him to escort an appealing female passenger around his ship. That wasn't like him. Gratefully, she wanted nothing to do with him, because he surprisingly found himself attracted to her. He felt off-balance and disliked finding himself in this new and unexpected situation.

At forty-three years old, he'd spent the last ten years mourning his deceased wife—the love of his life—and had no interest in other relationships. His amazing wife, an OB/GYN, was the person in the family who had taught women how to take care of themselves and be responsible for their bodies. Besides pap tests and delivering babies, Eira loved teaching women about their sexuality.

When she died, life had lost all meaning for him. With no love left to give, he'd never open his heart to another woman. He couldn't live through that agony again.

For him, his present position provided contentment—as much as his empty, guilt-ridden life could hold. His wife would have helped Kimberlee. But she was gone and that wasn't his job, nor his interest. That's what he kept telling himself.

Watching his passengers and crew, he noted everything promised smooth sailing. People were having fun and the crew was doing a great job helping passengers enjoy themselves.

He had nothing more to do until 5:30 a.m., when duty required he be on the bridge for a 7:00 a.m. docking in Key West.

Even though he looked forward to the nighttime solitude, he also felt, for the first time, the emptiness of being alone on a sex-filled ship.

KIMBERLEE MADE HER WAY TO THE LIDO DECK CONTAINING the pool and two hot tubs. The crew had locked up both the bar and grill immediately following the sail-away party, and cleared all remnants of celebration. As much as she enjoyed sharing the quiet space with the sea and night sky, she also found the shadowy emptiness slightly eerie.

She didn't know how to find the Captain. *This is what I get for not planning everything out better*. She stood stymied about what to do next. Should she stop one of the crew to ask for the Captain? Or should she just walk about the ship looking for him? And was this something she even wanted to do? And if she did find him, then what?

As she debated her next step, she heard his sensual, Norwegian accent behind her.

"I thought you were in your cabin, Kimberlee. Is everything OK?"

His caressing voice stroked her body like the softest silk, leaving her pulse pounding and a throbbing deep within. Bravely she turned around to face him, hoping to hide her neediness. And, also, wanting him not to notice how fearful she was of rejection.

Now was her chance to grab hold of her new life—to make herself some lemonade. She tried to tell him, but just got out "I...I...I..." while staring down at the deck. Where was the courageous Kimberlee when she needed her?

Trying again, she jerked her head up, looked him straight in the eye without flinching, took a deep breath, and said with determination, "Captain, you know this isn't the best cruise for me. But I am on this ship and I want to make the most of the opportunity. So, I want..."

She watched his face shift into a granite mask with narrow, icy eyes staring back at her. He asked harshly, "What do you want, Kimberlee?"

Oh, he knows I'm going to ask him about sex—and he's pissed.

Clinging to her courage, she told him bluntly, almost defiantly, "I want to climax. I've never had a climax and I don't know who to ask." Clenching her jaw, she stood her ground regardless of how vulnerable she felt and how displeased he appeared.

I just want to disappear. Oh Lord, get me out of here. Scotty, beam me up.

Carefully studying his reaction, she observed a shadow of annoyance flit across his features and his lips thin with suppressed irritation. She knew immediately she had really, really pissed him off. What now? She should turn around and head back to her cabin with her tail between her legs.

Initially, he stood statue-like, unmoving. Then, as if stalling for time, he asked, "Are you a virgin?"

With a heat spreading up her neck, making her face feel flushed, she said, "No. The few times I've had sex were… uneventful. Well, not horrible, but not good either. Rather quite boring. A waste of my time." *Just stop talking. Shut up. Time to leave, Kimberlee-girl. Cut your losses and get the hell out of here.*

"You understand Captains aren't supposed to have personal relations with passengers? I could get fired."

"I know. I'm sorry I even asked. Please forget this conversation. I know I will." *In one hundred years, if I'm lucky.*

Quickly spinning around to head back to her cabin, she needed to move as fast as her trembling legs could carry her. Before she took her second step, the Captain said, "Wait, Kimberlee. You're a beautiful woman. I'm sure there are men on this ship who'd be thrilled to be with you."

She almost doubled over as if he'd punched her in the gut. *I'm not some hopeless female who would be grateful for any asshole.* Looking over her shoulder, she declared in a tight, fury-choked voice, "I'm not that desperate." *So fuck off.* "I'm sorry I bothered you."

Without looking back at him, she gathered her tattered self-respect and began walking away, hoping he wouldn't see her tears of humiliation.

In three long strides, he caught up to her. "Kimberlee, wait."

When she didn't stop, he lightly rested his hand on her shoulder. She jerked her body away from his burning touch. And kept walking.

IF HE WERE HONEST WITH HIMSELF, THE CAPTAIN KNEW HE'D relish holding this fabulous woman in his arms while she experienced her first orgasm. Torn between his needs as a man and those of the ship's captain, he almost turned away. But something about her pride, her vulnerability, and her courage spoke to him in a way that no other woman had in ten years.

He knew none of the men on the ship would appreciate her bravery, intelligence, and even her innocence. Most likely they would abuse that innocence. With this last troubling thought, he shut down his analytical left brain. In a few steps, he once again caught up with her. Without thinking of what he would do, he said, "Stop, I'll help you."

But who in the hell's going to help me?

Warfare taught him once he decided on a plan of action, he didn't second-guess himself. That invariably led to mistakes, and even loss of life.

He only knew she heard him because of a slight hesitation in her step, before continuing her march onward. "Kimberlee, stop. Let's talk." This time she did, but kept her unyielding back to him.

Putting his hands on her shoulders, he slowly turned her to face him, finding himself looking into vulnerable, hurt eyes. For a moment, they both stood quietly observing each other. Operating on instinct, he said, "I didn't mean to hurt you. I want you to know the joys that await a beautiful woman like yourself. Sometimes I say dumb things."

She nodded. Without needing a verbal response, he grabbed the opportunity she offered, saying, "Wait for me. Sit here. I'll be right back." Gently, he guided her to the nearest chair.

By the stiffness of her body, he could feel how she struggled with wanting to flee and her desire to trust him. He saw fear seep into her eyes. But he also observed a tremor of desire flash through her voluptuous body.

He was grateful she obeyed his request and he hoped she'd know he wasn't a danger to her. Waiting only long enough to make sure she stayed seated, he turned toward the bow of the ship and strode a few steps away.

Keeping his back toward her, he removed his personal phone, speed-dialing Ramil's number. They had been crewed together in another cruise company and friends for the past eight years. When Ramil answered the phone, Johan spoke to him in a combination of Tagalog and Norwegian. While no one was near, both past-navy men naturally protected their private conversations.

He asked Ramil to buy a Hitachi Magic Wand in the ship's sex toy shop and book a grotto. He knew by Ramil's moment of silence he was surprised, but there was no judgment in his voice when he responded.

Almost godlike, Captains maintained total responsibility for the ship and all souls aboard. They lived in a bubble of emotional isolation on their vessels, where personal loyalty and trust remained in short supply. Throughout the years sailing together, he'd remained grateful for Ramil's steadfastness and allegiance.

This was the first time he'd made such a request, putting his career in his friend's hands.

Returning after the short call, he found Kimberlee standing next to the railing, looking out to sea. He could tell by her death grip on the handrail, she struggled with her decision to remain or to bolt.

Moving directly behind, but not close enough to touch her, he said, "We can stop now. There is no reason for you to force yourself to do something that's not right for you."

Without turning around, she said, "There're lots of things in life we don't want but may be good for us in the long run. Regardless of how much I want to be with you, I don't want to get you in trouble."

"I appreciate your concern. I'm capable of taking care of myself and my career."

Before he could say another word, she asked, "What languages were you speaking? I didn't hear much, but I could tell it wasn't English."

"I used Tagalog, a language of the Philippines, and Norwegian. I met Ramil eight years ago on my first cruise ship. As different as we appear, we view the world similarly." Stalling for time until his phone vibrated telling him all was in order, he continued, "He was the officers' room steward when I was a second officer. Over time, as we got to know each other, he taught me Tagalog, while he learned Norwegian. Sharing late-night beers, we developed fluency in each other's language, finding we both had natural linguistic abilities."

"I envy your language skills. Growing up in Iowa, foreign languages weren't high on my educational list. I guess, he's used to your requests by now?"

Irritated by her assumption that he'd fucked passengers on a regular basis or even at all, he answered curtly. "No.

This was the first time I've asked him to do this." Before he could tell her he'd changed his mind, his phone vibrated.

Ramil had everything in place. It was now or never.

She must have sensed her mistake and his annoyance. "I'm sorry. I shouldn't have said that."

Accepting her apology with an abrupt nod, which she couldn't see, he asked, "Do you still want to go downstairs?"

He watched her head jerk yes. Then she took a deep, unsteady breath and rotated around to boldly face him, resolve filling her eyes. "If you're still willing, Captain, let's go downstairs."

CHAPTER THREE

*B*oth remained silent, standing wide apart. The elevator made the only sound: the ding as it passed each deck.

Fiddling with her earring, the only thought flitting across her mind was how grateful she was that she had gotten a Brazilian wax two days before the cruise.

As they walked out onto deck three, he said, "Normally, we shouldn't have been together, but at this time of night most passengers are locked away in their cabins."

When they entered their grotto, the Captain once again held the door open for her. After closing it behind them, he turned the dead bolt. She stiffened hearing the lock loudly click into place, filling the stillness of the cabin. Imposing an iron will on herself, she remained rooted to the floor, not even turning around when he spoke to her in a calming voice.

"Kimberlee, these rooms can be used for BDSM play, but they don't have to be. Some passengers use them just as private space. Please turn around and look at me. You're safe with me. I'll stop whenever you ask."

She swiveled around to face him.

"Do you know what a safe word is?"

"Yes," she said, frowning at him. "I'm not stupid. Just inexperienced."

"I didn't mean to imply you're stupid, but you're in new waters. I don't know what information you have. What word do you want to use?"

"Orchid. It's my favorite flower. But I really don't think I'll need it. If we don't get into kinky stuff, I'll be fine."

"Perfect. We won't do anything kinky, I promise you. Now remember, if for any reason you get scared or I do something you don't like, say your safe word. I'll stop."

"I know or I wouldn't be with you." She said this last statement without hiding her annoyance at the way he talked down to her. At the same time, hunger for unfulfilled fantasies roared awake, making her insides clench with unexpected yearnings.

Her friends would understand. In this moment, this man and night belonged to her.

GENTLY, THE CAPTAIN PUT HIS HANDS ON EITHER SIDE OF HER flushed, oval face, looking deeply into her wide, desire-filled eyes. Unhurriedly, he bent his head to lightly brush a kiss on her clenched mouth. Then he rested his lips on hers, letting Kimberlee get comfortable with him. When she sighed with her growing arousal, he traced the soft, richness of her lips with his tongue, leaving them relaxed and moist.

Lifting his head, he kissed her forehead, eyelids, and down her throat as she tilted her head back for him. She moaned her pleasure when he reclaimed her lips.

As he felt her body unlock, he deepened his kiss with a craving that contradicted his outward calm. Catching him by surprise, his balls jerked up and his dick pulsed against his constricting trousers.

This wasn't supposed to happen. He expected to feel nothing. Certainly not his cock leaping to life.

As he deepened his kiss, her breathing became rapid and irregular. She parted her lips in offering, letting him explore her moist silkiness with his tongue. The aroma of her arousal filled his senses, making him want to shove his tongue into her wet core. How he'd love to suck on her needy clit.

After ten years of celibacy, he throbbed from all the explicit things he wanted to do to her luscious and willing body.

Suddenly, without warning, she grabbed the front of his uniform, pulling him closer, begging into his open-mouth kiss, "I want more. Oh, please give me more."

Her plea stripped away the last of his limited defenses. Growling, he forced his tongue farther into her mouth, just as he wanted to shove his cock into her.

He felt, as much as heard her deep moans of desperation. She was his for the taking.

NEEDING TO FEEL ALL OF HIM, FRANTIC FOR HIM TO FUCK HER senseless, Kimberlee clutched her arms around his neck, grinding her drenched pussy against his rock-hard dick. Greedy shivers raced along her nerves, unlocking long-repressed passion.

Not enough. More.

Finally, she felt safe demanding all the sex she'd spent her life fantasizing about.

Briefly ending their kiss, the Captain bent his head to bite the side of her neck, nip on an ear lobe, and suck the pounding pulse below her jaw. Her hard nipples pushed into his chest; her aching desire found no relief humping him.

Amidst the hurricane of want rampaging through her, she still heard the Captain's moans. *Oh yes*, h*e wants me*, registered somewhere in her fog-hazed mind.

By now, her body was flushed hot and feverish, her clothes constricting. As if recognizing her desperate need, the Captain quickly pulled her tie-dyed silk cashmere T-shirt over her head and unzipped her jeans, which he helped her step out of. His wonderfully experienced hands swiftly remove her lacy black bra and boy shorts.

She stood stripped of all defenses, held tightly against him. He seemed to understand how both her body and soul wanted to hide their nakedness. Amazingly, he recognized how her plump figure caused her embarrassment.

Then all modesty vanished, swamped by overpowering craving.

JOHAN CRUSHED THIS MAGNIFICENT, NAKED WOMAN IN HIS arms. Holding her tightly in his safe embrace, he let his hands roam over her body, wanting to feel every inch of her inside and out. Impatient to explore her pussy, he backed up to the love seat behind them, never taking his mouth or hands off her. Only after his legs knocked into the couch did he turn Kimberlee around so her back was pressed against his chest. He sat down with her sitting between his spread thighs.

He lifted first her right leg over his thigh, then her left leg over his other thigh, coaxing her open. He slowly moved both his legs wider, exposing her to his probing fingers. He locked her body so she couldn't move, commanding she abandon herself totally to him.

She leaned back into him, whimpering and showing her

trust. Nothing seemed to matter, not even the buttons on his uniform pressing into her naked back as he trapped her forcefully against him. Her guttural groans and the delicious scent of her soaked woman's flesh told him how desperately she needed him to fuck her.

"You're so amazing, Kimberlee," he whispered in her ear as he nibbled on the lobe. "I love touching you. Looking at and smelling you." *God, I wish I could taste you.*

All the while, his hands freely explored her unprotected body. He only stopped to forcefully pinch a nipple, moving on to flick a finger across her engorged clitoris. "And someday, I'm going to bury my face in your fantastic pussy. I'm going to eat you until you can't even scream for mercy."

He wanted his words, as much as his hands and cock, to brand her as his.

Vigorously squeezing her other nipple, he whispered in her ear, "I want your body, mind, soul. When I'm through, you'll never want another man."

Saying that, he moved one hand down to her woman's lips, gaping wide open for him. He plunged in his index finger. Her tightness immediately gripped him. Sucking him deeper.

She felt perfect in his arms—as if she belonged there.

As HE STROKED HER DEEPLY BURIED SEXUAL FIRE, HIS OWN passion exploded, breaking free of his decade-long numbness. With a shocking desperation, he wanted to gorge on her until nothing remained of either of them.

But tonight was for her, so he'd find a way to keep his raging boner under control. He would jack off later.

God, I hope I can wait that long.

He put a second finger inside her, but found she was too

tight for a third. Instead, he used his thumb to rub her begging, distended clitoris. Holding her locked in this spread-open position, she had no escape. He demanded total surrender—with no place to hide from him or herself.

By the way she thrashed in his arms, he knew she desperately needed something, but didn't seem to know what. Thankfully, Ramil had placed the vibrator in an easy-to-reach location.

Removing his fingers from inside her and releasing her distended nipple, he removed the cord from the Magic Wand, turned it on low and put it into her hand, helping guide it to her pulsating nerve center.

Slipping his fingers back inside to stroke her G-spot, Johan said, "Kimberlee, hold your vibrator and put it where it feels good."

He held it with her as she moved the silicone, vibrating head around. Then suddenly, she felt a powerful grabbing deep in her pelvic muscles. The pleasure-pain blasted up her body, gripping all her muscles and exploding throughout her.

Throwing her head back against the Captain's shoulder and arching her back, Kimberlee opened her mouth in a silent cry, then screamed as her first orgasm engulfed her.

With the force of her climax, her vaginal muscles slammed down on his fingers, trapping them inside of her.

As her body began relaxing, he started removing the vibrator. Kimberlee instantly tightened her hold exclaiming, "No!"

The Captain immediately replaced it just as her second orgasm hit. He held her tightly, kissing the side of her neck, brushing his lips against her temple, biting her. All the while, he whispered how magnificent she was and urged her to let go…to keep coming.

He continued holding the vibrator with one hand and stroked her G-spot with the other, driving her to multiple orgasms.

Kimberlee's overwhelmed mind lost count of how many times she came. She just let her body take over—trusting both herself and him.

With a soft moan, she slumped back into the Captain's embrace and released her toy without a thought of where it would fall. Luckily, he still held it. Turning it off, he put the vibrator on the couch beside them.

BRINGING HIS LEGS TOGETHER, THE CAPTAIN TURNED HER sideways on his lap, cradling her in his arms against his chest, pressing light kisses on her face, neck, and shoulders. He could feel the muscles in her body relax with exhaustion. Within a few minutes, he sat listening to her softly breathe as she trustingly slept with her face buried in his neck.

Sitting quietly, holding an exhausted Kimberlee in his protective embrace, he thought about what happened. After eight years on cruise ships, what had caused him to destroy his strict rule of no sex with passengers? He prided himself on holding this value sacred. Now it lay shredded. He felt angry at himself. How could he have been so weak?

But if he were honest with himself, he'd do it again.

Of course, he still had the fucking issue of her being a spy for the hostile takeover. Tomorrow, when he had time, he'd Google her to see where she worked. Just his luck, she'd be a mole for those bastards. Now, he had a raging cock to take care of.

And sleep.

Leaning his head against the back wall, eyes closed, he knew he had to get Kimberlee dressed and returned to her cabin. Letting his mind drift, he acknowledged how he loved the feel of her in his arms, the smell and taste of her on his fingers. What was he going to do with her?

The numbness he'd lived with after his wife's death felt less heavy, less imprisoning. He wondered if his deceased wife, Eira, was telling him it was time to move on with his life? If so, he wasn't ready. He didn't want a romantic entanglement. Loving brought too much pain. He also didn't deserve a second chance, because with the first one, he'd failed.

CHAPTER FOUR

*K*imberlee slowly awoke to her body being shaken. She heard a voice telling her she needed to wake up. Strong arms encased her. Her nose remained buried in a wonderfully musky-smelling neck. A very masculine neck with slight bristles of late-night beard growth. In that moment, she rocked peacefully with the motion of the sea.

Joy flooded her, leaving her aware of the new woman she'd become. She snuggled closer into him, releasing a contented sigh. Wanting to stay that way forever. Wanting to find a way to bottle such fabulous feelings and package his amazing lovemaking powers.

With another shake, stronger this time, she gave a little moan of frustration at having her cocoon disturbed. Slowly opening her eyes, she looked out at the world, feeling satiated and blissful.

Then, like having an ice bucket dumped over her, she looked into hard, cold, blazing eyes. In that moment, something shriveled and died in her. Like Eve tossed out of the

Garden of Eden, she felt naked and exposed by the anger radiating from him.

Words she was about to say died on her lips.

"Kimberlee, you need to get back to your cabin. This should never have happened." He spoke in a harsh voice without hiding his displeasure.

Desperately trying to reorient herself, she took a moment collecting her thoughts. Mumbling, she replied, "I'll go. I need to get dressed."

Sliding off his lap, she stood on trembling legs. Her newfound delight was smashed to smithereens and her trust betrayed.

Still sexually exhausted and half asleep, she moved slowly. With an exasperated sigh, he grabbed her clothes saying, "Here, put these on. We've got to go."

Being treated so rudely and unfairly made something snap in her. Standing there proud and naked, with hands on her hips, she looked him straight in the eyes saying in her best boardroom, putdown voice, "I realize you shouldn't have been with me. But you did make that choice. I didn't force you. So, don't you dare take your anger out on me. True, I shouldn't have asked you, but you didn't walk away... Did you?"

Without waiting for an answer, she continued, "Now, you've turned me into the bad guy, a dumping ground for your hypocritical self-righteousness. Well, fuck you."

I'm not going to cry. I'm not.

Watching her put on her clothes, he said, "You're right. It was a mistake for me to bring you here. I have a ship to run. I'm not a sex therapist. I—"

Not letting him finish, she immediately shot back, "No, you aren't. But to be honest, as wrong as this was for you, it was extraordinary for me. And I'm not sorry. Unlike the few men I've been with, you weren't a wham, bam, thank you, ma'am. You cared about my needs at the expense of yours. And for that I'm grateful.

"I am sorry you hated being with me. You can regret tonight all you want, but I won't feel guilty. Well, maybe a little for imposing on you. And leaving you unfulfilled. But I still wouldn't have changed anything—except your cruelty.

"I knew this would be only a one-night stand. I'd accepted that. However, I will not accept being made to feel like a horrible person—demeaned and stripped of all dignity."

WHAT COULD HE SAY?

She was right. He'd dumped his self-disgust on her. He could have said no. Instead, he'd had one of the most sexually arousing evenings in ten years. He'd missed the joy of giving a woman pleasure. Fucking had its place, but so too did the delights of holding a completely exhausted and satisfied woman in his arms.

Should he have given this night up? Of course, he should have. But then he'd never have known the paradise of hearing her, watching her, feeling her, smelling her come. Bringing her to her first climax. The only thing he didn't do was taste her. But he could guess how wonderful she would have been —a delicious feast.

Now, he'd never know.

In the midst of analyzing how badly he'd fucked up, he suddenly noticed she was already dressed, heading for the door. Then she abruptly stopped, looking around. Seeing what she wanted, Kimberlee marched over to her Magic Wand, grabbing it.

Remaining still for a moment, she asked, "Where's the box?"

Instead of answering her, Johan went over to the closet and reached for the top shelf, retrieving the requested item. Still in silence, he handed it to her.

She snatched it out of his hand, put the sex toy back in, and walked out the door without looking back. She had just discarded him from her life.

If only I could dismiss her as easily.

For a moment, he stood rooted in place, shocked how this once demur woman had morphed into a pissed off Amazon warrior. Without a word, she'd communicated he was useless to her.

Well, he did deserve it.

For a few moments, Kimberlee swayed with exhaustion outside her cabin door, gathering the necessary courage to face her friends and all their questions.

Right now, her psyche ached with pain and fatigue, making it impossible to figure out how to fix a horrible mistake. She had tomorrow. No, it was already tomorrow.

Sleep first. Then, she'd talk with her friends about how to move on.

She wasn't sorry about what happened. But she deeply regretted how something magical had been destroyed.

The one thing she knew for sure was how every muscle in her body ached. All she wanted was her bed and to sleep for eternity.

At least she knew she could come.

When she opened the door, three concerned faces and voices greeted her.

"Kimberlee, where have you been?" an anxious Lori, a TV executive producer, asked, wringing her hands.

Paulette, a senior vice president of retail and operations for the US division of a French fashion house, said half joking, "We thought you might have fallen overboard. We've been so worried about you."

"My God, Kimberlee, you look awful," Bonnie, the ophthalmologist, exclaimed, rushing over to her. "What happened? Are you OK?"

Although her friends wanted answers, she had none to offer. All she sought was a safe place to curl up and hide. She needed to lick her wounds. Much later, she could tell them her story. "I'm fine," she lied. "I just need sleep."

Bonnie looked at the box in Kimberlee's hand and asked, "What's in that box?"

She hesitated, not wanting to get the Captain in trouble. But then she realized the box had a picture of her sex toy on it. "It's my vibrator."

Three shocked faces looked back at her. Then all three women exclaimed at the same time, "*Vibrator!?*"

Paulette was the first to find her voice and asked, "Where in the world did you get a vibrator?"

With hesitation, she admitted, "The Captain gave it to me."

For a moment they just looked at her in stunned silence. Bonnie spoke up, saying, "Oh my God, you fucked the Captain! Is he any good?"

"Holy shit, the Captain! We're your best friends; you need to share him with us. I bet he can take all four of us on," Paulette chimed in.

"The Captain? The Captain! Only you would find the most divine man on the ship," bemoaned Lori.

Kimberlee just stared at her friends, not sure what to say or how to tell them about what had happened. She hurt emotionally and was too wiped out physically to face a grilling.

During her walk to the cabin, she'd admitted to herself the Captain's anger and rejection hurt as much as losing the long sought-after partnership. Her self-confidence lay in tatters. She knew she'd angered the one man she wanted to shine for.

She didn't say a word, just looked back at them.

Being the medical doctor of the group, Bonnie asked in her clinical voice, "Kimberlee, are you OK? Did he hurt you? Please talk to us. Tell us what happened. We're here for you. We love you."

That's all she needed, the safety and genuine concern of her friends. With Bonnie's caring questions, Kimberlee dropped down on her bed, overwhelmed by feelings of loss and failure. Tears rushed to her eyes.

And then sobs.

For all the years they'd known Kimberlee, her friends had only seen her cry once—when she was refused partner and had lost hope for the future. They knew she came from tough Midwestern stock, so a crying Kimberlee meant something drastic had happened.

Lori immediately sat on the bed beside Kimberlee, hugging her until she quieted. Paulette handed her the box of tissues which she'd gotten from the bathroom. Nobody said anything. They just sat silently, patiently waiting for her to regain control.

They knew sometimes being a friend meant sharing in silence.

Before answering, Kimberlee took a deep breath, swallowing the remaining tears. "No, he didn't hurt me. Just the opposite. He showed me I'm not an ice queen and I have a wonderful body made for coming…and coming. He just hates me for making him break his vow of no passengers."

Her three companions quietly waited. Kimberlee would eventually tell them her story. She just needed time to get her thoughts together and gather her ragged emotions.

Slowly, she began telling them about her life-changing evening. She started with the drunk man, talked about her tour of the ship and grotto, how she met the Captain the second time, described her mind-blowing climaxes with an incredibly skillful lover, ending with how he woke her up with anger and disgust.

In a shaky voice, she told them how her own fury had gotten the better of her when she told him off.

As an afterthought, she added how she took her own pleasure and gave nothing back to him. The entire night had been just for her. She wondered if she'd been a less selfish lover, he might not have been so ugly.

Her friends sat in round-eyed astonishment, but not interrupting. In between yawns and deep sighs, an exhausted Kimberlee lacked the energy to censor herself, giving them all the intimate details.

At the end of her account, men-wise Paulette spoke up, "Kimberlee, you did nothing wrong. From your story, the Captain didn't expect anything from you. He never took his clothes off and didn't ask you to do anything for or to him. So, you're not at fault. I'd say the issue is with him. And as you figured out, he's pissed at himself for having sex with a passenger. He's a big boy and knew exactly what he was doing. If he didn't want to be with you, he wouldn't have. Nobody's going to force that man to do something he doesn't want to do. I'll guarantee you that."

The other two nodded.

Kimberlee sat and looked at her friends, who were like loving sisters. She trusted them and knew they were far more experienced than she was when it came to men and sex. So, maybe she hadn't screwed up…at least badly.

Eventually, they had nothing left to discuss. Fatigued from the excitement of cruise day, boarding their ship, and the events of the evening, four weary women gratefully fell into their beds.

FINALLY, SITTING ON THE COUCH IN HIS CABIN DANGLING A glass of brandy from his hand, a drained Captain Johan brooded about the evening's events. What was it about Kimberlee that drew him to her against his better judgment? On the surface, she appeared like nothing special, yet he found himself surprisingly attracted to her. He'd just have to get un-attracted. There was no place in his life for her.

His tired and overly stimulated body filled him with painful restlessness. If docked in port, he'd have gone for a long, grueling swim, releasing his agitation. That wasn't an option this time of night or with his ship sailing in the middle of the ocean. He hoped when he finally slept it would release some of the unwanted tension.

Then, he remembered how poorly he'd treated Kimberlee when he'd shaken her awake. Guilt made him grimace with self-disgust. She wasn't at fault. She'd done nothing wrong.

It shouldn't have been me. I should have said no. I shouldn't have punished her for my weakness.

He recalled her joyful smile when he woke her, cuddled in his arms. How right she felt. And how he treasured the look of wonder and gratitude she gave him. Her lovely, glowing eyes spoke of sexual satisfaction and a newfound confidence.

His guilt-driven behavior extinguished all that beauty.

Never had he hurt a woman…until now. He was raised by his parents to treat women with respect. He married his best friend and dearly loved her. Yes, there were times in his marriage he'd gotten angry, but he'd never verbally abused or treated her with a lack of respect.

Kimberlee had called him cruel. She was right. This just compounded his self-directed disgust. He owed her an apology.

How disappointed Eira would have been with him. In fact, she would have been furious. She was so protective of women.

In the back of his mind, he also knew he didn't deserve another loving, intimate relationship because he hadn't protected the woman he loved. Kimberlee, with all her radiant beauty and sweet innocence, wasn't meant for someone like him. She deserved a man who would protect her and give her a wonderful life in New York City. His life was here on this ship. Love was no longer an option for him.

She might also be a spy. The answer should be a quick internet search. He could then decide what to do with her, because he couldn't toss her off the ship.

As much as he'd like to.

Tomorrow, he'd figure out how to fix the Kimberlee mess. Right now, sleep.

He needed to be alert for mooring in the morning. Usually he enjoyed the challenges of docking, maneuvering around other vessels in a busy port, making sure his ship could easily depart in an emergency, and keeping the craft safe when dealing with strong or unexpected winds that could slam him into the dock or another vessel. In the morning, he'd hopefully get his enthusiasm back.

But, he still didn't know what to do with her…and his ball-clenching horniness.

*F*our physical and emotionally drained women slept in, almost missing the delicious breakfast buffet. Eating al fresco on deck eight's aft patio, their conversation bounced between Kimberlee's experience the previous night and what they should do in Key West.

Recently-divorced Bonnie kept taking quick peeks at Kimberlee, ensuring she was OK. Lori, with her long, black hair clipped up from her neck, handed out a list of must-see sights they needed to choose from, hoping to distract Kimberlee from last night's disaster. Paulette, often reached over, giving her brief hugs of loving encouragement.

For their first full day at a port no one had visited before, they decided to walk around town, starting with Duval Street, the shopping and tourist area. They would include Ernest Hemmingway's 1831 Colonial Spanish house, Harry Truman's Little White House, and must-have key lime pie for lunch. Otherwise, they would keep their options open, doing what caught their fancy and having fun together.

Disembarking, Kimberlee felt a sense of relief getting away from *him*. She almost didn't want to return, but knew she had to. It wasn't like her to run away from difficult situations.

Her friends talked among themselves as they strolled around town, allowing her to join in as she wanted. Sometimes she listened to their chatter, but mostly, she thought about her life and future. And what she was going to do about Captain Johan.

Today was one of the Sundays she normally spent at the battered women and children's shelter on the Upper West Side. Twice a month she volunteered working in the kitchen, teaching math to the kids, and when necessary, providing legal advice to the women. Even on Sundays when she should be in the office working, her firm supported the time off. It was good PR showing how employees supported their community. Plus, having grown up in a family that wanted to make the world a better place, she needed to make a difference in people's lives.

Then her mind flipped back to last night. Maybe the fault wasn't hers. Maybe Paulette, who practiced serial monogamy, was right, the Captain had his own issues which had nothing to do with her. Even so, after the vulnerability of being naked in his arms, she still felt hurt and humiliated by the horrible way he treated her.

And pissed.

Would she have given up the magic of that evening in the grotto? No, being hurt was a small price to pay for finally learning about her body, gaining sexual experience, and having all those stunning orgasms. She wouldn't give this experience up for anything. Even if he was a jerk.

Admitting how important her evening had been, she finally stopped beating herself up and focused on the positives of the experience. For her, life was too short to dwell on the negative. She was raised to count her blessings and that's what she needed to do.

After a full day exploring Key West, the four weary friends grabbed a cab back to their ship. As they got closer to port, Kimberlee's anxiety returned in full force. Although appreciative for what she'd learned from the Captain, she still had hurt that needed healing. Would she have to see him? If she did run into him, how would she react, knowing how intimate they'd been?

She had kept nothing hidden from him. And if she were honest with herself, she loved the feelings of being in his arms while he remained fully clothed. How could something so simple be such a turn on?

Her friends kept reminding her with the Magic Wand, she didn't need him anymore, so she needn't see him again. Departing the ship in five days, she could enjoy being with them and the delights of being in the middle of paradise.

DURING HIS FIRST DAY IN PORT, JOHAN HAD A FEW EXTRA moments of private time. Because they were still sailing in the US, he didn't have reams of immigration paperwork to fill out, as he'd have when they entered foreign waters.

In the limited space of his front room, he paced back and forth in front of his computer, afraid of what he'd find when he researched her name. Eventually, he forced himself to sit at his desk and conduct his Google search. He needed to know what accounting firm she worked for. Could she be a spy for the bastards making the unsolicited bid for his cruise company?

It was too late undoing what had happened between them; he could, however, make sure he protected his ship and himself. If she was one of those greedy bastards, he'd easily render her harmless. This may be simply money for her, but for him, it was a war for survival.

Even the simple act of typing in her name made his body sizzle with sexual need. His cock stood at attention at the memory of having her naked body exposed to him, pliable and desperate. No matter what he found, this one night would remain seared in his memory. Of course, he'd have decades of visions helping him whack off once she was safely out of his life.

Googling her name, he saw immediately she worked for the enemy accounting firm. How stupid he was, getting taken in by her innocent act. Now she had the ammunition to destroy him, as she would, their holding company, SeaWinds Corporation. What an ass he was. How could he have fallen for her performance, except that she was so good at what she did.

How many other men had been taken in by her routine?

The only thing left for him to do was call corporate and tell them he had a spy on board. When he finally got Barry, the general council, on the phone, he kept his description short—leaving out the best-forgotten events in the grotto. After telling Barry what he'd discovered on Google, Barry asked two simple questions. "What office does she work for? And what level is she?"

"New York. And she's a senior manager. Why?"

"Well, Johan," Barry replied, "that accounting firm is humungous, only the few senior managing partners know what other offices are doing. In fact, her office would be so big, she really wouldn't know what anyone else was working on. She's too far down the food chain to know accounts in Miami, unless it's one of her clients. I'd say you have nothing to worry about. She's just above grunt level, so the odds of her being a spy are slim to none."

"Oh."

Barry continued, "Has she been asking probing questions about operations or financials?"

"No."

"Then forget about her. She's there for BDSM games. She's just one more passenger we need to encourage to spend money. Don't lose sleep."

"Thanks for the info. Goodbye, Barry."

"Save your energy over this one," Barry said. "Have a safe trip. Bye."

Johan carefully replaced the receiver back on the phone, which connected directly to headquarters.

As he collapsed back in his chair with eyes closed, relief coursed through his tightly coiled body, as if he had just dodged a bullet. This entire episode lasted only a few minutes, but felt like an eternity.

He sent a silent thank you out to the sea gods that he didn't have a spy on his ship. But then again, if she had been, he'd have a reason to hate her.

What the numbness couldn't hide was his guilt at the way he'd treated her. She had done nothing wrong—an innocent in this entire mess. He'd been the bad guy, assuming the worst of her.

She was exactly who she said she was, but I didn't believe her.

With the espionage issue eliminated, he needed to still keep his distance. Loving and losing Eira taught him that love only caused pain. Should he become sexually active, he'd keep his feelings separate from where he shoved his cock. This way he'd be safe from having his heart broken again.

With that question out of the way, he still faced the

ongoing corporate buyout. Sure, he could find another captain's position, but that wasn't the issue for him. Memories of a past hostile takeover flooded his emotions. Thirty years ago, another bastard company destroyed his family's independent fishing business in their greed to suck up all the little, self-supporting companies. And now he had to go through this debacle again.

With that last thought, he left his cabin, heading for the bridge.

BECAUSE THE MS *APHRODITE* SAILED AT 5:00 P.M., THE women were on board by 4:00 p.m. They feared being left at the pier. Cruise ships followed a tight schedule, which meant they left people behind who weren't aboard at departure time. They didn't want to be one of those dreaded pier-runners, with the entire ship at the railings cheering them on as they ran for the gangway. How mortifying.

Back in their comfy cabins, they sat talking about life on their floating home. Everyone loved the intimate sitting area next to the floor-to-ceiling window and door leading to their balcony. When planning this trip, the women had discussed room arrangements. They had enough money to put two people in a veranda suite with a balcony, which was better than trying to fit four of them in one cabin. Lori and Kimberlee shared one, with Bonnie and Paulette in another. While they didn't have connecting doors, they were next to each other, so they could keep their doors open, visiting back and forth. The queen-sized bed divided into two twin beds, giving everyone personal sleeping space. They had a small round table for room service and a large walk-in closet.

Best of all was their marble bathroom with a tub, two

sinks, and a walk-in shower. Thankfully, it had a glass door—not one of those yucky, plastic shower curtains that stuck to you and held the scum from bathing. While it was called a suite, it certainly didn't have the space of upscale hotels. Even at 300 square feet, they had plenty of room for a week. Nobody felt crowded.

They were putting the final touches on their makeup before dinner when Captain Johan's voice came over the public-address system. He announced that everyone was back on board, so they would be departing at 5:00 p.m. or 1700 hours. He told passengers the outside temperature, wind velocity, what the ship's speed would be, and how they would have smooth sailing during the night. With that, he wished everyone a pleasant evening.

Kimberlee froze when she heard his voice fill the cabin. Her heart pounded while her lungs gasped for air. Her body refused to move. Even if she could flee, she had no place to go, but over the side. So, she stood listening to the same sensual speech that whispered intimate words about her body —as his hands and mouth tortured her with incredible pleasure.

Within seconds, all three women surrounded her with protective support. No, they wouldn't let her stay in the cabin. She wasn't a terrified little rabbit. She was a smart, talented woman, who should be proud of herself. Not even a sexy Captain was worth abandoning her pride. She was going to face the world with self-respect. She wasn't going to let a Neanderthal male defeat her.

Fifteen minutes later, they dragged Kimberlee up to the Aphrodite Lounge on deck ten at the bow of the ship. They'd already put out to sea. As they sailed through the darkening Caribbean waters, the women had a spectacular view through the floor-to-ceiling windows. In fact, they observed the same scene the navigational bridge officers saw as they guided the ship from one deck below.

The friends sat contentedly sipping their cosmos, listening to predinner piano music and discussing their day. Halfway through their drinks, Lori announced she had read some interesting statistics about female orgasms. All heads turned toward her with expectation of something titillating. Being an executive producer for a television company, fascinating facts often found their way to her desk.

"You won't believe this, or maybe you will. I discovered from two major news network reports a British study that found about eighty percent of women fake an orgasm about half of the time. They did this to help their partners climax faster, boost the men's self-esteem as a lover, or because they were bored and wanted the sex to end ASAP."

"I'd vote for bored," Paulette chimed in.

Nodding, Lori continued, "Also, about twenty-five percent of women fake climaxing ninety percent of the time."

"That's probably because they've never experienced a real orgasm and that's all they knew," commented Paulette.

"Well, of course," Bonnie, the blue-eyed, blonde of the group said. "I do it all the time, because men won't give up until they think I've come. And they don't know the difference between a real or fake orgasm. Remember that scene with Meg Ryan in *When Harry Met Sally* when she demonstrated to Billy Crystal how easy it is to fake a climax?"

Lori told them, "Research has shown that most women only reach that earth-shaking orgasm with clitoral stimulation, not vaginal. And most men only focus on our pussies for their pleasure. They think that the longer, the deeper, the harder they fuck the better it is for us."

"They're probably looking for our G-spot, which they can't find," filled in Bonnie.

An embarrassed Kimberlee declared to the table, "Well, I don't know where mine is."

With that announcement, all three women began talking at once, describing how she could find her G-spot. Oblivious to the room around them, the friends sat with heads together discussing sex and men.

CAPTAIN JOHAN STRODE INTO THE APHRODITE LOUNGE. After his ship departed safely from the dock, he visited the public rooms, talking with passengers to discover how their day went and what their plans were for the evening.

Walking around the area chatting with people, he glanced toward the windows. His body halted mid-step. There was Kimberlee with her friends engaged in a lively conversation. She was the last person he wanted to see, but knew it would happen sometime. He contemplated his two options—leave immediately or continue talking with passengers. He'd sailed in enough storms to know some things couldn't be avoided.

He'd stay and let this fiasco play itself out.

Watching her laugh, he saw a vivacious and sensual woman glowing with life. Definitely not the innocent, angry woman from last night. With mounting uncertainty, he contemplated his next move. Not sure what that should be. He hated not having a clear plan of action. But at least, he wasn't dealing with a spy. *Be grateful for small things.*

As Johan continued making his social rounds, he acknowledged, regardless of his stay or leave decision, he'd have to do something about his randy cock demanding to fuck her. Obviously, he wasn't as indifferent to her as he thought. Regardless of what his body wanted, last night would never happen again. Never.

Drawing closer to their table, he must decide if he was

going to stop and talk or avoid them. Shit, he detested being indecisive. It rarely happened.

I had to eventually meet her. This is as good a time as any. I need to get this over with. It's not life or death.

Watching her, hunger grabbed him by the balls. By force of will, he barely managed to keep his cock under control. *Stupid me for underestimating last night.*

Sex with her should have been a physical exercise that faded fast. But no. The feeling of her tight pussy grabbing his fingers still haunted him. Her honeyed scent continued to fill his nostrils.

He had to get out of there—now. Instead of escaping in self-preservation, his guilt for how he treated her spurred him on. To say what, he didn't know. Like the proverbial moth to a flame, he walked directly to Kimberlee.

He saw how engrossed they were in their conversation, remaining unaware he'd joined their group. Standing by the table, he heard the ladies talking about the best vibrator for orgasms—they all agreed that the Hitachi Magic Wand topped their list. *At least, I got that one right.*

Not wanting them to think he was eavesdropping, he quickly said to bent heads, "Good evening, ladies."

Four pairs of startled eyes flew up, fixating on him. Those same eyes turned into hostile hardness, making him know he was unwanted. Drawing on his military training, he presented his emotionless façade, hiding his discomfort. Too late to retreat, he asked in an impassive voice, "How was your day in Key West?"

One friend recovered first. "It was good," she replied. No one else said a word. They just sat glaring at him.

Kimberlee lowered her gaze to the table, the smile vanishing from her lovely face. Regretfully, he knew he'd caused her discomfort. He should never have stopped at their table.

He'd give anything to bring back that smile.

When everyone remained silent, he filled the awkward quiet saying, "What time is your dinner reservation?"

This time another of her friends spoke up. "We're having dinner in the Rose Restaurant at six thirty."

It's now or never to say something. Make it never and get the hell out of here. Instead he said, "Kimberlee, would you have an after-dinner drink with me?" Knowing she wouldn't answer, he added, "How's eight thirty?" Where did that come from? He was just making the whole situation worse. Hopefully she'd turn him down.

Kimberlee's head shot up, staring at him in wide-eyed shock—not uttering a word.

The first friend jumped back into the uncomfortable stillness saying, "Yes, Captain, eight thirty would be fine for her."

Now what? "Good. I'll meet you outside the restaurant. Have a good dinner, ladies."

With a slight nod, he abruptly turned around and exited the lounge, needing to put space between himself and them.

What he couldn't do was free himself from wanting her. Yes, he must make amends for being a jerk, but he also had to guard against a repeat performance. That meant not acting on the hunger roaring through his veins straight to his dick.

CHAPTER SIX

*E*scaping the fiasco he created, Johan fled down one flight of stairs to the navigational bridge. During his rapid descent, he asked himself what stupidity made him approach their table? And even worse, what temporary insanity made him invite her for an after-dinner drink?

Entering the bridge, he checked all was smooth sailing. Then, he went to the tray in the back of the room, selecting sandwiches for dinner. The galley kept the bridge officers supplied with fresh snacks twenty-four seven.

Truth be told, he didn't look at which ones he'd grabbed. Right now, food wasn't a priority, except for nutrition. He needed to get his thoughts straight and his cock back under the control of his brain.

Because of his agitation, he skipped eating with his officers in their dining room. Rather, he took the overloaded china plate into his cabin. Seizing his smartphone, he tapped the music app, automatically linking with the Bluetooth speakers. Most of the younger officers listened to Metallica, R&B, or 80s rock. When he wanted to think, he turned to Norway's famous son—Edvard Grieg. Right now, the *Peer*

Gynt suite filled his small cabin with the power of the stunning fjords. No matter how much he loved the tropics, he still carried the splendor of his country in his soul. Grieg's music transported him to those glorious inlets, offering needed sanity.

Instead of dwelling on what an idiot he'd been in the lounge, he reviewed this afternoon's call to Barry. At the moment Johan learned Kimberlee wasn't a spy, well, most likely wasn't; a huge weight lifted from his shoulders.

But he couldn't banish the guilt. He'd treated her badly—that wasn't him. She was the innocent in this mess. Instead of owning his idiotic decision to have sex with her, he used his anger as an emotional Taekwondo kick to her gut.

He'd turned himself into the victim, wanting to think the worst of her.

As he contemplated his stupidity, a knock sounded on his door. Turning off the music, he opened it, inviting Ramil in. Usually at this time, they'd spend a few moments sharing a beer and discussing the day. Tonight, Ramil handed him a cold lager Bokke asking, "How you doing?"

Sitting back down, Johan replied, "Like shit. Last night was a fucking mistake. It should never have happened."

After taking a swig of his beer, Ramil asked, "How many know?"

"I'd say her three friends."

"Well, my guess is they won't blow your cover."

"No, I don't think they will, but I can't let it happen again. No matter how much I want to. I'm an ass for allowing last night to happen. And I'm even more of a fool for inviting her to have a drink tonight."

With that last announcement, Ramil stopped mid-swallow from his beer. He quietly studied Johan. Setting his bottle on the coffee table, he said, "It's about time you came back to the living. The grief never leaves, but it does soften. You're still a man with male needs. Unfortunately, you're also the captain who signed a contract forbidding relationships with passengers. Be careful."

"I keep telling myself that, but...but even knowing I can be fired, I'm drawn to her like a magnet."

"I'd say more like a starving man at a banquet," Ramil's voice carried no judgment. "Just remain on guard. Protect yourself."

Their conversation moved on to discussing their day and plans for tomorrow, until Johan needed to leave for his ill-fated drink.

They walked out together. Before turning in the opposite direction, Ramil said, "Your wife wouldn't have wanted you to live your life without love." With that, he left the Captain, walked back to his cabin, and situated below the waterline.

Contemplating what Ramil said, the Johan acknowledged he didn't want to live a life barren of love and joy. But she wasn't the person he should practice with.

It had taken him a decade to begin the healing process. He'd barely put his crushed heart back together again. He couldn't risk further damage to it. Even the simple act of caring about another, would reopen his wound. The price was too great to pay. As long as he stayed above emotional entanglement, he'd remain safe from pain.

When Johan arrived at the restaurant's atrium on deck four, his talk with Ramil had him once again thinking with his big head. True, he still had a knot twisting his guts, filling him with misgivings about his unwanted/wanted drink with Kimberlee.

His uncertainty about how to handle their meeting increased his irritation with himself...and the woman involved. He prided himself on being in control. Now, he faced a dilemma, leaving him irritated at his loss of self-discipline.

A few minutes early, he could observe the dinner scene. While chatting comfortably with the hostess, he surveyed the dining room, passengers, and service. After two years on this ship, he still enjoyed hearing about her evenings and what she might need.

On past cruises, he'd had plenty of after-dinner drinks with passengers. Usually, corporate asked him to charm them or sell to potential investors. So his appearance waiting for a diner caused no undue interest.

He may have looked perfectly in control on the outside, but internally he grappled with what to say when he saw Kimberlee. He also struggled with wanting the forbidden. The turmoil between his values as Captain and his needs as a man created an unwanted war within him—for which he had no successful strategy.

Looking into the dining room, he saw the four women sitting at their table deep in conversation. *Maybe they were convincing her not to join him for our fucking drink.* That would solve a lot of problems.

KIMBERLEE USED THE MEAL TO STRATEGIZE A PLAN FOR HER after-dinner cocktail. Before she could bring up the topic, Paulette, with her charcoal, short Vidal Sassoon cut, immediately began the discussion. She'd lived in Paris for five years, so she had a more worldly approach to sex.

"You have plenty of single men on this ship," she began. "All we have to do is find you one good specimen who isn't intimidated by vibrators and smart women."

"That's right," Lori added. "The Captain isn't the only male on this ship. You can do better, if we look around." Of the four women, she was the only one involved in a long-term relationship.

"I know you're right," Kimberlee interjected. "I've been evaluating the men I've seen, but none interest me. Yes, there are some nice-looking ones, besides the entertainers, but they just don't do it for me. To be honest, every man I've studied falls short compared to him. None of them turn me on the way he does."

Bonnie said, "OK, so you want the Captain."

"But he doesn't want me. And even if he did, he can't be with me because I'm a passenger."

Bonnie continued, saying, "He's not the first captain who's been with a passenger. We just have to make him really, really want you. Nothing gets a man's hormones pumping like a little competition. I guarantee he won't want to share you."

Paulette added, "Bonnie's right. None of the men may turn you on, and they don't have to, but you need to make the Captain think they do."

"But he doesn't want me," she declared. "He doesn't want me."

"Kimberlee," Bonnie said quickly, "not so loud. The table next to us looks like they're listening. Whether he wants you or not, you still need to protect his reputation. We don't want him fired because of us."

"Oh shit, I'm sorry. I completely forgot about that no passenger clause in his contract. I'll be more quiet. Thanks."

Picking up where their conversation had been briefly paused, Paulette said, "He doesn't want to desire you, but he does. You just need to help him recognize how much."

And so, the conversation flowed through the repast. By the time they'd finished dessert, Kimberlee almost became convinced there was hope for one more glorious night with him. She just didn't quite believe it.

During their lively discussion, Kimberlee's thoughts drifted to the Captain and sex. Yes. No. Maybe. She couldn't decide what she wanted. Half of her said to go for it; she only had five more days on board. The other half told her to walk away. She knew her friends would be no help because they would support her, regardless of her choice. She was on her own.

The one thing her companions stressed was how she should trust herself.

She wanted to enjoy her dinner, but instead picked at her perfectly prepared truffle-encrusted lamb chops. Her mind whirled in turmoil and her stomach clenched with apprehension making eating anything more than small bites impossible. She knew if she was wearing her new IWC watch, she'd spend the entire dinner staring at it, wanting the hands to move faster or was it slower?

By eight o'clock, she wanted time to stop altogether.

Finally, when the witching hour of eight thirty arrived, it was time for the drink…and talk.

Leaving the restaurant with her friends, she found the Captain waiting outside the entrance, standing self-confident in his masculinity. His black-clad physique emphasized the powerful muscular body beneath. The light from the crystal chandelier overhead made his reddish-golden-brown hair gleam.

He looked back at them with his expressionless, granite-chiseled Captain's face. She could read nothing from his shuttered thoughts.

Trust myself.

"Good evening, Captain," Lori said, looking him directly in the eye without a smile.

"Good evening, Captain," Bonnie repeated in her best frosty voice, staring straight at him.

Paulette shot him a hard look and followed with a harsh tone in her voice. "Bonsoir, Captain."

But Kimberlee didn't say a thing. She just gazed at his left ear with a mask-like face drained of all color.

"Why, Captain," Bonnie said, "I thought captains were supposed to wear their professional white uniform. What happened to yours?"

As if he were used to this question, he replied, "During my limited free time I like to blend in as much as possible. True, I'm always on duty, even when sleeping. For a few hours, I'd like a rare moment to myself. A cruise ship's crew has no privacy day or night. The ship and passengers always take priority before our personal needs."

Kimberlee gave him a sideward glance, amazed how he lived a life totally consumed by his ship—awake and asleep. How sad. She'd never thought about what a captain's world was like.

They really didn't have a life of their own. And they probably didn't make a hell of a lot of money for all the time and responsibility they shouldered. That's not the way she wanted to live—no privacy twenty-four seven and no time to call her own. And no shopping at Bergdorf's.

Intrigued about his life, she waited to hear what he would say next.

Instead, he immediately asked, "Will you join me for that drink, Kimberlee?"

She nodded, still not looking at him directly. And disappointed he provided no further insight about himself.

"Walk with me to the Dolphin Club."

Not even a "please."

"Ladies, have a wonderful night. You have a lot of

evening activities to explore on ship." With that, he turned to Kimberlee.

Hearing her racing heart pounding in her ears, she surreptitiously wiped her damp palms on her Dolce & Gabbana calf-length cotton dress as she took the few steps to his side. Coolly nodding at her with his stony face, he turned toward the stern of the ship.

Together they left her friends standing in the restaurant's atrium, worried looks on their faces.

Kimberlee, who had no idea what to say, kept hoping he would talk. Instead, he remained frustratingly quiet as they walked up one flight to deck five. In the painful silence, their short climb seemed interminable.

When they entered the club, a small band was already playing, with a few couples on the dance floor. Going up to the bar he asked her, "What would you like to drink?"

"I'll have a Grand Marnier, thank you."

"Hello, Belmiro," said a cordial, smiling Captain to the bartender. "I'll have one Grand Marnier and my Hennessy VSOP, please."

He can smile and say please to his crew, just not to me.

Trying to distract herself from her increasing irritation with his rudeness, Kimberlee noticed that Belmiro's name tag listed Portugal as his home country. "Belmiro, where in Portugal are you from?"

"Lisboa," he replied handing the Captain both drinks. "Have you been to Portugal?"

"Yes, I was in Lisboa for business about three years ago for two weeks. You come from a beautiful city. And are a very gracious people to accept the way we mispronounce and misspell your city's name. Until I was there, I'd called it Lisbon, like most English-speaking people. When people mispronounce US cities names, they usually get a not-so-gentle correction. Most Portuguese default to the incorrect one, so as not to offend the person they're talking with."

Avoiding being alone with the Captain, she continued, "You're a long way from home. Do you miss it?"

"I do miss my family, but I also consider the *Aphrodite* my home now. This is a great way for me to see a new part of the world and work with wonderful people from different countries."

Nodding, the Captain said, "After a while, the ship feels like home and the crew like family. I couldn't live anywhere else."

Hearing the Captain's words, Kimberlee knew they had little in common—a cruise ship and New York City were universes apart. Having this thought took some of the underlying anxiety out of trying to build a relationship. They had no future. This would be just a simple sexual fling for her.

If he were willing.

The Captain held the door open as they walked out to the aft patio. Closing it reduced most of the music, letting the stillness of the night enveloped them.

"When we're in international waters outside a country's laws, this pool deck becomes a nude bathing area. But at night, people are at dinner, seeing shows, or their own entertainment. We should have this space to ourselves."

Kimberlee looked around with curiosity. She found herself in a lovely area with a miniature swimming pool, almost like a plunge pool, and two small hot tubs. Placed around the pool were plenty of loungers. In the back area, tables and chairs filled the space. Overhead, an awning-like cover protected people who didn't want the sun or to hide from the rain.

She watched the wake formed by the ship. *What an amazingly peaceful place. I can understand what draws him to living on the sea.* Just standing outside with the light breeze and the sound of the ship gliding through the waves began relaxing her.

With a light pressure on her still rigid back, he guided her toward a corner table on the port side. As he held a chair for her, Kimberlee sat down, making sure she didn't brush against him.

Sitting in strained silence, they each sipped their drinks, looking out to sea through the dark night. She frantically searched for something neutral to say, but nothing came to mind. *Just say something, Captain. Anything.*

Finally, he broke the silence between them.

CHAPTER SEVEN

*A*s if hearing her thoughts, Captain Johan said, "I owe you an apology for last night. I violated my responsibilities as a Captain and then took my anger out on you." He stopped, watching her. When she sat quietly staring at him, he continued, almost as if filling the void.

"In the eight years that I've been on cruise ships, this is the first time I've been physically intimate with a passenger. I wish I could deny my attraction to you, but I can't. You're a beautiful, passionate woman."

Your turn. Don't force me to do all the talking. "To be honest, holding you in my arms felt right."

She didn't reply, so he continued, "I'm sorry for what happened. We met at the wrong time and in the wrong place."

With that last statement, he watched an incensed Kimberlee blaze into life. Her eyes shot flames of anger at him. She squeezed her liqueur glass so hard he feared she'd shatter it or throw the remaining liqueur in his face.

"Well, I'm not sorry. Last night was as much about me as it was about you and your vaulted values," she said in an outraged voice. "This was one of the most glorious experiences I've ever had. I refuse to feel guilty. But I am sorry that you found being with me so unpleasant. I'm also sorry I was so selfish and didn't worry about your needs."

Caught off guard by her furious outburst and by the spunky woman who replaced the innocent one of last night, he had no reply.

She continued before he could figure out the right words.

"You made this experience all about you, but I'm in the equation too. You could have asked me how I felt rather than telling me how bad it was for you. I'm sure, Captain, that you know a lot about ships, but you seem to have limited knowledge about women. I may know more about mergers than I do about men, but I don't understand how you could have treated me so callously. Yes, I may have left you sexually frustrated; however, you never told me what you wanted. Even though you haven't cared enough to ask me what I want, I'll tell you."

Stunned, his pragmatic mind struggled to find a way to defuse her anger but came up empty. At the same time, he needed to hear what she wanted from him. So, looking into defiant, accusing eyes, he said nothing, letting her continue.

AFTER TAKING A DEEP BREATH, KIMBERLEE SAID, "I MAY never have another chance to learn about sex, men, or my body the way you can show me. I want to walk off this ship five days from now a wiser and more experienced woman. I can't do it alone, even with my new vibrator.

"Yes, that's a problem for you with your no-passenger clause. However, you already broke that last night. In Iowa, we say it's a waste of time closing the barn door after the horse has left. You left that barn door open last night, so closing it now doesn't eliminate what happened between us.

It makes you a hypocrite. If our drink tonight is for you to apologize, then you have, and I can go.

"My friends are already looking for another man for me. One who won't treat me like a criminal and make me feel shitty about myself.

"They tell me there're lots of experienced men on this ship who care about pleasing women. With three of them looking, I'm sure they'll find someone who'll treat me with respect…and be a quality lover at the same time. You don't have to be concerned about me anymore."

She glared at him with the same steely look she gave opposing counsel in negotiations.

HIS BODY FROZE WITH DISBELIEF. THE THOUGHT OF ANOTHER man touching her left him feeling as if he'd been kicked in the solar plexus. She'd knocked the wind out of him without a touch.

He had nothing to say. He could say nothing. She had every right to find another man. Yes, she did. The fuck she did.

Fine, let her go.

No. I don't want another man near her. I'll beat the bastard to a pulp. She's mine.

For the first time, he was torn about being Captain. He wanted his ship. And he wanted her. He knew what he should tell her, but the words refused to come out. He should get the hell up and walk away, but his body wouldn't move.

HE STARED BACK AT HER. SHE SAW A MAN WATCHING HER OUT of hard, narrowed eyes. The look that told his crew "I'm the commander. Do what I say." That gaze had no effect on her, because she'd stood up to tougher adversaries and got what she wanted.

Silence. Only the sound of the ship sailing through the sea filled the space between them.

She didn't have anything else to say. She'd said it all. Her body slumped in the chair, feeling limp from the emotional outburst. Plus, she needed to regroup her thoughts and energy, preparing for the next round.

She also knew that silence was a powerful negotiation tool, so she waited, curious for what he'd say. She didn't have long to wait.

"You're innocent in this mess. Yes, you had the right to ask. It was my choice alone for what happened. With the thousands of people coming on this ship, I was eventually bound to meet someone who attracted me. As in control as I am, my libido seemed to have a life of its own with you. I can't control the weather and it seems I don't have control over my sexual needs when they relate to you."

Within a few seconds, he added, "You're correct, I know ships better than women. Once my wife died, I shut myself off from relationships. I guess it shows."

Wife?

"I see I shocked you mentioning my wife. Let me tell you about myself. Then, maybe we can start over. I'll try not to bore you with too much detail, but I want you to understand who I am. I want you to make an informed decision about where we go from here. And what you want from me."

"Thank you. I do want to know about you."

"I grew up just above the Arctic Circle on the coast of Norway. My father and his father, all the way back through the generations, were cod fisherman. When not in school, I was on a fishing boat. I was the first person in my family to graduate from college. I attended the Royal Norwegian Naval

Academy and then on to the Royal Norwegian Navy Officer Candidate School."

As he talked, the evening's warm Caribbean breeze picked up force, blowing Kimberlee's hair into her face. She brushed it back, never taking her eyes off him. Yes, she wanted to know all about this man, who came from a world so different from hers. But then, maybe cod fisherman and Iowa farmers weren't that far apart. Whether it be sea or farmland, both worlds depended upon planet earth for their livelihood. And the whimsical, uncontrollable forces of nature.

Pride filled his voice and his eyes glowed with self-confidence…then the shine faded. Looking down at the table, he paused before continuing.

"When I graduated from the academy, I married my childhood sweetheart, Eira. She was going to medical school to become an OB/GYN.

"Ten years into our marriage, she was driving home from a late-night delivery, when three drunk Brits forgot they weren't in England and were driving on the left side of the road. Their speeding car crashed head on with Eira's, killing her and ending her four-month pregnancy. When I lost them, something inside of me died.

"I was serving in the Persian Gulf when she was killed. There was nothing I could have done to protect them. Yet, I still feel horrible guilt for not being there when they needed me.

"Truthfully, I don't deserve a second chance."

Pausing a moment, he added, "I have nothing left to offer you. Well, that's not totally true. For this coming week, I can give you a safe environment to discover your sexuality and what a stunning woman you are. If you are willing to trust me."

. . .

THE ANGER INSIDE HER SEEMED TO FRAGMENT. TEARS CLUNG
to her lashes as her heart ached for the pain he must have
felt…and still did. Nobody should face such a horrible loss.
She couldn't imagine how she would have lived with that
kind of agony.

She couldn't take away what happened to him. She
couldn't heal him. She could, however, show him that she felt
his pain. Instead of hiding her tears, she looked straight at
him, letting him see how much she ached for him. Not with
pity. No, never that. But with compassion from one human
being to another.

He reached across the small table, using his index finger
to wipe the tears as they slid down her cheek. His own eyes
were wet from the decade-long torment, which he'd kept
locked deep inside his soul.

What could she say? Really nothing. Sometimes pain was
so great that mere platitudes wouldn't bring comfort. But she
wanted to try. "I'm so sorry, Captain. I can't imagine how…
how awful this must be for you. I don't have words."

He kept his finger on her cheek to catch the next tear as
they gazed at each other without defenses. The intimacy from
the night before stripped them of need for speech. His eyes
expressed the rawness mirrored in her heart. Sitting together
in stillness, she only heard the sound of the wind rustling the
canvas overhead and the sea against the ship.

The vessel's soft outdoor illumination let her see him in
the moonless night without the harsh glare from indoor lights.

As much as she wanted to believe they'd magically
resolved their issues, she didn't completely trust him. Not
after the way he treated her. A heaviness lodged in her chest
leaving her conflicted about what she should do. She had no

fears physically, but with such profound intimacy, she remained psychologically vulnerable to his unpredictable moods—especially his guilt for being with a passenger. Even with Hope being her middle name, she wasn't stupid. Their shipboard romance had no future. So, what to do?

Shifting her gaze from his eyes, she stared down at the table. Within moments, she decided to risk one more night. She had nothing to lose, but oh, so much to gain.

How long they sat this way, Kimberlee wasn't sure. Sometime in the peaceful intimacy, she looked back up at him, spontaneously asking a question that popped into her mind. "With this horrendous loss in your life, how did you end up on a sex ship of all places?"

She watched the Captain's face relax with a slight smile. As he lifted his finger from her still damp face, he slowly stroked her cheek sending spiraling desire flooding through her. How easily her body responded to his caress. How she craved more of his touches.

"I stayed in the navy's special forces unit for two more years, volunteering for dangerous assignments. But no matter how many risks I took, I always made it home in one piece.

"I just wanted to get away from war and death. When one of the large, premium cruise ship lines sent out job openings for bridge officers, I took it. The sea is a part of me. I'll never leave it.

"After six-years of working on different size vessels, my oldest brother and his eight business partners asked me to captain the ship they were refitting in drydock—this one. Having been celibate for eight years, working on a sex ship was like any other cruise ship for me."

Kimberlee's eyes widened. She stared at him, stunned by his revelation. "Then I'm the first woman you've been with since your wife's death?"

"Not only have I been celibate for these past ten years, Eira was the first and only woman I've been with."

She leaned forward, clearly surprised by his revelation. It took a few seconds before she asked, "Well then, where did your experience come from?"

"Eira, wanted to help women more than just the typical OB/GYN medical practice. She wanted to support them taking responsibility for their health and sexuality. So, she read all the books she could find on women's sexuality, because medical school only discussed sex from a physical, technical, and medical perspective. I read the books with her and we experimented together, learning from each other."

Kimberlee experienced a sudden burning sensation at the back of her throat. How could she be jealous of a dead woman? But she was. He really had an amazing relationship with her. There was no way she could compete. Repressing her jealousy, she asked, "Why me, after all this time?"

CAPTAIN JOHAN LOCKED HIS EYES ON KIMBERLEE'S questioning brown ones, struggling to give the unvarnished truth. "I've asked myself that same question. And I don't have an answer. After five years in the special forces, I've learned to trust my instinct and not second-guess myself... That trust saved my life and my team's life on many occasions.

"You came into my life and I wanted you in my arms. It seems that simple. But of course, it's not. Truthfully, I planned to avoid you for the rest of the cruise. But after seeing you in the lounge, I knew I couldn't abandon what we had."

He watched how motionless she sat, as if scrutinizing his every word—deciding whether she should stay or walk away.

Not knowing what she'd choose, he continued, "I'll manage my conflict between being this ship's captain and creating a temporary relationship with you."

Seeing the flare of fury in her eyes and her lips twist with dislike, he quickly added, "Sorry, this was an unfeeling way of telling you yes, I want to continue what we have. After ten years being alone, I've forgotten the niceties in relationships. Plus, as you bluntly pointed out, I know ships better than women."

She continued to glare at him.

Releasing a deep sigh, he said, "Remind me not to face you across a negotiating table. You'd make mincemeat of me with your lawyering skills."

No response. She was letting him find his own way out of this mess. Well, he had nothing to lose, so he might as well keep talking, digging himself into a deeper hole.

"Now, the question is, where do we go from here? I do know regardless of how this relationship evolves, I want honesty between us."

"You've certainly been honest. Thank you. Now it's time for me to go."

As she began to stand, he reached out and took her wrist in a firm, but not painful grip.

She froze. "I'm more experienced with spreadsheets and the legal issues in mergers than I am with men and sex. It's best I let you find another woman who has more to offer."

"Wait. You have a lot to offer. I never meant to imply you didn't. We have five days left. Give me another chance. You have the right to walk away any time."

KIMBERLEE FOUND HERSELF CAUGHT IN THAT AWKWARD position of being half out of her chair and bent hovering over the table. She inelegantly plopped back down in her seat, firmly pulling her hand out of the Captain's hold.

An icy anxiety froze her. She faced an internal approach-avoidance struggle…wanting to escape his bigger-than-life presence, but also wanting what he offered.

OK, Kimberlee-girl, what's more important, protecting your self-worth or exploring your sexuality with a Norse god? No-brainer.

Regarding her with searching intensity, his piercing eyes belied the casually, neutral tone of his voice. "Now that you know something about my background, tell me about yourself. What took an Iowa woman to New York City?"

I'm one of those unique people raised in a loving and happy family. I'm from central Iowa. My parents met in Walmart where my father is still a pharmacist and my mother has returned to being a cashier now that my brother and I are out of the house. I'm the first woman in my family to graduate from college."

"We have something in common there."

With increasing confidence, Kimberlee continued, "My mother's father was a butcher and couldn't afford sending her to college. My father's father worked at a Case—that's the red tractors—dealership. So my parents are proud of me and what I've accomplished. I've got a wonderful younger brother, who I adore. If I can, I want to help him financially with his education to take some of the burden off my parents. Of course, they'd never ask for my help, but I want to support my family any way I can."

As she talked, a small smile tilted the corners of her lips up, showing how loving she felt toward her family. Feeling encouraged by his nod of interest, she expanded about her life.

"For as long as I remember, I've wanted to be a partner in

one of the Big Four accounting firms. I need a career with good compensation, so I can help my parents when they retire. They have spent so much on educating both of us, I'm afraid they won't have money for retirement. I want to return their generosity and love."

As an experienced negotiator, Kimberlee knew one way of getting a truthful answer was to throw someone off with an unexpected question. Using this tactic, she said, "OK, what do you have in mind for our five-day relationship?"

TAKEN ABACK BY HER ABRUPT CHANGE OF TOPIC AND DIRECT question, he didn't know how to answer. He stared at her for a moment, then responded with the first thought that entered his mind. "We could try traditional lovemaking. Nothing kinky."

He saw a spark of apprehension flare in her eyes. "Does that mean no vibrator?" she asked in a panicked voice. "I'm not giving up those fabulous, mind-blowing, earth-shaking climaxes."

With twinkling eyes and a trace of amusement in his voice, he said, "We'll use whatever you want. This is your time."

"What about your time? What about your wants?"

"Men have been designed simply and straightforward—a cock looking for a hole or hold. We're uncomplicated, with not much hidden. At forty-three years old, I know how my body works. For me, my pleasure comes from experiencing your pleasure with you. Knowing that you're sexually satisfied is my goal—if making love has a goal."

· · ·

Kimberly sat quietly for a moment staring out to sea. He knew she had heard him because of her swift intake of breath and he watched her nipples harden into glorious peaks.

Across the table from her, he sat motionless, his whole being waiting for her response. He wanted to reach down to stroke his rock-hard cock but forced himself to keep his hands on the table. He didn't want to freak her out. She wasn't ready to watch him jack off. Not yet, anyway.

Slowly, she looked back at him, her soft brown eyes turning dark with passion. In a husky voice she said, "I'll trust you, Captain. I don't know what else to say. I'm out of my league."

"Thank you," he said softly, startled by her faith in him. "I won't abuse your trust."

Pushing himself up from the table, he rose in one fluid motion, telling her he needed to make a call. Moving to the railing, he speed-dialed Ramil, hanging up after a brief multi-lingual conversation.

Then, he walked over to Kimberlee, holding his hand out to her. Taking it, she let him pull her to standing. When their eyes met, a sexual heat sizzled between them that neither could or wanted to hide.

Roughly, he pulled her to him, forcing her arm behind her back, pinning her needy body against his powerful one. Whispering into her hair, he told her with a groan, "I want to taste every inch of your body. I want you helpless, cumming with my mouth sucking your clit. I'm going to bury my cock deep in your tight, wet pussy, fucking you until the world explodes." He hid nothing. Exposing his vulnerability and craving for her.

Claiming her lips in a hard and searching kiss, he begged her to join him in the grotto.

CHAPTER EIGHT

*A*lways the gentleman, the Captain held open the door to their grotto. Filled with both trepidation and anticipation, Kimberlee still noticed they'd entered a different room from last night. The tightness constricting her chest eased knowing he didn't keep a cabin reserved for his sole use.

Thank heaven she wasn't part of some sex assembly line, as she might have been with many of the men of her acquaintance.

Her relief vanished when she thought about his expectation. Even if he hadn't been sexually active for ten years, he was still much more experienced than she was. She should have read those erotic romances Paulette recommended. She'd have greater knowledge about what to expect and what to do.

His caressing voice broke into her reverie. "Kimberlee, do you take birth control pills, or should I use a condom?"

"I'm on the pill." *Not that I've needed them. Thank heaven I didn't stop taking them when I'd planned.*

"Good. Remember you don't have to do anything you

don't want. Your safe word is orchid. Use it if you need to." He added, "Is there anything you don't want?"

"I guess I'm not experienced enough to know what I don't want. All I've known is 'typical sex,' which for this ship is boring. I'm willing to try new things, but I just don't know what those would be," she said, then hesitated before going on, "I would like my vibrator, but it's in my room."

"Ramil brought a different one. Hopefully, you'll like it just as well."

"That was the call you made?" she asked.

He nodded.

She then said, "How did he get everything so quickly?"

"It turns out, when I left to meet you, he took the initiative to reserve this grotto and buy a vibrator from the ship's sex store." Pausing for a moment, he added, "I guess he knows me better than I know myself. I was only planning on having a drink. I never expected for us to be here…but I wouldn't change anything. I want to be with you. I want to make love with you."

Placing his strong, capable hands on her shoulders, he continued, "I think you're a beautiful, stunning, sexy woman." He then lightly brushed a kiss across her nose.

No man had ever called her "beautiful" or "stunning" or "sexy" before. Many other adjectives, from bland to disparaging terms, had been used. Even wearing the most expensive designer clothes, men didn't find her appealing. Too pudgy. Not glamorous. Definitely no sex appeal.

Kimberlee wanted to believe him. His words acted as a great foreplay technique, because her body temperature shot up a few degrees.

Leaving her for a moment, he walked over to the night-stand checking out the newest sex toy, which Ramil had plugged in for charging.

Standing in the middle of the small room not knowing where to look—certainly not at the BDSM bed—or what she should do, she waited for him to make the next move. She just stood twirling her gold earring.

Holding her breath, she watched him stride toward her, returning his calming hands to her tense shoulders.

She gazed up, hoping he'd recognize trust was all she had to give.

"You're a gorgeous woman," he said, cradling her face then giving her parted lips a tender kiss.

That was all the encouragement she needed to shed her remaining fears. Immediately, she threw her arms around his neck, pressing her eager body against his—spontaneously rubbing her hungry sex against his rigid cock.

When he moaned, her confidence soared knowing he wanted her almost as much as she did him. Deepening her kiss, she opened her mouth wider—begging him to explore her with his searching tongue.

Shutting down her thinking brain, she just wanted to feel. Not miss any of the wonders he offered. She might not have this amazing opportunity again.

Tentatively, Kimberlee touched his tongue with hers. Then, she boldly thrust into his mouth, discovering him as he was her.

He sucked on her tongue, pulling it deeper in, using his teeth to tenderly bite.

Enclosing her tightly in his arms, he bit her neck, telling her how he wanted to enslave her with his hands and mouth. He cupped her breast, firmly squeezing it until she arched her body demanding more. His rough palm skimmed her puckered nipples through her dress until they became so sensitive she gripped him for support.

"You've got such beautiful breasts," he whispered huskily in her ear.

"They're too small," she exhaled between moans. "I wish they were bigger."

"Oh no, they're perfect. I wouldn't change anything about you," he replied, squeezing the nipple harder. "I want you just as you are."

Hearing those words, she felt beautiful. In this moment, nothing existed but letting his passion consume her.

Without thought, she quickly unbuttoned and slid off her dress, while he reached around to unhook her bra, sliding it off her arms. Immediately, she reached down to yank off her silk panties.

Totally naked. Finally free of all physical and emotional restraints. She'd flung off her Midwestern judgments about sex, leaving them on the floor with her clothes.

This was what she'd fantasized sex should be. Some dreams do come true.

GIVING HIMSELF OVER TO THE PASSION OF HER KISSES, HE felt currents of desire shoot into his balls. Needing more, Johan walked her backward a few steps to the bed. With his lips fastened against hers, he murmured for her to lie down. When she sat on the side without moving, he lifted her legs onto the mattress. Still consuming the moist softness of her lips, he guided her backward, laying her on her back.

Pulling away from their drugging kisses, his mouth tingled from where her teeth had clung to his lips—as if trying to prevent him from leaving.

Stepping back, he stood beside the bed, looking down at *his* naked beauty. *Herregud, you're magnificent. Made for love.*

Quickly stripping off his clothes, he allowed her to inspect every bare inch of him—letting his rampant hard-on show how much he wanted to fuck her.

He watched her passion-hungry eyes feast on his naked body. As she spread her legs wider in a plea for him, he saw how her pussy muscles began opening and her love juices seeping out, filling the room with her scent.

She softly said, "You're a gorgeous man...like a Norse god, but on a Greek goddess ship. A fantasy I didn't know I had. I've gone to heaven—or is it Valhalla?" Then in a louder voice, "Please don't wait. I'll beg if you want."

WHEN SHE REACHED OUT HER HAND, HE IMMEDIATELY grasped it, stretching out on the bed beside her, pulling her into his arms. He wanted to taste her, to feel her clit against his tongue, to pump his cock inside her until she cried for him to never stop.

It took all his self-control not to throw himself on top of her, shoving his dick inside. Instead, he drew upon years of military training for self-control, putting her pleasure before his. With demanding hands, he caressed her flushed body, following each stroke with a kiss, a nibble, a lick. He sucked then bit each nipple as one hand reached down caressing her trembling, engorged folds. She was wet and wide open...all for him. He knew from watching and listening, she wanted him, but she hadn't lost all control. And he wanted her mindless with need.

Sliding down her body with his lips, he stopped to feast on her distended clit. Settling between her spread thighs, he began drinking her nectar. Her fabulous taste and smell sent an explosion of desire through him, making him struggle against spewing his seed over the bed.

He loved feeling her pussy juices smear his face.

Needing to force her beyond anything she'd experienced before, he slid one then two fingers into her tight channel, angling forward for her G-spot. He wanted to shove another finger up her ass but knew she wasn't ready for that yet. Next time he would take his time exploring that hole with great thoroughness.

From last night, he knew many of her pleasure points, but not all. As passion-drugged as his mind was, he still sought to strip her of every inhibition. He needed her every fantasy exposed to him. All defenses demolished.

"Oh yes," she cried, jerking her hips upward, giving his greedy mouth more access to her thrashing body. She shoved her hands into his hair, forcing his face deeper into her soaked core.

He watched how shamelessly she brought her knees up to her shoulders—exposing herself. Hiding nothing.

He couldn't last much longer. He reached for the little vibrator, turning it on as it fit naturally in the palm of his hand. He placed the toy over her pelvic bone, so the tip rested on her clitoris.

Within five seconds, he felt her muscles clench in multiple deep contractions, racing up her body. Then she arched up from the bed, forced into a silent cry. Holding the toy in place became difficult because of her fierce spasms. But he milked her orgasm, never letting up, not letting her pull away from his mouth, hand, and toy.

"You're so gorgeous coming. I could suck on you all night."

But he really couldn't. When her second orgasm washed through her, he dropped the vibrator on the bed, gathered her in his trembling arms and thrust his cock into her wide-open, soaked pussy. Her violent contractions continued even without the toy, her muscles fiercely clamped around his engorged dick, pulling him in deeper. Within minutes, he felt his penis thicken and lengthen as he too roared out his climax, shooting every drop of his hot cum deep into her.

With his softening penis still embedded inside her clutching sheath, Johan rolled over to his side, taking Kimberlee with him nestled in his arms. He held her close as her body continued spasming around his cock. Releasing a contented sigh, he buried his face in her neck, kissing her and telling her what a glorious woman she was… How wonderful he felt deep inside her… And graphicly explaining all the intimate ways he wanted to bring her pleasure. He wasn't sure what language he used—and didn't care as long as her moans never stopped.

As they sailed through the night, he showed her the various ways they could make love, as if the *Kama Sutra* was his guide, allowing her to explore each position and what worked best for giving her multiple orgasms. Eventually, he lost count how many times she came.

He just loved hearing her pleasure, smelling her honey, and feeling her body explode around his cock, on his face, or in his arms.

KIMBERLEE ALSO LOST COUNT OF HER CLIMAXES. CUDDLED IN his strong, protective arms after one more body-twisting, "exotic" position, she reflected on her stunning and mind-altering lovemaking. After this evening, her life had irrevocably changed. No longer was she the same woman who walked aboard this ship.

I'm a new Kimberlee. I've learned how sex is passionate, playful, and filled with laughter. I've always thought it was serious business—a performance I got rated on. No more. Sex celebrates life…and who I am. Thank you, Captain, for your beautiful gift.

Just as she began slipping into sleep sometime in the early morning, her last thought was, *I have years of lost climaxes to make up for. This is a good start, but only a start.*

When the morning light from the porthole woke her, Kimberlee realized she was alone in bed. She wasn't sure when he'd left, but a little violet Svakom Echo vibrator and one red rose lay on the pillow beside her. No note. But she knew he was thinking of her.

CHAPTER NINE
CRUISE DAY 3

*B*y the time Kimberlee walked into the cabin, her friends were getting ready for a new adventure; this was a sea day. As much as everyone wanted to hear the delicious details about her adventure, they needed to get breakfast. So an in-depth discussion had to wait until they had their al fresco fruit, yogurt, and freshly scrambled eggs. They found the best place for breakfast was the aft patio outside the buffet. Nothing like eating while watching the wake as the ship plied the glorious blue Caribbean.

Paulette was first out of the cabin and found four invitations in the plastic mail holders beside their stateroom doors. She handed each envelope to the person named on the front. Opening hers first, her face lit up with pleasure. "Listen to this, ladies. We have an invitation for a bridge tour this afternoon at 1500 hours."

Counting on her fingers, Lori translated, "That's three our time."

Shaking her head in wonder, Paulette said, "Wow, most ships rarely give these tours, or if they do, they charge beaucoup bucks. This is because of you, Kimberlee. You've really won the Captain over."

Was it really? Kimberlee wondered. She'd love to think he included them in the tour because of her relationship with him—even if it was forbidden. Smiling to herself, she stood a little straighter with pride for her connection with the Captain. But, she still worried about his job security. Hopefully, the company couldn't be stupid enough to dismiss him because of her. Not far from her consciousness, the fear hovered in the back of her mind. *We need to be more careful. I don't want anything to happen to him.*

Suddenly, a voice penetrated her musing. Ever the organized one, Bonnie said, "This means we need to get back to our room from the pool by two, so we can make ourselves presentable. Let's eat breakfast quickly and get out to the Lido deck. Hopefully, we can find four lounge chairs together. You know how cruise ships have problems with pool chair hogs."

"Especially on sea days, everyone is looking for the perfect spot. We'll be lucky to find even one chair, let alone four together," Lori said.

With bathing suits on and matching cover-ups over, they hurried to breakfast on deck seven—and Kimberlee's abridged description of her evening with the ship's commander. Whether they were hungry or fascinated by her evening's descriptions, they remained quiet, only asking a few questions at the end.

Without embarrassment, a tired, glowing Kimberlee gave them the basic details they longed to hear. Then off the friends went to the pool, where they found four lounge chairs together up on deck nine, overlooking the Lido deck below. Maybe there were more people at the nude pool area than they had expected…which was why they found their sought-for chaises.

Being a sea day, they all had their book or e-reader, plenty of suntan lotion, and wide-brimmed sun hats. While delicious piña coladas were their drink of choice, the women made sure they also drank plenty of water to keep themselves hydrated.

As she knew they would, her friends wore tiny, sparkling, stylishly sexy bikinis. She, however, sunned in her tankini, with a thigh-hiding skirt. *Oh, I'so jealous of them in their bikinis. I wish I was built differently, but I look just like the rest of my family. All of us are constructed like the German farmers we've come from.*

Even with a sexually satiated body, she still considered herself chubbily unattractive—especially when comparing herself to her friends. By now, she should have become used to looking asexually nondescript, but it still hurt.

How she wished the fates had designed her differently. She didn't need to look like a contestant on *America's Next Top Model*, but at least less like a farmhand. With all the choices available to the Captain, she still couldn't understand what he saw in her. The men in her New York world wouldn't waste their time with the likes of her. They had too many gorgeous women to pick from.

In the midst of feeling sorry for herself, she started studying the variety of women around the pool. She realized the loungers contained bodies in every imaginable shape and size. And they all seemed comfortable in their skin. What really surprised her was how most of those sunbathers wore quite skimpy bathing suits, even those with lumpy, bumpy figures. Maybe she'd been living in the Big Apple too long, adapting Madison Avenue's definition of beauty.

Perhaps, she could use the next four days to pump up her self-confidence in who she was in the nontechnical areas of her life. Even after just two nights with Captain Johan, she walked with more pride and assurance. Her friends were right, this cruise had been the best antidote for her feelings of self-defeat. If her firm didn't want her, another one would.

During their restful time in the sun, the gentle rocking of the ship and soft breeze lulled the friends to sleep for short, needed naps. This was the kind of day they had been longing for on their cruise. In a way, she regretted their bridge tour, because she wanted to stay out until the sun sunk into the ocean.

Exactly at noon, the Captain's voice came over the speakers for their midday update. On sea days, he gave a short briefing to passengers and crew about the weather, wind, and cruising speed. Closing her eyes, she let his voice flow through her, igniting memories of their extraordinary nights together. Thankfully, her little skirt hid a spreading dampness between her thighs. She'd thought after being up most of the night making love, she'd be sexed out. But no, just hearing him became almost like having him touch her.

Bonnie had set her smartphone for a two o'clock alarm, making sure they would be on time for their exciting and exclusive bridge tour. Even with their longing for more sunny deck time, everyone still looked forward to seeing the navigational bridge.

Would he be there? By two forty-five, the women were up in the Aphrodite Lounge on deck ten waiting for their tour. With them were seven other people excitedly talking about the coming bridge visit.

The bartender, Terrence from Zimbabwe, handed everyone a flute of champagne along with bite-size canapés on a tray.

"Thank you, Terrence," each woman said, taking their glasses of champagne.

Her friends skipped the canapés, leaving Kimberlee looking longingly at the food. Then with a guilty rush, she grabbed one, swiftly eating it. *Ah, that was delicious. Just what I needed to absorb the alcohol. Maybe just another one wouldn't hurt.* She reached for another treat. They really were quite good, and small so not a lot of calories.

Standing about the same place where they sat the night before, the friends looked out the wall-to-wall window watching the bow of the ship plow through the sea, Bonnie said with a relaxed, dreamy voice, "They certainly know how to get the small things right. This is a lovely way to begin our tour."

"You're right," Paulette responded with a sigh as she took another sip of bubbly. "So often the little things make the difference.

The women quietly discussed how much they liked their little ship, what they were doing for dinner, and their plans for the following day at their second port.

Exactly at three o'clock, the third officer arrived to escort passengers down one flight of stairs to the bridge.

With an equal mixture of curiosity and anticipation, they passed through a door labeled CREW ONLY into the off-limits officers' area. Right outside the bridge, on their right, was a cabin with a brass plate beside the door identifying it as CAPTAIN.

"Oh my," Bonnie said, "I can't believe these two tiny rooms are where the Captain lives. You'd think such an important person would have a super suite with a huge balcony. Instead, he's got a small window and narrow balcony off the bedroom with barely space to move."

"His front room looks more like an office than a sitting room," Lori agreed. "There's nothing but charts, papers, computers, and phones. Nothing personal on the walls or photos on the end tables. That man certainly doesn't have a great living environment."

Whispering in Kimberlee's ear, Paulette said, "No wonder he takes you to the grottos. He can't entertain anyone here. You have no privacy with all the officers outside your door listening."

Kimberlee wanted to sneak in to look around and see, particularly, what his bedroom looked like. Unfortunately, she needed to stay with her group. So she kept walking. *Well, this certainly isn't a place that I would want to live. It's tinier than most New York apartments.* She felt totally defeated realizing that even if she wanted—which she didn't—she couldn't have a home with him on this ship.

Just before entering the bridge, she glanced down the hall to her left. There stood a crew member dressed in a house-keeping uniform, staring back at her. For a brief moment their eyes met and he smiled. Quickly returning his smile, she rushed forward through the bridge door before it shut, locking her out. And then it dawned on her, that man must have been Ramil, the Captain's friend and the officers' room steward. Well, now she knew what he looked like if she needed to find him.

Once on the bridge, everywhere visitors looked they saw either large floor-to-ceiling windows or walls and desks covered by computer monitors of every shape, size, and design.

Even though the MS *Aphrodite* sailed with the most advanced technology—the same on navy warships—the offi-cers also used paper nautical charts, which they maintained by hand as a safety backup.

In a strange way, there was something fascinating, even magical, about the room. All lives depended upon the officers and what they did here. Yet, this room remained a mystery to passengers.

When she heard the word "Captain she immediately began paying attention to the conversation occurring around her. People were talking about the authority of the Captain, the highest-ranking officer and master of the entire ship. She learned not only was the Captain held accountable for the safety and working order of the physical vessel, but also for the welfare of all souls aboard—both passengers and crew.

In addition, the Captain had a responsibility to protect the environment according to corporate policy, local regulations, and international maritime laws. The friends learned how conscientious the crew was for guarding the health of their nautical world.

What a huge responsibility. I can't imagine the education and training he had to go through to perform this job.

All the visitors remained fascinated about their Captain. They wanted to understand the vast and varied duties weighing heavily on his shoulders twenty-four/seven. As Kimberlee listened in awe at Captain Johan's job responsibilities, she began realizing there was no other job like his in the corporate world...even an airline pilot didn't have twenty-four-hour accountability for the plane or 700 people, let alone 9,000 souls found on the mega ships.

How did he manage living with all these obligations day and night for months on end? The ship was his only world. He'd never have time for anyone else in his life. His first love was this ship. She was nothing more than a blip on one of his many radar screens.

A blip that had only four more days.

What people spent the most time discussing was how cruise ship Captains needed extraordinary leadership skills in a multicultural environment under extremely stressful conditions. The visitors expressed surprise at how someone with maritime engineering and technical training could also have the sophisticated people skills necessary to deal with conflict management, irate passengers, people rude or abusive to crew members, and other passengers. Plus, he dealt with the emotional breakdowns which came with cramped living conditions. Of course, he also had to handle marital conflicts and drunken, stupid behaviors.

"Why would anyone want this job?" Lori murmured to her friends. "The pay isn't great, and he spends his time kowtowing to passengers who feel they own the ship because they paid for a cramped cabin."

As the group continued on their tour, they learned how the ship had cameras everywhere, even where eyes couldn't see. At any time, the officers could select what they wanted to view on the multiple TV screens attached to the back walls. "Hopefully, we don't have cameras in our cabin," Bonnie whispered. "Given what we're doing tonight, I don't want all these young, delightful men watching us."

When the three women smiled in agreement, Kimberlee narrowed her eyes, tilting her head to the side, trying to figure out what everyone was talking about. Obviously, people had plans she wasn't aware of.

As the tour came to an end, Kimberlee felt disappointed the Captain hadn't joined them. She'd kept listening for his delightful voice, quickly looking over her shoulder when she heard accented English. But it never was him. How she wanted to see him in his command center. *Power is so sexy,* she sighed inwardly. *Especially if that power comes packaged in a delicious white uniform with a sexy body and magical hands and mouth.*

The four women exited the bridge with their group.

Paulette and Lori each took one of Kimberlee's arms, quickly leading her back to their cabin.

"Hey, wait a minute," she complained. "What's all the rush to get back to the cabin? I thought we could get our evening cocktail upstairs in the lounge."

Without saying a word, her friends just kept her moving down the halls to their room. Once inside, they quickly bolted the door.

CHAPTER TEN

As soon as the cabin door locked behind them, Kimberlee's friends pushed her onto the love seat. With a smile lighting up her face, Bonnie whipped out a box she'd hidden under the bed and handed it to her confused friend.

No one said a word. They just watched her as she took the carton.

Still not understanding what was happening, Kimberlee opened the gift only to find inside a 10.7-inch realistic, silicone dildo.

"What the hell is this?" she demanded in a voice filled with disbelief. "I don't need this thing." Implying that she had the Captain to do a better job. Sitting there, she glared at her friends with a mutinous, tight-lipped expression.

"No, Kimberlee, don't be silly. This isn't for you to masturbate with. You have your new Magic Wand that works much better. This is for you to learn how to give him a blow job," Lori replied quickly trying to defuse a developing crisis.

Lori continued in a soothing voice she used to calm difficult situations, "We're just trying to help you. We aren't making fun of you. Just the opposite. We want you to have a wonderful time with the Captain…and we want you to feel confident when you're with him. Plus, you know, assurance in one area does generalize into others."

"Besides," Paulette chimed in, "we want you to shine the next time the two of you are together."

Kimberlee sat deep in thought, looking straight ahead without focusing on anything. The other women sat motionless, waiting to see what she had to say.

Slowly she said, "All right, I'll agree sucking cock isn't one of my talents. You know I'm not well versed in most aspects of sex. Blow jobs have never been something I needed to know, because up until now my limited sexual experience has been quickies. So yes, I could use a few pointers."

"That's my girl," Bonnie said, giving her another bright smile with a hug.

Kimberly held up her gift, turning it in different directions, inspecting it. Sensually stroking it as she contemplated how little she really knew about what to do with a penis. She wrapped her fist around it, experiencing what it felt like jacking it off. *It feels almost natural.*

Everyone sat there mesmerized, watching her hand pump up and down. Giving it a soft squeeze. Using her forefinger to play with the little eye at the tip.

Releasing a deep breath, she didn't know she'd been holding, she looked up at her friends with laughter-filled eyes. "It feels almost real, but it looks like it belongs to a *Star Wars* giant from a different solar system. Thank heaven men don't walk around with something like this weighing down their pants."

Choking back their amusement, her companions nodded. "Glad that crisis was averted," Lori said.

"Yep, looks like we have an eager student," Paulette agreed.

Contemplating the massive dildo in her hand, Kimberlee realized she would enjoy the power that came from knowing skillful cock-sucking techniques. Plus, this was valuable knowledge she could use once she left the ship. She might as well apply the same brainpower on blow jobs that she gave to analyzing mergers and acquisitions. In fact, sucking cock should be a lot simpler than investigating the financials of a company.

Before they could begin their tutorial, Kimberlee waved her new toy in the air. "Does it have to be this big? His certainly isn't."

"Are you telling us he's got a small dick?" Lori asked with a shocked voice.

"No. Don't tell us he's got a teeny weenie," Paulette responded in an uncertain tone with confusion clearly written on her face.

Kimberlee quickly corrected their confusion. "It isn't small for me. In fact, it seemed big until I saw this one."

Trying to reduce her friend's confusion, Bonnie clarified saying, "We got you this big one to practice on, so when you're faced with the real thing, it won't be intimidating. In fact, his cock would seem small to you and easier for you to work on."

Paulette added, "Just make sure you don't make a slip and call the Captain's a teeny weenie in comparison to this one."

All of them broke out laughing imagining his face if Kimberlee made that verbal comment to him.

"If you ever say that," quipped Lori, "I want to be there to watch his expression. Now that would be priceless."

As their mirth died down, Doctor Bonnie jumped in, wanting to provide factual, anatomical information. "Don't worry, men aren't built like this silicone monster. In fact, women don't use giants like this unless they're in porno films made for men's sexual entertainment. Men think this is what we want, a gigantic cock shoved up our pussy, but that comes from their own fantasies."

"Some men want to believe that women get off on gigantic cocks, when our greatest pleasure mainly comes from our clitoris. As you've been finding out," Lori added.

Paulette pointed out, "I really don't know any woman who would use something like this. I certainly wouldn't."

Digesting this new information, Kimberly's body began tingling in anticipation of her coming lesson and how she would apply it. She flashed her friends a big smile. "OK, let's get on with this," she said. "I have a performance to give tonight."

Once again, Bonnie took over giving basic information on penis, balls, and other parts of the male anatomy, answering all her friend's questions with factual, medical school descriptions.

Kimberlee listened intently, realizing no one had ever given her a detailed lesson in male sexual anatomy before. Sex ed in school only focused on the basic male equipment and operations, nothing that would have been useful in real life. And because she didn't study sex sites, she missed out on valuable information.

Starting with the head of the dildo, Kimberlee practiced sucking, licking, nibbling as her friends cheered her on.

"You know ladies," she said in between a mouthful of dildo, "there's no feedback. This thing is lifeless. I don't know when I should do more of something or less. I guess I need to spend just as much time watching his reactions as I do focusing on my techniques."

Everyone nodded. When she got through with the captain, he'd be enthralled to her, his defenses in tatters.

"You go, girl," Lori said, cheering her on.

Paulette, who remained focused on technique, used a moment of silence to suggest a delightful addition—to blow over his wet cock head.

With that suggestion, Kimberlee licked her hand then blew on the damp spot delighting in how tingly it felt. "Boy, does that feel great. Maybe he could do that to me."

"If he doesn't already know it, he will after you do it to him. I'm sure the captain is a fast learner," said Lori. "An ice cube in your mouth will add a boost of excitement."

"Or," Bonnie chimed in, "a hot washcloth would take everything to a whole new level.

As suggestions kept flowing, they discovered that each of them learned something new from the others. While this educational demonstration was for Kimberlee, everyone benefited.

By the time for dinner, Kimberlee felt quite pleased with herself and confident that she could give the Captain the blow job of a lifetime. *Maybe we should just skip dinner and go for the sex.*

This evening they were dining in the small Italian restaurant, Casa Dei Piaceri—House of Pleasures—on deck eight across from the Rose Buffet. They heard from other guests how good the food was and wanted to give it a try. Of course, coming from The Big Apple, they knew what great Italian food was, so they looked forward to tasting what the ship offered.

LATER THAT NIGHT THE WOMEN LEFT THE RESTAURANT AFTER a delicious Italian dinner and much discussion about sex, sex, and more sex. They found the Captain in the atrium waiting for them. He had an easygoing and relaxed manner—exhibiting natural, bone-deep confidence that came from commanding a ship. After the bridge tour the friends now understood the massive demands he confronted day and night…and how his self-assurance came from facing and being triumphant over never-ending natural and human storms.

They were, however, surprised to see him, because he had neither invited Kimberlee for an after-dinner drink nor had he asked them where they were having dinner.

"Good evening, Captain," they all said in unison.

"How was your dinner?" the smiling Captain asked, who only had eyes for Kimberlee.

Paulette answered for them. "We were pleasantly surprised. While it wouldn't pass for fine dining in New York, it was equal to our favorite neighborhood trattoria."

Seeing a shadow replace his warm welcome, Kimberlee realized they had inadvertently insulted him by saying his ship's best restaurant wasn't up to their fancy New York standards.

Before she could fix the situation, Bonnie spoke up trying to soften the comparison. "Of course, our wine this evening was excellent. We had a wonderful Amarone."

Kimberlee took a deep relaxing breath, glad that Bonnie changed the topic for them. She quickly asked, "How did you know we were having dinner here?"

"Cruise ships have some of the most sophisticated computer systems. We need to know where passengers are at any time. I looked up your name and it listed what restaurant and when you were dining."

As if Paulette realized she may have been too harsh about the specialty dining room, she quickly spoke up, "Thank you for our bridge tour. I found it fascinating. It's something passengers should take at least once to understand the magnitude of what's required in people and technology for a cruise vacation. I know I took all of this for granted."

Three other voices quickly said, "Yes, thank you."

But Kimberlee was the only person he continued watching.

In a momentary conversation lull, his wonderful voice filled the silence, asking, "Kimberlee, will you have a drink with me?"

"Yes. Thank you." *I thought you'd never ask.*

"Is deck five aft, OK?"

"Yes. I prefer sitting out there. I think it's one of my favorite spots on the ship."

With a smile that brought back the twinkle to his smoky-blue eyes, he looked at the other women. "I hope you ladies have a fun evening. As you've probably discovered, there's a lot to do on this ship."

With a nod, he turned toward the stern with Kimberlee beside him.

CHAPTER ELEVEN

*A*s the two walked up one flight of stairs empty of passengers, the Captain remained silent and an enthusiastic Kimberlee kept up the conversation. "I loved the bridged tour. I had no idea what it took to navigate a cruise ship. And we only saw the tip of the iceberg. Thank you."

She saw the corners of his mouth turn up slightly, telling her he valued her comments. In response he said, "I'm glad the timing worked for you to join the tour. This was for our top loyalty program passengers. Luckily, we had spaces open."

FOR THE FIRST TIME IN YEARS, THE CAPTAIN FELT AT A LOSS for words. He was amazed by her display of self-confidence and enthusiasm. Where had this come from?

Watching her like he would the sea—the currents, the swells, the winds, and the effects on his ship—he began feeling adrift in unknown territory. He found the new, bubbly Kimberlee both exciting and baffling.

Looking into her shining eyes, he was about to ask how her day had been, when she beat him to it. "How was your sea day?"

Without waiting for an answer, she continued, "I missed not seeing you on the bridge. I thought the captain would have given the tour. Personally, hearing you talk about your job would have added an extra layer of information and depth."

He almost didn't answer, being lost in the depths of her laughing brown eyes.

Quickly recouping, he replied, "When captains lead the bridge tour, passengers want to spend hours asking questions about the ship and our personal lives. It's much easier having one of the newer officers take over. It also gives them practice talking with passengers, plus nobody wants to overstay their visit with a junior officer."

Nodding, she added, "You also get an hour for yourself."

By now, they were sitting at their special table on the aft deck five. He even had their drinks waiting in front of each chair. This way, they didn't have to stop at the bar, but could head directly to the privacy outside.

"Well, not really," he replied. "I had paperwork backing up. I had to get rid of the growing mountain."

Even engaged in this innocuous conversation, he enjoyed observing her natural sparkle and lively spirit. Shifting in his chair to make room for an expanding cock, he reached out to caress her smile-filled face.

She tilted her head as if wanting to feel his entire hand cupping her cheek. Then, she reached up to hold his hand in place. They sat that way in comfortable silence, enjoying a natural intimacy.

He loved the softness of her cheek. The feel of her silky

skin, like the feel of her pussy. If he kept thinking this way, he'd never be able to leave the table.

Hating to break the spell linking them, he knew they needed to talk about their evening. "What would you like to do tonight?" he asked with an intimate, passion-roughened voice.

"I'd like to give you a blow job."

Sucking in a quick breath, he barely got out, "Excuse me. Did you say…blow job?"

"Yes," Kimberlee replied, with a glowing smile of satisfaction filling her face.

Frozen in place, he just stared at her in shocked silence. *Oh God, I can't take this. I'm going to explode right here. And where did this new woman come from?*

"If I might ask, what made you interested in blow jobs?"

To answer his question, she launched into a description of how her friends gave her a 10.7-inch dildo to practice on and how they schooled her in what to do with it. And after practicing on something so large, he'd seem small in comparison.

"Does that mean…you find me…small?" he asked.

"Oh, no. It means I won't find you intimidating. You definitely don't have a teeny weeny."

"Excuse me. Did you just say teeny weeny?" *For heaven's sake, stop repeating what she said. You sound like a fool.*

"I didn't mean to. It's just an expression that Paulette said jokingly. She wasn't talking about you. Just that you won't be as big as the dildo, so it would be easier for me to suck you after practicing on it. She certainly wouldn't know how you're built."

Stunned, he sat a moment digesting what she had just said. The evening wasn't progressing the way he had envisioned. He hated surprises. That's why he kept informed on the latest weather information and forecasts. He needed to prepare his officers, ship, passengers, and himself for anticipating and responding to the unexpected.

Except, at this moment, he found himself unprepared for dealing with the spirited woman sitting across from him. With only four days left, he needed to be at his peak performance, making every moment count.

Stalling for time, he refocused the conversation from having his cock sucked to something more controllable. "Have you been to a Chippendales show before?" he managed to sputter.

She shook her head. "No, but I've wanted to."

"Perfect. The show begins in ten minutes. Let's go see it." Finally, he was regaining a modicum of composure.

"You don't want me to suck your cock?" she asked in an innocent voice.

"For God's sakes, Kimberlee. I'm only a man. If you keep it up, I'll fuck you over this table. I only have so much self-control. And now it's demolished."

Giving him another cheery smile, she said, "Well then, tell me about the show. I can give you a blow job afterward."

"You're baiting me. Be careful. You might end up with an unexpected catch you can't control," he said, eyes boring into hers. He'd finally given up keeping his dick under control. All he could do was keep himself from constantly shifting in his chair. He'd never find a comfortable position.

"Well, is it working?" she asked, taking a long sip of her drink, then licking her lips with her tongue.

"Yes." Skipping a beat, he added with a warning in his voice, "Do you want to see the show?" A part of him hoped she'd say no.

"Yes, I do. We do have all night." Then she said, "Providing, you don't require a lot of sleep."

"I can manage. Thank you. First, I need to explain the show to you. It's not like the big Vegas reviews, but more like the original smaller strip shows. The women love them and because we're in international waters, there's no need for the men to cover their private parts with a hat."

Her eyes lit up showing immediate interest. Laughing, he said, "There will be plenty of penises for you to check out." And then he observed her face flush with embarrassment, as if he'd read her thoughts.

"Do you also have women performing?" she inquired, changing the conversation.

"Yes. We alternate evenings between shows by men and by women. Though, everyone seems to go to both. And then at eleven, we have the passengers perform BDSM scenes that everyone can watch. The theater fills up quickly with this program."

He said the last bit carefully watching her response. He saw her shoulders slightly tighten and her eyes look down at the table. *Ah, she's not as liberated as she thinks she is. And how she wants me to think she is.*

Picking up her drink. she replied with a pseudo-confident voice. "Then let's go to my first strip show." She never mentioned the BDSM performances.

Smiling to himself, he nodded, keeping his expression neutral. There was still much for her to experience. And for him to show. He looked forward to taking her to places she'd never go on her own. Maybe experiences she'd never even thought of doing.

Standing up, he offered her his hand. Even though she grasped it naturally, she still wouldn't meet his eyes.

The tension flowed out his body. He experienced relief being back in control. Looking forward to the evening, he planned to see how far he could push her.

They walked up the one flight of stairs to the intimate theater. This time her bubbling enthusiasm sounded more forced—which added a lightness to his steps. He detested being off-balanced. And now knowing her confidence was only superficial, he could relax and enjoy the rest of the evening.

Reaching into the pocket of his black jeans, he felt his mini, finger Fukuoka vibrator, which Ramil picked up for him. It would be easy to reach when the time was right.

Entering the Dolphin Salon, Kimberlee savored the warmth of his hand on her lower back as he guided her to a love seat against the back wall, in a dark, far corner of the theater. Taking her seat, she said, "I'm glad you've found us a private place. I was worried about being in a public setting together."

"I personally asked for Belmiro to serve cocktails this evening. While I don't have the same relationship with him as I do with Ramil, I've grown to trust him these past two years."

Looking around, she observed many of the seats were already filled with both couples and small groups of either women or men. Obviously, these shows were well attended.

With a quiet sigh, she released the tension locked in her body, which she unconsciously held after he mentioned the BDSM show. Even if she couldn't give her blow job performance, she loved the natural ease they felt in each other's company.

But right now, she planned to enjoy her first strip show. And, of course, the delicious man who escorted her.

She liked the small, intimate feel of the theater. Understandably, there wasn't the stage space for a Vegas-style review. As she was thinking about the design of the theater, the already dimmed lights reduced to a soft safety level—leaving their corner in deep darkness.

Recorded music filled the hall. On the low stage, five gorgeously built young men strutted out wearing the traditional Chippendales white collar with a black bowtie, white cuffs, and tight jeans that looked painted on.

How will they ever move in those?

Obviously, they had no trouble showing off their dazzling dancing skills. These were Broadway-trained entertainers and fanatical bodybuilders. "Oh," she sighed, "they really are glorious men. What fabulous bodies they have." Though she hoped he didn't think she preferred those kinds of men over him.

At the end of the song, the eye candy left the stage. After a quick change, one glorious young man returned dressed as a fireman for his striptease performance. About halfway through his number, Kimberlee was clapping and hooting with the rest of the audience.

CAPTAIN JOHAN ENJOYED WATCHING HER PLEASURE AS Kimberlee stared mesmerized by the gyrating, uniform stripping, billboard-perfect fireman. Leaning back in the love seat with a slight smile, he observed her more than the action on stage. Her uninhibited joy and spontaneous laughter bewitched him, intensifying the throbbing in his ever-ready cock.

He wasn't sure how long he'd last in this show. Already his fantasies began creating scenes for when they were alone. So many things he wanted to do, but he knew she wasn't ready…yet.

Her alluring mix of innocence and uninhibited freedom

spoke to him in a way no woman had before or after Eira. It was almost as if his wife was—not fading—but making space for another. Before he could pursue that thought, the next entertainer strutted on stage.

Dressed as a cowboy, he showed off his athletic dance, and gymnastic prowess in a cowboy hat, chaps, cowboy boots, fringed vest, and fringed jockstrap.

Just at that moment, a memory of Eira reduced his throbbing hard-on. At least, he could now enjoy the show without a painful dick demanding to burst through his jeans.

In the middle of the energetic performance, the Captain noticed Kimberlee had become totally enthralled with the stripping, half-naked wrangler and had forgotten about him, even though he sat beside her.

Feeling left out, he leaned over, whispering in her ear that she should come and sit between his legs. Without hesitation, she positioned herself between his open thighs. Just before she sat down, he pulled up her halter-dress so that her black lacy panties were on the love seat, with her dress bunched up behind her.

Even though they sat in the darkest corner of the theater, he still made sure the rest of the dress covered her. He wanted to lift her legs over his thighs as he did the first night, but needed to protect both of them.

Still, he had her where he wanted—open and exposed to his exploring, experienced fingers.

Watching the arousing cowboy strip show, he held her tightly against his chest with one arm, while running his free hand up and down her sensitive inner thighs under the shelter of her clothing. Then, he slipped his hand under her barely-there panties to explore her wet pussy with a single-mindedness to make her even more aroused until all she wanted was him—forgetting the titillating performance.

He sensed her trust and surrender when she collapsed against him, resting her head on his shoulder, giving her body totally to his demands. Watching her eyelids lower halfway, he knew she continued watching the titillating show, even when moaning her pleasure. He savored the way her body naturally drew his fingers deeper into her needy, soaked core.

Watching her struggle to reach her orgasm, he decided she could use a little extra aid. He reached into his pants pocket to retrieve his tiny finger vibrator. While the fingertip massager needed to be used with other stimulation, it still provided a gentle, soft buzz that added that extra sensation she needed.

Between his mouth softy biting her neck and fingers fucking her, the Fukuoku quickly did its job. Within seconds, he could feel Kimberlee's body shudder as an orgasm seized her, waves of pleasure surging through her.

He could tell she no longer cared what happened on stage or around her as she arched back into his arms, giving him total control over her. The music of the show drowned out her groans, allowing him the freedom to push her beyond a life-time of rigid self-control.

She was so gorgeous as she shuddered, slicking his fingers with her love juices. While he wanted to lick his fingers, he didn't want to stop pushing her. There would be time enough the rest of the night to suck and taste her.

As Kimberlee collapsed against him, he felt her powerless to resist the force of his hands and mouth. He could tell her entire world constricted into a single point of need—for him and the extraordinary ecstasy he gave her.

How he thrilled holding her in his arms, feeling her body uninhibitedly climax and freely letting him explore her. She'd never know how much he needed her—how long he had waited to cradle a passionate woman against his sex-starved body.

. . .

UNAWARE OF ANYTHING BUT HIS HANDS AND MOUTH, Kimberlee solely focused on her own ecstasy—letting waves of rapture surge through her. Leaning against him, she could feel his steel-hard erection press into her butt crack. Even that simple stimulation aroused her to wanting more of what he could give her.

If I'd only known how glorious sex could be, I'd have been on this ship years ago.

Time lost all meaning. She didn't care what happened on stage, or the rest of the world. Nothing mattered, but the feel of him dominating her every sensation with his powerful body. His demanding hands became slippery, coated with her pussy juice. Sweat slicked her skin making her want to strip off her dress, but couldn't…not yet, not here.

She knew on some deep molecular level, after the last three nights, her life had irrevocably changed. She'd never be the same—but didn't know who she'd become. Somehow, she would find a way to live without her Captain. Maybe, she'd have to learn to live with inadequate sex—no sex would be better than shoddy, inferior sex.

THERE WAS NO WAY HE COULD LAST THE ENTIRE SHOW. He needed to get them out and into their grotto. Now.

Unfortunately, she was in no shape to walk on her own. So, he'd have to chance taking her downstairs himself.

While a naked cowboy performed on stage in only boots, chaps, and a hat, Johan told Kimberlee they were leaving. Waiting longer enough for her nod, he straightened her clothes and managed to get her up on shaky legs. Just then, the theater went dark between sets, allowing them to slip out unnoticed.

After all her climaxes, he knew she'd have difficulty walking down three flights of stairs. Hopefully they wouldn't meet anyone in the elevator. Thankfully, the sea gods granted his wish.

They'd barely walked into their grotto, when he pushed her against the closing door with the force of his body. Trapping her there.

Bringing her arms above her head, he pinned her hands against the shut entryway. He bent his head, whispering in her ear, "This is what happens when you play with fire."

Continuing, he told her what he wanted. After stripping off every fiber of clothing, he wanted her kneeling on the edge of the bed with her ass in the air and her pussy open to him. He wanted her knees wide apart and head buried in the covers.

Looking into her passion-glazed eyes, he asked, "Do you understand?" She nodded.

"No. I want to hear you answer me."

"Yes."

"Not good enough. Try again."

"Yes, I understand you want me doggy style on the side of the bed."

"Still not good enough."

"You want me doggy style with my ass in the air and my pussy wide open for you."

"Good girl. Let's get you stripped," he said, removing her clothes. Quickly the black lacy underthings lay on the floor with her dress.

"Now, what are you supposed to do?" he commanded in a flat voice, cool and controlled in its authority.

Without looking at him, she walked the few steps to the

bed. Kneeling on the edge, she stuck her face in the mattress, shoving her ass up.

Standing directly behind her, he used his hand, pressing down her back so her bottom jutted higher. He then applied both hands, pushing her knees wider, until he saw her spread open just as he wanted.

Her bright pink, swollen folds lay exposed and open for him, with nectar glistening. Begging him to fuck her.

He barely had time to get his pants unzipped and his cock in hand before he thrust into her hot, wetness. "Herregud, you are magnificent," he growled in a choked voice.

Forcing his body back under control, he took deep breaths, slowly releasing the air. She might be ready for him, but he had one more part of her body to explore before he shot his wad. After sucking on his index finger to lubricate it, he spread her butt cheeks, revealing her tight, virgin asshole. It was his for the taking.

By her strangled moan, he knew she understood what was happening...and she didn't use her safe word. Taking his moist finger, he rubbed the fluid around her clenched sphincter, watching it slightly relax with his stimulation. Using a bit more pressure, he pushed forward, rotating to relax her. Then, with more insistence, his finger popped through the barrier. Sinking deeper, he circled his digit, watching as her hole loosen even more for him.

By now, her groans filled the room. As he began fucking her with both finger and cock, her hips rocked back and forth, as if begging for more. With her face hidden in the covers, she cried out as pleasure escalated. Reaching around, he rubbed her clit. Just touching it made his dick lengthen and thicken. His sensitivity intensified until his balls squeezed and he became lost beyond stopping. An electric current shot up his spine, his gut muscles shook with contractions and the world went blank. Cum exploded into her.

Within seconds, his arms and legs went limp. Feeling light-headed, he collapsed on top of her with a groan. Too wiped out to move, he lay there. Slowly, his penis shrunk and slipped out. All he wanted was sleep…with her in his arms.

CHAPTER TWELVE
CRUISE DAY 4

Mmm, you smell so good. Kimberlee burrowed her nose deeper into the pillow Captain Johan had slept on the previous night. Except, as she began waking up, she realized he was gone and once again she was alone in their grotto. Except for one red rose on the pillow.

She figured he left for the bridge sometime during the early morning. He always made sure he was there an hour or more before the ship docked. Today they were docking in Costa Maya at 7:00 a.m.

While she missed his warm and vibrant presence, she also relished the privacy to relive the amazing evening. With a lazy morning-after stretch, she recalled the sexually extravagant evening at the Chippendales show. How could one man know so much about a woman's body—her body to be exact? He had shown her not all men were inept lovers, but then her sample hadn't been large.

Then there was the issue of how could she abandon all caution and dignity to a man she'd only known for a few days? A man who really didn't want to be with her because of his professional responsibilities and cruise ship ethics. Also, his dead wife still controlled his heart—leaving no room for her.

Suddenly, images of their time in the grotto slammed into her thoughts. Her face became hot as she remembered what they did. Or rather, what he did to her.

"Oh my God, no," she said out loud as she buried her head under the pillow. She didn't want to think about it. But all the hiding in the world couldn't change what had happened. She got what she wanted, but it wasn't what she expected.

She'd fantasized about wild, uninhibited, fabulous sex. Obviously, she wasn't as free and brave as she thought she was.

Even though her parents had taught all sex was acceptable between consenting adults, she'd just discovered some things were more acceptable than others. But not so unacceptable she needed her safe word.

For her, anal sex had existed in the not-OK pile. Now, she wasn't so sure anymore. *Of course, it had to be with the right person.*

Obviously, it was natural for him. And if she were honest with herself, the whole experience took sex to an entirely new level.

No one warned her how sensitive the anus was. They certainly didn't teach that in sex education.

The problem she faced was even if she'd wanted to stop him, she couldn't have because she'd lost all coherent thinking. By the time she'd left the theater, she had no will, but sex —wanting to drown in sex. It was as if her rational brain had shut down, hijacked by the rampant needs of her body. Sometime during the show, she'd crossed some kind of line where only pleasure existed.

Truthfully, she'd become like the white rats she'd learned

about in University of Iowa's Psych 101. With electrodes implanted in their tiny brains' pleasure centers, they became addicted to pressing a bar, which electrically stimulated their cortical reward circuits. They would keep slamming down the lever rather than drink water or eat their favorite rodent food. They pressed until they lay exhausted on the bottom of their cage, unable to lift a paw or twitch a whisker, but still tried to reach that bar. They would die before giving up their source of pleasure.

Well, she knew how those little creatures felt. In her own way, she'd tumbled to the bottom of her Captain's cage. *Forget food, just give me his hands, mouth, and cock. I'll die blissful.*

OK, she and white rats developed into far different species, but their limbic brains did have some similar designs. While she lacked whiskers and a long tail, she did have a neuro-pleasure center producing dopamine. This neurotransmitter kept her craving the Captain, like the white rats endlessly pushing their bar.

Thankfully, with distance from him and needed sleep, her control had returned. She could finally pick herself up from the bottom of the pleasure cage. First, she required nourishment. Starving to death wasn't in her travel plans.

Now, it was time to get up and head for her cabin. "Oh shit, what time is it?" she said to herself as she searched for her watch. "Oh God, no! It's seven oh five and my friends are probably waiting for me." The group had a beautiful day of snorkeling in front of them. Quickly throwing on clothes, she headed back to her cabin.

As she walked-ran to her room, an amazingly sexy, but impersonal voice came over the ship's sound system. She stopped abruptly to listen to his morning announcement, relishing the sound of his speech. Just remembering the erotic, passionate words he whispered all evening blasted fierce lust through her body. And her newly discovered body part.

Don't you dare let yourself tumble back to the bottom. Your brain's bigger than those in the little white rats. You can make it until tonight.

"Good morning, ladies and gentlemen. This is your Captain from the bridge. We docked in Costa Maya this morning at six forty-five and have completed customs. You can now go ashore. You have a great day for your excursions and shopping. A perfect temperature for all your beach activities. We depart at 1800 hours or six this evening. Please remember we must leave on time. Have a wonderful and safe day in sunny Costa Maya."

When she opened the door to her cabin, just as she expected, her friends sat inside, waiting for her with poorly concealed excitement. She sighed, knowing they'd demand full details. One in particular which she wasn't ready to reveal. Maybe it was her traditional, Methodist upbringing, but some things she'd rather keep to herself right now.

In a false, upbeat voice she said, "Good morning, everyone. Sorry I'm a little late. Let me quickly change and we can go to breakfast."

They just sat there staring at her. No one moved.

"OK, what do you want to know?"

"How did you like the Chippendales show?" Bonnie asked.

"How did you... Oh my God, you were there!"

Paulette replied, "I saw you just by accident. You were well hidden in a dark corner."

"You were spying on me," Kimberlee wailed.

"No," Lori said. "We weren't spying on you. You and the Captain were well concealed in the back of the room."

"It was just by chance I saw you," responded Bonnie with her soft, calming voice that usually worked with upset patients. "We were sitting in the center when I turned around to see how many people were in the audience. That's when I happened to notice you off in the back, dark corner. We weren't looking for you. You know how much we care for you and would never do anything to harm you.

"In fact, when we realized it was you, we immediately looked away to give you privacy."

Doctor Bonnie brought some calm to the volatile situation. Somewhere in her emotional distress, Kimberlee knew her friends wanted only what would make her happy—the way loving sisters would. Holding that thought, she took a deep, soothing breath. Then a second. And a third. She acknowledged to herself that her friends wouldn't have spied on her. With a few more inhalations, she finally sat down on her still-made bed.

Looking down at her tightly gripped hands in her lap, she said, "Well, I guess there's nothing more for me to say."

Without looking up, she felt the bed shift with another person sitting down beside her. Lori put a caring arm around her. Lori had a huge, loving heart hidden under all her technical know-how. Few people ever saw it, but she knew Lori would do anything to help any one of them.

With a sigh she released her stress, resting her head on Lori's shoulder. *This is what friends are for.*

The tension permeating their cabin evaporated as the women reaffirmed their deep bond for each other. Once again in sync, they quietly talked while Kimberlee jumped into her bathing suit and cover-up for their fun-filled day. Within a few minutes, they walked out the door for breakfast and their big adventure snorkeling in the glorious Caribbean Sea.

While eating breakfast at their favorite al fresco spot, the three friends listened to Kimberlee explain how she never got the chance to apply her newly learned blow job skills. Instead, she gave them a radically shortened and censored version of the evening. She appreciated that as much as they wanted the details, no one asked.

With breakfast and conversation completed, they were ready to meet their snorkel guide.

Lori researched the perfect excursion. Nobody wanted to be crammed on a catamaran with a bunch of loud, partying passengers, which meant they needed their own boat and guide. They wanted to bring a picnic lunch provided by the ship, but local law wouldn't allow food from the ship on shore. So, they'd find another way to obtain nourishment.

Walking down the gangway, they discussed their options for a late lunch after snorkeling. They could have their guide recommend a place to buy a picnic lunch, stop at a small or local café, or grab a bite back on the ship.

The day was theirs to decide what they would do—a luxury that rarely existed back home.

THE PASSENGERS MAY HAVE HAD A PLAYDAY, BUT CAPTAIN Johan had a workday. For all sailors, there was no greater safety concern at sea than fire—which could have catastrophic consequences on a ship. To protect his passengers, crew, and vessel, the Captain made sure all personnel focused on the three p's—prevention, preparation, and practice.

Today, while passengers enjoyed themselves in sunny Costa Maya, he held the crew's twice-a-month fire drill. This meant when the fire alarm sounded, each crew member went to their assigned station. Some people actually donned fire-protection suits and handled fire hoses and extinguishers. Elevators stopped and fire doors slammed shut.

The officers on the bridge observed the monitors, making sure all fire doors were fully closed and all personnel were in their designated places. The entire drill lasted thirty minutes, allowing the crew to return to their regular duties, take needed time off to sleep, or to spend time on shore.

For Johan, he took his limited free time leaning on the veranda railing outside his cabin thinking about the hostile takeover his brother was fighting...and Kimberlee.

The messages coming from corporate explained how their self-protection strategies were winning. They had the financial wherewithal to fight this battle. If he could, he'd destroy those bastards, but that wasn't his job. He'd leave the fight for their legal team. Even so, some of his suppressed rage began seeping out. *God, it hurts how a greedy corporation wants to destroy our ship. For them it's money. For us, it's our lives.*

But Kimberlee presented a totally new issue for him. What did he want from the relationship? No matter how he analyzed it, he could find no comfortable answer. Realistically, he should end it now. But time with her brought him pleasure beyond belief. Guilty pleasure, but awe-inspiring pleasure nevertheless.

Just thinking about their last three nights together, he felt a craving churning deep in his groin. Hunger for her made him silently groan. He relished how each time they were together she gave him her body with complete abandonment. How last night in the theater, her drenched pussy gripped and rippled around his fingers as he kept thrusting in and out of her...how he wrung nonstop orgasms from her sweat-glistening body, never letting her rest.

Then there was their time in the grotto. Had he moved too

fast? Did he push her too hard? How was she feeling this morning? Unfortunately, he couldn't have been with her when she woke up, observing how she was. Or being available for them to talk. He'd learned from Eira how women needed the emotional and mental lovemaking of intimate conversation, along with the physical closeness. Frustratingly, he wasn't able to give her that.

Eira. He wasn't ready to let her go. Probably ever. And he only had a few days left with Kimberlee.

Even as great as the sex was, he also relished sleeping with her. How he enjoyed the feel of her trustingly curled up in his arms. For ten long years, his bed had remained empty and cold, with this morning the first time his hard-on wasn't for pissing. It was for her.

With that last thought, he softly moaned. He wanted her now. He wanted his face buried in her pussy. Torment in his crotch swept upward, filling his body with overwhelming need. His enormous and sensitive cock took on a life of its own—demanding attention.

I've got to stop thinking about her... But then his mind returned to her, like sunflowers naturally turning to face the sun. Where was she now? What was she doing? Was she thinking about their time together?

What should he do tonight?

CHAPTER THIRTEEN

*D*own at the pier, an eager Kimberlee awaited her first snorkeling venture. Unlike her friends, who chattered about their expectations, she observed the action unfolding with a quiet curiosity. Everything was so new—not just this excursion, but her entire vacation. Of course, being with the Captain topped the list of novel experiences. And after last night, even her body felt different, almost like it belonged to someone else. If she could, she'd have stayed on board analyzing the unanticipated, crazy turn her world had taken. Feeling like Alice falling down the rabbit hole, she needed time digesting the bizarre adventures turning her well-planned and controlled life upside down.

Reaching up to play with her earring, she found an empty earlobe. Just to be safe, no one wore jewelry on this day trip. Instead, she fiddled with her newly bought gear. Originally, she wanted a full-face mask, but decided on the traditional, separate mask and snorkel. Even as a snorkeling newbie, she wanted to feel a part of the ocean, not have her entire face locked behind a cover. She'd long dreamt of learning to scuba dive, making this excursion the first step on that road.

Wearing her fifty plus UV long-sleeve swim shirt, she received instructions on how to use the new equipment, including spitting into the mask, then rinsing it in the sea to prevent fogging. Finally, with everyone strapped into their life vests, it was time to board their tour boat. Of course, this was also her first boating trip, except for a rowboat on a small lake.

Yet, all wasn't right in paradise. The sensual beauty of the Caribbean kept her newly awakened, passionate body in a state of arousal. Rather than drawing her thoughts to the here and now, the physical and sensory exquisiteness of the aqua-blue sea, the tropical humidity, and the caressing breeze heightened her craving for *him*. The surrounding environment had trapped her in a vortex of lustful greed and need.

Even if she couldn't control her body, she'd damn well manage what her mind focused on. With determination, she forced her thoughts onto their coming adventure. She wasn't going to let *him* highjack her day with friends.

Lori had thoroughly planned this excursion for them. She found a highly recommended guide who led small, private dive groups but would also take snorkeling passengers. Because this was Kimberlee's first experience, her companions wanted something easy and beautiful. Once in the boat, the master and first mate took them to an area where the dive boats had already disgorged their divers to the depths below. Thankfully, their guide dropped anchor away from the scuba crowd.

It felt as if the sea belonged only to them.

While one man stayed in the boat, the guide remained in the water to ensure everyone's safety. He put them into pairs of buddies. Within a short time, Kimberlee felt comfortable and secure floating on top of the sea, observing the stunning, varied life below.

In her life vest, Kimberlee could observe the magnificent underwater world—for the first time. To her delight, turtles swam beneath, a moray eel slithered into a sea bottom hole, stingrays glided around, and of course, a large variety of colorful tropical fish surrounded her. To attract the fish, their guide brought stale rolls with him. Once he scattered small pieces of bread in the water, she was inundated by gorgeous fish of every imaginable size, color, and design.

She even became self-confident enough to tear off small pieces of bread to hand feed them. A few times, she didn't withdraw her fingers fast enough, so she had a few sharp nibbles. Nothing that hurt or punctured the skin, but still surprising. A perfect touch for making her experience unique.

Paulette, the fashion expert, wasn't about to let her friends use a "stinky, dirty, yucky mask and snorkel" which hundreds of people had stuck on their germ-infested faces. Also, no pre-used fins for them. Therefore, a week before their cruise, she herded everyone to a dive shop on the Lower West Side, so when they jumped in for their aquatic quest, they all had new, specially fitted equipment. Of course, Paulette made sure she color-coordinated her mask, snorkel, and fins with her bikini. The other three women only cared about fit and comfort; color wasn't important.

But they did have sexy, sparkly bikinis, while Kimberlee had her blubber-hiding tankini. Brains couldn't make up for a lack of beauty or a great figure. She was who she was. And her friends loved her for it.

Maybe it was time she began liking herself. The Captain certainly found her attractive. Didn't he? He wouldn't have risked his career for a total looser. Would he?

Having grown up in Iowa's farming country and now living in the steel and concrete canyons of New York, she was thrilled drifting through paradise—an experience she'd long dreamt about. After seeing her first *National Geographic* magazine with tropical photos, she'd fantasized about swimming in the glorious, blue Caribbean—a world to explore, but no way to discover those exotic destinations. Somehow, the cornfields left her feeling trapped. Moving to New York and traveling to clients around the world filled much of her hunger for adventure. Now this cruise had opened a new door for her—in more ways than one.

Frustratingly, being immersed in the caressing sensuality of the water, her body's overstimulated nerve endings remained on high arousal. Not even the refreshingly cool sea could dampen the sexual furnace she'd become. *I guess, I'm still on the bottom of that cage, even when floating on top of the ocean.*

When four exhausted and famished women finally climbed back aboard their boat, it was time for a late lunch. Their guide suggested they grab some food from a mom-and-pop beach snack shop. He guaranteed they would be fine with the meal—tummy-wise. And they were.

After picking up their lunches, they motored to their picnic spot on a private strip of beach. The guide took them to a small cove with soft golden sand where they could talk and enjoy a simple meal of lobster tacos and huitlacoche quesadillas. Sharing a delicious lunch, everyone enthusiastically recounted the wonders of what they'd seen. In the excitement of a delicious beach picnic, even Kimberlee forgot her fixation of the Captain…at least momentarily.

This was heaven. The day offered everything she'd hoped for. What she hadn't bargained for was how the sea would become like a sensual lover…a reminder of the man she left on ship.

As they ate and talked, Kimberlee found her mind jumping between their conversations about snorkeling and her fantasizing about her Captain. Yes, now he'd become hers.

Thoughts concerning work also snuck in, specifically about the denial of her long-desired partnership. That rejection devastated her. Yet for her, hope springs eternal. She needed the opportunity to fix a major client issue and maybe they'd change their mind. Somehow in her mind, she got the idea that once she got the promotion, her social life would pick up momentum. With the right credentials, she'd finally find Mr. Right. Regretfully, he wouldn't be on this ship. If only she could have both—the partnership and the Captain. But that was not reality.

And now she was down to three nights left on this ship and in his arms.

Toward the end of lunch, she began realizing how frustrated she'd become with their sex life. Her three sexual experiences with him focused mainly on her. It was one-sided, with him always in control. Plus, she'd not had the chance to try out her newfound blow job skills. Something had to change. And change it would.

This was the perfect time to talk with her friends. They were all relaxed and happily fed. "Ladies, I need your help. I've been thinking about sex and the Captain." Three pairs of eyes turned toward her in expectation of what she had to say.

"I need to shake things up, but I'm not sure how to do it. The last few evenings the entire focus was on me—and I've loved it, but something is missing. Lovemaking should be a two-way street, not one-way. I need to do something different tonight. Suggestions?"

The companions sat quietly thinking.

Bonnie spoke first. "Well, this is a sex ship. Maybe you should turn the tables on him. I'm not sure how, but between the four of us, we can come up with ideas. We're intelligent and creative."

Being the fashion expert, Paulette began brainstorming about clothes. "He looks fabulous in his captain's whites. When I think about him dressed up, my mind immediately goes to watching him undress. Taking those whites off just for me."

"Perfect," Bonnie said.

"You can tell him that tonight you want to be in charge," Lori added. "How dominating do you want to be?"

Kimberlee thought for a moment then replied, "Very dominating. I want to shock him. I want to push him out of his comfort zone, as he did me. But I'm not sure he has one."

"Oh, I guarantee you, all men have a comfort zone they don't want to leave," Bonnie said.

The three women began describing enthusiastically the boundaries men maintain to protect their self-worth. What amazed Kimberlee was how different men were from each other. What one man refused to do, turned another on. Really, not any different than women.

Would he be willing to go outside his comfort zone? Would she? The women then began talking about the various activities she could instigate. She was amazed by the variety of their experiences. While she would never be a sexually free spirit, she still wanted to break out of her shell. The last three nights had produced cracks in her traditional barricade. Now she was ready to break it wide open.

In the boat back to the pier, the increasing afternoon wind and noise of the motor made conversation difficult. Kimberlee used this time to mull over what she wanted to do, what she would say to the Captain, and how she would say it.

Her mind kept returning to a toy she'd seen in the ship's

sex store. Would she dare buy it? Could she even use it if she owned it?

Like the Captain, she also trusted her instincts. So, yes, she would buy it. But she still wasn't sure what she'd do with it. And maybe she would never know until the time came.

By 3:00 p.m. when four tired, wet, sandy, and salty women walked up the gangway, she knew she would write him a letter and what she'd say. But not how to give it to him. It would have been so much easier to send him a text, but with her phone on airplane mode to eliminate huge roaming charges and wanting to minimize the high Wi-Fi fees, she'd have to settle for using the old-fashioned mode of communication.

She'd find Ramil and have him give the invite to Captain Johan.

First, she needed a shower and then she'd write her note inviting the Captain to join her for the evening in the grotto—which she would personally reserve.

This would be the night to spread her wings—not just her legs. And who knew, maybe he'd fly with her.

CHAPTER FOURTEEN

*C*aptain Johan leaned on the railing of deck nine, gazing out to sea. He loved this time of night—the quiet—with passengers finishing dinner, ensconced in their cabins, watching the show in the Dolphin Salon, or enjoying their socialization in the various bars pulsating with live music. For this moment, the ship and the sea belonged to him.

Every opportunity he got, he'd spend it outside. As a kid working on cod fishing boats, the sea and sky became like oxygen to him. People didn't realize how much of his job he spent inside—either working in his cabin or on the bridge.

He hated his one stint sealed on a submarine. He needed the freedom living on top of the sea, not trapped on the bottom, never knowing when he'd again inhale fresh air into his starved lungs.

Letting the familiar roll of the ship rock him, he felt for Kimberlee's note in his pocket for the umpteenth time. At five that evening, as he was preparing to depart, Ramil delivered the letter to him on the bridge. Strange how only a few readings had seared the words in his memory. She told him, "Wear your captain's dress whites and meet me in grotto three forty-three at nine. For this evening, I'll be in charge. You shouldn't have too big a dinner."

Was she being serious or playful writing that last line? Or both? Just to be safe he skipped dinner altogether.

She reserved the grotto herself. What could she possibly be planning?

To be honest, he was both intrigued with this different person, but also a little wary of what she wanted and if he was ready to relinquish control. He'd never viewed himself as a submissive; he was more of a Dominant. Well really, he was neither. He and Eira enjoyed role-playing, but it was more kids trying out their newly discovered sexuality.

While he could still sense Eira's presence, she no longer felt as strong. *Are you leaving me, Eira? I'm not ready to let you go.*

Returning his musings to this evening's meeting, he knew that for most of the passengers on this ship, sex and BDSM were serious business. The majority of couples cruised with the MS *Aphrodite* to try out new, thrilling sexual experiences. A few people on the ship were hard-core BDSM practitioners, but they were the exception.

As she requested, he wore his dress whites. Even relaxed, he felt small tingles of anticipation gripping his balls—both looking forward to their meeting in one hour and feeling, surprisingly, a little uncomfortable.

He'd never really thought about control in a sexual relationship. But reliving his three nights with Kimberlee, he had to admit he controlled their time together. He picked the place, the sex toys, and what they did. Not that they were in a Dom/sub relationship. It was just how it naturally evolved.

Thinking about her note, he realized she must have viewed herself in a submissive role. And now, she wanted to reverse the power imbalance. Being secure in his sexuality and masculinity offered him the freedom to let her take charge of their evening.

Maintaining control sometimes meant giving up control to another. But would the chemistry still be there when they reversed their roles? And what toys would she want to use? Would he want to use them? So many unknowns—and he hated unknowns.

Feeling the warm evening breeze brush against his neck, he took a moment from his swirling thoughts to enjoy the sway of the ship and the whoosh it made gliding through the darkening sea. He belonged to this life.

Staring down at the wake, he reaffirmed his dislike of surprises...an incongruent situation for a captain who lived with constant unpredictability from the sea, the weather, the ship, the passengers, and the crew. Now this evening offered him another uncharted world to navigate.

Sighing, he rolled his neck from side to side, releasing the growing tightness.

Returning to the Dom/sub relationship, he knew most people thought being a Dom meant aggressively controlling the other person. They were wrong. It meant understanding the physical and emotional needs, as well as the fantasies, of the sub. It wasn't brute force applied to the partner, and never without their consent.

Johan recognized Kimberlee needed freedom to explore her sexuality and the greater her sense of personal control, the more comfortable she'd be sharing it. He wanted to keep her trust. So, tonight was an important moment for them.

Of course, he had another issue to deal with: she'd be leaving the ship in three days and he hadn't decided what he wanted from her or from this relationship. He knew captains had landside liaisons and marriages. But he was jumping ahead of himself with this thinking. He'd worry about the future once he knew what tonight brought.

So far, their relationship had remained off the public radar. He'd been lucky. Hopefully, that would continue until she left. He didn't need to explain his actions or his stupidity to the company's CEO. Thankfully, her friends had kept silent.

Like the water flowing against the ship's hull, minutes also slipped by. Finally, it was time for him to head down to her reserved grotto. With an odd mixture of emotions, he arrived twenty minutes early. He spent the time waiting, watching the sea through the porthole; the water never lost its fascination for him. It also relaxed him, better than booze. *But maybe not as much as sex.*

When he heard the click of the keycard opening the door, he immediately turned around facing it. Naturally, he remained standing in his role as captain.

She entered, quietly closing the door behind her without breaking eye contact with him.

KIMBERLEE NEVER KNEW IF THE CAPTAIN RECEIVED HER invite, but hoped it was delivered and he would meet her. She hadn't requested an RSVP. And he hadn't responded—one way or the other.

As she walked closer to the reserved grotto, worry gnawed away at her newfound sexual confidence.

What if he didn't get it? What if he won't meet me? What if he doesn't want a strong, independent woman? What if he doesn't want me after reading my note?

The answers to her questions remained hidden behind the locked door.

Standing a few seconds in front of the closed cabin, she took deep breaths trying to calm the escalating anxiety. They helped a little. After one more inhalation, she forced herself to apply her keycard.

Without knowing what to expect, she opened the door and walked in.

There he stood, in his whites, waiting for her.

Profound relief swept through her, forcing her to hold on to the door because her wobbly legs made it difficult to stand.

Closing the door, she reached behind, turning the deadbolt without breaking eye contact.

"Thank you for coming. I was afraid you wouldn't. Please sit down." She indicated the chair closest to him.

She immediately sat on the love seat, knowing he wouldn't sit until she did. And then instantly wished she had taken the chair because the couch brought back graphic memories of their first night together. Looking back into his eyes, she saw them darken with passion, showing he too remembered their initial time in the grotto on a similar sofa.

Within seconds, her fears transmuted into a craving. She almost abandoned her plans, throwing herself into his powerful arms, begging him to consume her with his gifted hands and exquisitely talented mouth. But something held her back.

He sat rock-still, intently watching her with lust-glowing eyes, which held a fire deep in their depths. He knew her inner struggle and wasn't going to make this evening easy. She was on her own.

She moistened her lips, debating how best to present her case.

Drawing on her Midwestern strength, Kimberlee sat with a strong, straight back, holding her hands loosely in her lap. Looking back at him with a calm, fearless expression, she presented a woman who had control of both herself and the situation. Regardless of what she experienced inside, she knew how to portray a self-assured and determined person on the outside.

You know what you want to say. Now tell him.

Even though she wasn't cold, a shiver snaked up her body. While she thought she'd done a good job hiding it, she read in his watchful gaze that he knew what she was experiencing. Did that man miss anything?

She inhaled a calming breath to regroup before speaking. "As I was snorkeling today, I acknowledged my frustration with our relationship," she said in a steady voice. "It was one-sided. You gave, and I received. I want to give you pleasure as well as receive it."

Refusing to show her unease by fidgeting, she held herself rigidly still. "I'm new to this and not sure what I want to do or what I want you to do," she continued. "Thank you for coming tonight and showing your trust...and being flexible in our relationship."

Still he sat there watching her without making a sound. Just observing.

Damn him. He's forcing me to do all the talking. Fine. I'll show him.

She wanted to cross her arms in front of her chest but rejected showing any signs of weakness. Almost as if her hand had a will of its own, she found herself reaching for her earring but quickly brought it back down.

Offering her best upbeat boardroom smile she continued with the prepared speech. "I also want to explore your body as you have mine."

Searching how to tell him her thought process, she added. "Because I have limited time on this ship, I want to walk off with more knowledge and experience than I walked on with.

So, tonight I want to discover more of who I am sexually by understanding who you are sexually."

Still no word from him.

She stared at him, trying to detect what he was thinking. Even with dread and excitement battling inside, she maintained silence, knowing he would eventually break the stillness.

He momentarily dropped his eyes to the carpet, then immediately looked back at her.

Taking his own deep breath and slowly letting it out, he answered, "Being with you gives me great pleasure. I'm not a fancy man. I don't need sophisticated games. I enjoy holding you in my arms, feeling you cum, and knowing I've satisfied you. There's nothing more to tell you."

Hearing his words sent relief streaming through her body, washing away the tormenting tension.

With greater self-confidence, she asked, "How do you feel about taking a more passive role?"

"If it gives you pleasure, then I'm willing to sail with you. Where do you want to go?"

"I really don't know, but I do want to take the lead and be in control. Do you have a safe word?"

"I don't need one."

"Well, in that case, I want you to please undress…for me —like those men did on stage last night. No music. Just you and me."

She stopped talking, but instead sat quietly watching him. Outside, she looked calm and cool. Inside, butterflies turned her stomach upside down, while at the same time, her panties became damp from a tingling and clenching deep inside.

They sat for a moment, neither saying a word, just staring at each other. The anticipation filling the cabin became thick, making breathing difficult.

Without taking his eyes from hers, he suddenly stood in one fluid motion, looking relaxed, self-confident…and oh so sexy.

His eyes began to glow with an unfathomable inner fire that pinned her against the couch. Even if she wanted to, it was too late to turn back.

Oh, her Captain looked so delicious standing for her in his dress whites. And she was going to taste him—everywhere. She wanted to feel his body quivering from her touch, just as hers did when he made love to her. Even if she didn't know what she was doing, she hoped she had the courage to try new things and push him beyond his comfort zone—wherever that was.

Because she was out of hers.

Dragging her gaze away from his unfathomable and captivating eyes, she leisurely looked down his Viking-proud, powerful body. Abruptly halting at his impressive hard-on. There his erection stood in all its glory—just for her—tenting his white dress pants in a show of obvious desire.

How glad she was that women's arousal wasn't front and center, letting the world see when they were turned on. Thankfully, he would never know how desperately she needed him…standing there just for her.

When she lifted her eyes back to his, she saw lust blazing in their depths, with an intensity she had never seen from any man. *Oh, thank you for showing me I'm a desirable woman.*

She sat quietly waiting for him to begin.

Slowly, Captain Johan began unbuttoning his jacket—starting at the top, one gold button at a time. Leisurely, he removed his jacket while leaving on his undershirt. He laid the coat carefully on the chair. He then sat on the bed, removing his white shoes and socks.

Nipples hardening and tingling, she leaned forward, wondering what he'd take off next.

She hoped his pants, but no, as if reading her mind, he did the exact opposite and took off his undershirt. If possible, his cock seemed to grow bigger. Calmly, he stood there, letting her look over his bare chest. She scanned his beautifully defined pecs with its dusting of golden-honey hair that drew her eyes downward as it disappeared into his pants.

By now, Kimberlee's body flushed with a scorching heat, turning her into a puddle of uncontrollable lust. She throbbed with the hunger to touch him, to caress every inch of his amazing body. She wasn't sure she could delay until he totally stripped. Maybe she should just rip his clothes off instead of waiting for him to finish.

Consuming him with her eyes, she watched his nipples became hard pebbles…his breathing quicken…the pulse in his neck throb.

Even with his fierce passion, he let her know he saw through her cool-as-a-cucumber facade into her own raging need.

This was no longer a game—for either of them.

Finally, he undid the gold buckle on his white belt, pointedly pulling it through one loop at a time. In the silence of their grotto, the sound of sliding out his belt filled the cabin with erotic hints of how he could use it. But not now; this was her time and she wasn't going to let him take over. He could regain his command later.

She held her breath as he reached down to unzip his pants, slowly revealing boxers that fit him as if they'd been painted on. He stood a few moments, letting her intimately peruse his body up and down, down and up. He then unhurriedly reached down with both hands to slip off his trousers, then briefs.

Shivering from a craving pulsing between the apex of her thighs, her mind froze with one thought. *Oh, yes!*

That was what she'd been waiting for; he was totally naked just for her. Standing there with his pulsating rod displayed proudly and unashamed. Yes, she'd seen him stripped down before, but something seemed different. She'd been consumed with the passion he'd created. She hadn't cared what he looked like—only what fabulous things he'd do to her next.

Now it was her turn. All thoughts of what she should do and how she should do it fled. This wasn't part of her legal training—nothing prepared her for this part of life.

After standing up, she strolled over to her naked Norse god saying in a strong and decisive voice, "Captain, please keep your hands by your side and don't say a word—not a fucking word."

Walking behind him, she reveled in remaining fully clothed, while he was bare of all protective armor.

For a moment, she just stood there contemplating his magnificent body. He couldn't see her, so she could look to her heart's content. Stretching up, she buried her nose in the back of his neck. How she loved his masculine smell— musky, a slightly citrus cologne, and a scent uniquely his own.

"You smell so good. Good enough to eat."

With that, she began licking the back of his neck, down his spine and back up. His body had a slightly salty taste. A light rumbling purr came from deep inside his chest.

She reached down and stroked his ass. Gripping each cheek, she kneaded the taut, firmly rounded butt. She ran her index finger down his crack, watching him shiver with goose bumps forming. Then she dipped her hand between his legs, rubbing that sensitive spot between his asshole and balls.

Next, she reached farther in front, lightly cupping his balls, giving them a soft squeeze. Arching his neck, he gave a low desperation-filled growl.

She could explore his back and backside all night, but she still had the front half to discover.

"Oh, you're magnificent to look at, touch, taste, smell. You're made for sex—wonderful, passionate, mind-blowing sex. You're my fantasy man come to life. Thank you," she whispered in his ear.

Still, he remained silent—as she directed. But she saw how his muscles quivered with barely controlled desire.

Walking around, she stood in front of him. Looking up, she found herself gazing into hunger-ravaged eyes. Silently, they stared at each other, knowing that some line had been crossed. Neither of them would ever be the same.

She began exploring his face, as if she was blind and needed to learn his features with her hands and fingers. He must have shaved a few hours ago so he wouldn't give her a beard-burn. Even with his smooth skin, she still felt the slight abrasion of new growth scraping against her fingertips. What delightful things that slight beard could do to her body.

As she slid her hands down, he tilted his head back so that she could caress his neck. Her exploration continued to his broad shoulders that carried the responsibilities of his ship. She caressed lower, moving her hands over his athletically sculpted chest with his golden-honey dusting of hairs. Rubbing her fingers over his pebbling nipples, she heard a deep intake of breath.

Then she squeezed them, hearing him hiss through clenched teeth.

"I see your nipples are as sensitive as mine. I didn't realize that. Your body has been a mystery to me."

Using her nails, she deliberately scraped them down his

abdomen, watching his mesmerizing, rippling muscles clench and quiver under her exploration. Until she reached his magnificent erection, which begged for attention.

Now she'd finally put her dildo practice into action.

With both hands, she took hold of his throbbing cock. It felt silky and firm beneath her grasp. Almost as if it had a life of its own. Gently pulling down the foreskin, she watched his penis's head pop out. Bending over, she licked it like the top of an ice cream cone. Velvety. Smooth. A drop of pearly pre-cum glistened on the tip. Licking it off, she found it slightly salty but not bad tasting.

Taking one hand off his engorged cock, she reached down to cup his balls. Rolling them lightly back and forth in her palm. Looking back up into his face, she saw eyes squeezed shut and a face that looked in agony. *I wonder if I look like that when he's pleasuring me?*

He had so much power over her and now it was her opportunity to control him. What an amazing feeling to dominate such a masterful man. What a gift he'd given her.

Kimberly knelt in front of him, spending time getting to know his mysterious male parts—his taste, smell, feel, and sensitivity. She sucked, licked, lightly nibbled, firmly squeezed—anything she could think of to push him beyond his vaulted self-control.

Still he didn't say a word. Just jagged breathing showing her how he struggled with self-control...and was losing the battle.

CHAPTER FIFTEEN

*D*uring this exquisite torture, Captain Johan clenched his jaw, praying to keep cum from spraying all over the room, which would have been humiliating for a man who prided himself on control.

Kimberlee's mouth, her hands, even her nose burrowing into his groin left him ravaged by need so intense he had trouble standing.

He wasn't sure what turned him on more—what she was doing or her uninhibited joy in how she was doing it. Maybe both...and so much more. Whatever it was, something had shifted in him. He could never be celibate again. But he couldn't be a tomcat fucking any pussy. Right now, however, he had no mental agility left to construct a new future.

All he could do was keep from blowing his load all over her.

He frantically thought about what he needed to do after docking his ship at six forty-five in Cozumel tomorrow morning. That helped, but barely. He thought about what customs papers needed to be filled out with what information. Ah, that was better. That was, until he heard her say, "Captain, please put this condom over my beautiful new butt plug."

Anal play wasn't new for him; he and his wife had explored all aspects of sex. But he knew it was for Kimberlee. For a moment he stared at her in fascination. He couldn't believe that this innocent woman could transform into an awesome sexual powerhouse.

With wonder, curiosity, and pounding lust, he reached out his hand for the butt plug and rubber.

KIMBERLEE LOVED HER ROYAL BLUE, VIBRATING, SILICONE-soft butt plug. What she was going to do with her Moregasm Contour Butt Plug when she left the ship, she had no idea. But for now, she was going to push it up the Captain's sexy ass.

She wanted him to feel as vulnerable as he'd made her. She needed to see him as helpless to her touch as she had been to his.

Without saying a word, he took both the sex toy and condom from her. His fingers briefly brushed against hers, sending a torrent of craving flooding throughout her.

Enthralled with his experienced hands, all she could do was watch, mesmerized as he tore open the package, then expertly slipping the condom over the head down to the base.

He handed it back to her, his eyes never leaving her face.

Taking the covered vibrator, she wasn't sure what to do next, but knew she wanted to make sure he was all right moving forward.

No longer pretending to be Ms. Sexually Self-Assured, her cool, controlled front vanished. In its place stood an honestly courageous and vulnerable woman wanting all that he and life had to give, but not sure how to reach for it.

Looking back at him, she let him see the longing in her eyes—along with the uncertainty of where they were headed.

Kimberlee shifted nervously from foot to foot. "I won't do anything you don't want. Are you OK with using this?" she asked, waving the butt plug in front of him.

Never a man for many words, he simply said, "Yes."

"Are you sure you don't want a safe word?"

"I'm sure."

Before she could say anything else, he reached out, pulling her into a protective and comforting embrace against his naked body. For a moment, she nestled there, relieved she had found a safe harbor.

And loved being held by this extraordinary, naked man.

Resting his chin on top of her head, he began talking in a caressing voice. Not caring what he said, she focused on the silky sound comforting her.

He began nibbling on her neck, firmly nipping on her earlobe, then he gripped her bottom—pulling her tightly against his rigid shaft.

Leaving her ear, he brushed a kiss across her lips. When her body demanded more by pressing against him, his kiss deepened, devouring her. His teeth held her tongue in place as he sucked on it. Just as she had sucked on his cock.

His strength and powerful passion sent explosive waves of yearning slamming through her. She wanted more than those kisses that left her burning and inflamed. She wanted...

That thought got interrupted when her sex-drugged brain registered his words. She heard him tell her this was her evening. That she had to take back her control.

Matching actions with words, he loosened his locking grip, letting her rest against him with her own weight.

Slowly, her brain reengaged, telling her she had a decision

to make: would she return command to him or keep it for herself?

I've come too far to stop now. Go for it, Kimberlee-girl.

She took one shaky step back, but still in his arms. When she took a firmer second step away, he dropped his arms.

In silence, they stood gazing at each other. The naked Captain facing a clothed Amazon warrior—proud, fierce, and ready for battle.

She wasn't sure where those next words came from. They just popped out. "OK, Captain, lie down on the bed with your knees to your shoulders."

After making her demand, she held her breath, not sure if he would do as she asked.

But he did.

Oh my God, what a sight to see him totally exposed to me.

She froze in shock. It was as if time stopped and the rest of the world fell away, leaving just the two of them. Struggling to pull air into her lungs, she could only stand there staring in astonishment and awe at the glorious sight.

He's all mine. Totally mine. He trusts me to do what I want.

The same way I've trusted him.

She'd never seen an asshole before, not even hers. And here this stunning man was letting her look at his.

It's amazing what trust and lust can do to a person's inhibitions.

Without hesitation, Kimberlee reached out her finger to stroke his hole. Oh, she loved hearing him moan. With her other hand, she caressed his inner thigh, lightly running her nails back and forth. Each time either hand explored him, his cock twitched, abdominal muscles contracted, and he emitted deep rumbling sounds.

What an amazing sense of power to give another such soul-blazing pleasure.

But then again, he definitely had power over her. Without him ever touching her, she still burned with uncontrollable craving. The simple sight of sunlight sparkling off the water, the smell of sea salt in the air, and the sound of his voice during public announcements all conspired to keep her shackled to him.

And now it's my turn to enslave him.

Kneeling on the bed, she bent down between his splayed knees running her tongue around his puckered sphincter. She felt his body violently jerk. She watched how he tried to keep his whimper from turning into a bellow.

Oh, Captain, I'm only just beginning. Let's see how long you can keep going.

Pressing her tongue into him, she sensed his struggle not to close his legs. Quickly, she shifted from caressing his thighs to keeping them wide open. Now she began applying steady pressure with her tongue, until it slipped past his tight butt ring.

She could feel him give up the fight for self-control and abandon himself to her.

Now she truly had him, his body totally hers.

She spent a few minutes moving her tongue back and forth, and around. She stopped only because his violent jerks told her he was going to shoot his wad—and that was something she wanted to watch.

Pulling out her tongue, she reached for her butt plug. She wanted to make sure it was well lubed, so she added a dab of gel. Replacing the plug where her tongue was, she studied his face as she moved it around the outside of his opening, adding easy little pushes.

Each mini thrust became firmer until she felt his channel's

resistance relax and heard a soft pop as the tip of the plug slipped in. By now, his groans filled the cabin. She continued carefully pushing until the base of the plug stopped any further movement. Slowly, she moved the plug around, changed directions, then backward and forward. All the time, she watched his face as it became overwhelmed by uncontrollable lust.

"Captain, I want to watch you play with yourself. I want to watch your cum shoot out of your cock and cover you with it." Reaching over, she took his right hand, placing it around his penis, moving it up and down until he took over. Then she reached down and pressed the button on the base of the plug. On came the lowest level vibration.

By now his groans became deep-throated sobs. When he began to move his left hand to cup his cock head, she held his hand down. "No. I want to watch your cock shoot your cum. I want to see it spray all over you. I promise to lick it up afterward."

With those words, he cried out, exploding onto his chest and face. His gorgeous cock spasmed until he had nothing left.

Kimberlee just sat between his sprawled legs watching this amazing man give his all to her—totally uninhibited and completely drained. Turning off the plug and gently pulling it out, she put his legs back on the bed, then moved to his side to lick up his cum as he lay collapsed on the bed, softly whimpering. When she licked him clean, she got a warm, wet washcloth from the bathroom to wipe him off, gently washing his asshole.

Dropping the washcloth on the floor, Kimberlee quickly undressed, lying down next to him. She may not have been as physically exhausted as he was, but emotionally she was drained of all feelings. She ached from unfulfilled passion. Her thoughts in turmoil from the intense intimacy.

Too exhausted to reach for her vibrator, all she could do was press her depleted, unsatisfied body next to his.

Just as her eyes began closing, she felt him roll toward her. Pulling her into his arms, he drew the covers over them. Nuzzling her neck, he whispered, "You're amazing. Tomorrow's my turn. Now, get some sleep. We still have the night in front of us."

CHAPTER SIXTEEN
CRUISE DAY 5

*S*ometime during the night, Kimberlee became aware the Captain aroused her with gentle caresses, as they lay curled together as spoons. "I want to love you," he whispered in her ear.

All she could do was nod. Immediately, he entered her pussy from behind, lightly stroking the front of her body, teasing her rapidly hardening nipples until she arched her back begging for more.

Holding her top leg up, he had greater access exploring her inside and out. Even half-asleep, she felt her body awaken to the command from his hands and the thrusts of his penis.

She moaned as her body burst into life. How she loved the way he bit her neck, sucking on it until her world narrowed to just him. "Yes. Oh, yes. You feel so wonderful. Please don't ever stop."

More awake now, she luxuriated in letting him direct what he wanted her to do—and what he wanted to do to her.

Her groans filled the cabin, with a craving that had become a roaring fire. She opened her legs wider, begging him to thrust deeper, while squeezing her clitoris the way he was pinching her engorged buds.

As if understanding her desperation, he aimed for her G-spot. Rubbing against it, he ignited a ferocious firestorm. Her body writhed with pulsating urgency. Now, only sobs and deep guttural cries reverberated around their grotto.

Reaching under the pillow, he pulled the little hand vibrator out, turned it on, then pressed the curve over her pubic bone with the tip on her pleasure center. Instantly, she came, her body shattering like a mirror splintering into thousands of shreds. Her vaginal muscles slammed down on his engorged cock, forcing him to erupt, flooding her with his hot cum.

Rather than falling immediately into a sex-drugged sleep, he kept her already stimulated nerve endings pulsating with pleasure, touching her and holding the little toy firmly in place. She knew he was forcing her to cum until she had no orgasms left. So with a sigh of bliss, she sank into a sea of engulfing ecstasy.

At this moment, there could never be too much fabulous sex. Like the white lab rat, she collapsed to the bottom of the cage, only craving pleasure.

Eventually turning off the vibrator, he placed her leg back down, cradling her closer into his protective body. They both fell back asleep with his exhausted cock still nestled inside her.

Around six thirty that morning, the bright Caribbean sun flooded through the porthole awakening her. For a moment Kimberlee didn't remember where she was but knew she was once again alone.

Well, not entirely alone. One red rose rested on his pillow beside her.

She still craved his touch, the feel of him in her. As if

nothing else existed but the pleasure he could give. *Oh great, I've become a sex addict and my drug of choice is the Captain. And all I want is more, more, more. How could my well-planned life have come to this?*

She needed to get up and back to her cabin. It was time for breakfast and a day at the beach. She and her friends had rented two cabanas for the day at a five-star resort on the shore of Cozumel. This was another one of the excursions she'd been dreaming about—just sand, sun, and sea. No computer. No phone. No demanding clients or partners.

Paradise! Well it would have been paradise if she hadn't experienced the joys of nonstop climaxing in his arms. These past few days put a different spin on what heaven on earth meant.

Later that morning, Kimberlee and her friends basked in the sun's heat on their comfy lounges under their side-by-side cabanas. Whether dozing or fantasizing, no one spoke. As friends, they'd always respected the need for quiet time, so the silence felt comfortable.

Besides, they were all talked out from breakfast. While the ladies wanted to hear the delicious details, this was one time she didn't want to share everything with them.

Her friends reinforced what a great student she was. And how thrilled they were for her. She'd found her sexual wings. *I can now soar like those seagulls overhead.*

Slathered in coconut-scented sunscreen, wearing floppy hats and designer sunglasses, they luxuriated in the joys of the moment. Hotel waiters kept them supplied with unlimited water and delicious, frozen mango margaritas. The light breeze, gentle waves rolling onto the beach dissolving into a sandy foam and the intermittent hum of small planes trailing ad banners lulled them into a drowsy semi-sleep state.

Every now and then, Kimberlee wondered what the Captain was doing. Was he thinking about her and last night? She hoped so because she didn't want things to be one-sided. Sometimes doubt nibbled into her contentment. Had she been too aggressive? Would he want to be with her again? Could he really find her appealing? So many unknowns.

As she lounged in the caressing humid air, her mind floated to other caresses—more intimate ones with a definite masculine touch. Her nipples hardened just thinking about his natural sexual magnetism. Electrical ripples pulsed through her, filling her with deep needs.

Letting the brilliant sun warm the outside of her body, her insides heated with the thoughts of orgasms and sucking on his asshole. She could become accustomed to the joys of Caribbean living with the roar of the ocean, cry of seagulls, and the ecstasy of an extraordinary lover.

Just then Bonnie announced, "I need to cool off. Who wants to go swimming with me?"

Silence.

"Remember we agreed no one goes in alone—for our safety." No one answered her, so lost they were in their own sensual worlds.

Opening her eyes, Kimberlee stood up. "I'll go in with you. I also need to cool down."

Though, I don't think the water will help the heat raging through me.

To walk across the burning, golden sand, they put on their flip-flops, leaving them above the water's edge. As she stepped into the sparkling turquoise water, the cool sea first shocked her overheated body, but after throwing herself into an oncoming wave, the initial shock passed and she reveled in the refreshing coolness.

Striking out with breast strokes, she and Bonnie swam out to deeper waters, rolling over and floating on their backs, letting the buoyancy of the sea support them.

Bobbing in the waves, Bonnie said, "I'm so glad you came with us. I know this was difficult for you, but now you seem to be having a wonderful time. While you might not have been sexually experienced, you're really an adventurous person. And we thought you'd find this trip enlightening. Of course, I never realized how educational it would be."

With her eyes closed in joy from the sun's warmth, the water's coolness, and the sea's gentle rocking, Kimberlee remained quiet for a moment. Then she said, "I'm so grateful to all of you. I wouldn't have been here if you hadn't pushed me. I owe you all so much. I'll never be able to thank you enough."

After this brief conversation, the two friends drifted in companionable silence.

Funny, she loved how erotic floating in water could be. She felt encased by the sensual liquid flowing over every inch of her skin—like a lover's touch that cocooned her in his embrace. How had she gotten to this sex-craved place— coming from a life of order, of single focused professional obsession, and of self-reliance?

Even if she wanted to, she could never go back to the woman she was but had no idea who she'd become. Well, she did know she loved feeling alive and free, as she did when making love with the Captain. Making love, fucking, having sex—she didn't know what to call it. But knew she wanted more. And now, she only had two days left with Johan.

Their day flew by in a haze of enchantment: a glittering sea reflecting the bright Caribbean sun, the lulling melody of waves and seagulls, and the delectable bliss of deep sexual fulfillment.

By the time they shuffled onto the MS *Aphrodite* for the ship's departure, they were sun weary, sticky from lotion, and covered with salt and sand. And totally content.

WHILE KIMBERLEE INDULGED ON HER BEACH OUTING, Captain Johan kept his mind focused on his ship…and mostly succeeded. He refueled for the next half of their cruise, conducted a medical emergency drill, dealt with engineering maintenance, and updated his captain's log.

By the afternoon, he thankfully had a few hours to himself. Standing on his cabin's narrow veranda looking out to sea, he allowed his knotted muscles to unwind, appreciating the few moments of privacy, grateful they docked port side. His view from the starboard balcony faced seaward instead of the teeming dock filled with thousands of inebriated, sunburnt cruise ship passengers.

The latest message from corporate expressed cautious optimism about their defense from the hostile takeover. Yes, the mega-cruise companies had big bucks, but they also needed cash to keep building bigger ships, with even more fancy amusement park activities and glitzy décor. The bean counters weren't stupid. They couldn't waste precious cash on filling pockets of outside counsel and accountants. In a month or two, they'd give up and life would get back to normal.

His thoughts drifted back to his teenage life in Norway when the bastard fishing corporations were sucking up the little guys. He couldn't help his father when they stole his livelihood. All he could do was watch the man he idolized turn to the bottle drowning his fury and despair. Until he destroyed his liver and life. He never wanted to feel that helpless again. Maybe that was a reason he went into the military, so he could face, fight, and destroy the enemy.

While his father had no protection from the voracious conglomerates sucking up the independent Norwegian cod fisherman, the company owning this ship had the financial resources and legal power to fight. And win they would.

The cooling tropical breeze carried a hint of salt and sea brine—scents that always brought him peace of mind. As the hectic activities of the day receded, he allowed his thoughts to focus on Kimberlee and their budding relationship. That was the sticking point. What he wanted didn't exist in a vacuum; he had to know what she thought. But then again, he wasn't sure what he needed.

If he was honest, he wanted her to stay on the ship so they could sort out their relationship—and continue their mind-blowing sex. Unfortunately, he didn't have a lot to offer a fancy lawyer from New York City. His captain's cabin had to be smaller than her apartment—even a studio apartment wouldn't be as tiny as his rooms. His salary wouldn't compare to what she earned. Plus, this was a sex ship.

He and Eira had been made for each other. Growing up together, they were two peas in a pod with similar backgrounds and views about life. She'd been his other half. When he lost her, his heart shattered for both her and their unborn child. He didn't have a place for another woman in his damaged soul.

Rarely would he think about the loss of their unborn baby. When he did, as now, agony detonated through him—so raw it immobilized his breath. In the dark of nights, he'd let himself wonder if it would have been a girl or boy. Who would that child have looked like? What would the personality be? Losing Eira had destroyed him, but he had memories to ease the despair. Their infant created by their love, haunted him still, without relief.

Heartache, an overwhelming emotion, always hovered in the background. It ate away at his well-being. It interweaved pain into every minute aspect of his life. Even things unrelated got poisoned by the haunting agony. Grief was like air; it's all around you, yet you can't see it, touch it, or smell it.

But now, he needed to get back to Kimberlee. What was he to do about her? Where did she fit into his life? His heart still belonged to another. He had nothing to give their relationship but great sex. She certainly deserved more.

With her, he was sailing blind, as if in a dense fog...and hated it.

They had to talk. Tonight.

Then there was last evening. He tried not to focus on it, but kept getting flashbacks that blasted electrical currents up his spine and down into his balls. It was one of the most erotic experiences he'd had. No question, stripping for her turned him on—more than he expected. Watching her eyes devour him made him understand what kept the Chippendales men performing night after night. He loved it.

The rest of what happened that evening, he tried keeping locked away, not ready to examine. Just the fleeting thought of her joy when she sucked his cock, how she ate his asshole, used the butt plug, and watched until he shot his wad gave him a throbbing hard-on. Maybe he should go back inside to jack off. It was one way to release all this painful pressure... and to make sure he didn't humiliate himself tonight when they were together.

But first he needed to select a private location and a special menu for tonight's dinner...and their coming talk. Next, he must write a note inviting her. Then, there was the question of whether she would join him. As secure as he was with his sexuality and command of his ship, she represented uncharted waters for him.

Between now and their meal, he had time to determine what he wanted to say. And what he wanted from her. Plus, what he was capable of giving.

Kimberlee found herself standing at the same railing on deck nine where she first met the Captain a lifetime ago. He'd left an invitation in the plastic mailbox outside her cabin, which she found on returning from their divine day at the beach.

In precise, engineering-like block printing on his captain's stationary, he invited her to dinner. He asked her to meet him on deck nine at nineteen thirty. She still couldn't get used to the twenty-four-hour time, but with quick calculation she knew he meant seven thirty.

While she waited for him, her mind examined how quickly she'd found the sea legs she never knew she had. Now, she easily balanced on a rolling teak deck, enjoying the movement of the ship and her body. Leaning against the high-gloss wooden railing, she gazed out at the darkening tropical waters thinking about what tonight would bring and what she wanted. Discouragingly, both remained shrouded in mystery.

For a person who had always known what she desired from life, this lack of clear direction left her frustrated, disoriented, and even a little fearful. Regardless of what this evening brought, she needed a clear answer to where the relationship was headed.

Well, she really didn't. It was a sex cruise to nowhere.

Watching the outward spreading wake, she found the gentle rocking of the ship comforting.

Her body, even her mind, begged for the Captain's touch, the sound of his voice and the smell of his skin. Lost in her sensual and sexually arousing thoughts, she only became aware of his presence when two muscular, masculine arms came around on either side of her, with weather-beaten sailor hands braced on the railing.

She immediately recognized his scent—that intoxicating combination of citrus, musty spice, and pure male. Instead of his off-hours casual black T-shirt, he was wearing a black dress shirt with button-down collar and black slacks. He almost blended in with the growing darkness.

Suddenly, the sexually adventuresome woman became shy and awkward; she kept staring out to sea. But no longer seeing it.

"How was your day?" he asked against her neck, his voice velvety soft with its sexy Norwegian-accented English. Tenderly biting her neck, he added, "We have a dinner date tonight al fresco in the Rose Buffet. We're sitting off in a corner and they'll serve us something simple with a nice white Châteauneuf. "I hope you're OK with me selecting the meal?" he asked. "It'll be freshly-caught fish prepared island style."

"Of course, I am," she lied, still looking out at the vessel's wake. She didn't like him ordering for her, but it was less invasive than dealing with hundreds of passengers jockeying for food.

And, she was curious what his selections would be. It would show how well he knew her.

She tilted her head so he could have easier access to her sensitive neck—a shiver ran through her as he accepted her intimate invitation.

Then like the softest of butterfly wings, he whispered in her ear, "Thank you for last night."

When she didn't answer, he added, "It was also new for me."

Kimberlee gathered her courage. "I don't know what came over me. I'm normally a traditional person. Not experimental at all. Maybe it's something about this ship that brought out that unknown side of me." She exhaled that last statement in a hushed, passion-filled whisper as his tongue circled her ear, then he nipped lightly on her lobe.

Wrapping his arms around her, he hugged her into his chest, planting a kiss on the top of her head. "Shall we go to dinner?"

With her head resting against his shoulder in trusting abandonment, all she could do was nod.

CHAPTER SEVENTEEN

They sat at a small deuce table in a corner of the aft patio on deck eight. Here they had the privacy for an intimate conversation. A welcoming bottle of white wine rested in an ice bucket. As he held her chair, she didn't pull away from touching him as she did the first time. Rather, she caressed his hand as she smiled up gratefully.

Sipping her crisp, cold wine, she searched her mind for how to begin—without any idea of what she wanted to say. But she needn't have worried because he began talking as soon as he had his first sip of wine.

"This kind of conversation is new for me. And as you've already noticed, I'm sometimes too blunt. I realize after last night I can't go back to being celibate. You've reminded me how important passion and sexual pleasure are. Holding your magnificent body, smelling your femininity, and watching you come fills me the way only the sea has. Now sailing is no longer enough."

For a nanosecond her breathing halted and her hand tightened around the stem of her wine glass. Rooted in place, she worried any movement would halt his talking.

He paused briefly, as if gathering his thoughts, then continued, "I know I can't offer a successful lawyer from New York City a life on a cruise ship, especially a sex-filled one. Even so, I don't want to see you go. If you have the time available, I'd like you to stay an extra week with me. I don't know what your commitments are."

Holding her gaze with his, he reached out caressing her cheek. "You'd be my guest, at no expense to you."

Stunned, she stared at him speechless. She wanted to throw herself into his arms and at the same time, she wanted to flee the dinner...the ship...him.

"I don't know what to say..." She stopped talking when Belmiro, the bartender from their first night together, brought their starter course: an exotic island salad with papaya, avocado, mint, pumpkin seeds, and lettuce in a lime and olive oil dressing. All the foods she loved.

"Thank you, Belmiro. I thought you were a bartender."

"I work multiple jobs. I'm even on room service when they've got a lot of orders. This way, I don't get bored. Plus, I meet a variety of passengers." Smiling at her, he left them to their private dinner.

Looking at her, Captain Johan said, "I trust him. He's private, does a good job, and keeps his own counsel. The crew respect him. And so do I.

Looking at him, she just nodded because, while she liked Belmiro, she had nothing to add.

With a lull in the conversation, she studied the specially prepared salad. It looked delicious. A joyous warmth spread through her, because he'd taken the trouble to plan this meal just for her.

With the first bite, she experienced an explosion of delightful flavors.

Smiling at him with pure bliss and gratitude, she said, "This is so lovely. Thank you. I'm really at a loss for words."

Returning to her salad, she used eating as an excuse to sort out the thoughts and emotions tumbling around inside. Yes, she wanted to stay with him on the ship. And no, she needed to get back to New York to sort out her career and future. *Let's be honest, I'm afraid. I don't want to be hurt. I'm out of my depth with him.*

For a moment, silence filled their table with only the sounds of their silverware against the plate, murmured conversations from other diners sitting off at a distance, the hum of the ship's engines, and the whoosh of the vessel moving through the sea.

Finally, he said, "Please tell me what you're thinking."

Taking two deep breaths and lifting her head to look directly at him, she said, "I've grown to enjoy this ship. Yes, I like the ports but there is something special about sailing. Something relaxing for me."

He nodded, which encouraged her to say more.

"I also love our sex...fucking...lovemaking. You've introduced me to a new side of myself and I too can't go back to who I was. I'm confused. I'm certainly no longer the person I was who boarded this ship, but I don't know who the new me is."

He sat there quietly, giving her space to think.

A moment later, she continued, "Truthfully, I do have an extra week of vacation I was planning to use for analyzing my future, as well as take extra yoga and Pilates classes. You're right, we don't have a future. However, I too don't want to give up what we have. So..." Their main course arrived, stopping her from completing the thought.

Belmiro removed her salad, replacing it with a plate of

simple grilled red snapper, rice, and a light curried mango chutney. "Freshly caught this morning," he said. "The chef stuffed it with spring onions and island spices, covered it with coconut milk, then wrapped the fish in banana leaves." He finished by warning them about small bones. "No matter how good Chef is at filleting, little ones can still get away. Bon appétit."

With her first bite, she closed her eyes in delight, appreciating the divine flavors. Swallowing, she looked back at him with a brilliant smile.

"Oh, Captain, this is heavenly. I've never had such a simple, but exquisite meal," she said before taking another bite. After she finished it, she went on.

"To be honest, I didn't like you ordering for me, but you created an amazing dinner. Thank you. You know me better than I know you. I would never have been able to order for you."

Smiling he said, "I'm really a simple person. I like fresh food, especially fish, having grown up in a fishing community with a fisherman father and a mother who is a great cook."

"I gather your mother is still alive. What about your father?" she asked.

Taking a while to answer, he finally said, "My father destroyed his liver with alcohol."

Staring intently at her, he continued in a neutral voice. "The big fishing corps destroyed him because he wouldn't sell out to them. He was fiercely independent and didn't want to work on one of those massive fish factories. Obviously, he couldn't compete, so he lost everything. I was a teenager when this happened. I was devastated. I couldn't help him."

"How awful for you and your family. I'm so sorry."

He just sat there staring at her with his cold, stony Captain's expression. Feeling uncomfortable by his lack of response, she began talking about herself. She ended her monologue with, "While our backgrounds appear worlds apart, we both grew up with similar family values—trust and loyalty topping the list."

During her soliloquy, she watched how his body relaxed and his face lost its unfriendliness. Eventually, he began asking questions, showing a genuine interest in the descriptions of her family life.

With an internal sigh of relief, her growing concern began diminishing. For a moment, she'd panicked having done something wrong. Her tummy tightened with worry when the sparkle vanished from his eyes and he stared at her with... hostility. But why?

By the time dessert arrived, they'd become relaxed and were once again enjoying each other's company. Belmiro served them bowls containing a scoop of homemade coconut ice cream with thin slices of bananas flambéed in rum and Amaretto.

I'm in heaven. He selects food as fabulously as he makes love. If only he wasn't a cruise ship captain...on a sex ship. My family would never understand. Shit, I don't even understand.

His voice brought her back to the here and now. "Where would you like to continue our conversation? I took your dinner choice away, so you pick where you'd like to talk.

That was a no-brainer. "For some reason I gravitate to that back area on deck five. I like being closer to the water. Let's go there," she said, in a voice filled with both joy and sexual promise.

WHEN HE ASKED THE QUESTION ABOUT WHERE SHE'D LIKE TO talk, the Captain wasn't sure what Kimberlee would say. He'd hoped she'd pick deck five because he too liked its proximity to the sea. Looking at her face aglow with delight from the dinner and where they would talk, he knew she hadn't totally rejected his offer. He still had a chance.

But a chance for what?

He knew when he'd started talking about his father, the energy shifted downward. As he studied her, he watched her confusion mount by his change. But, nothing about her behavior demonstrated guilt. Not only wasn't she a spy, she really didn't know about the hostile takeover. Or, she was an amazing actress. And he'd lost his ability to read people, which he doubted.

Now, time to go for their talk. Walking around the table, he held her chair, at the same time offering his hand. When she accepted, her touch brought him both a sense of rightness and a throbbing hunger deep in his groin.

He must have nonverbally communicated his craving to bury his face in her pussy, because she looked back at him with uninhibited passion and a soft blush spreading up her neck.

Never taking his eyes away from hers, he said in a husky voice, "It's taking all my willpower to keep my hands and mouth from making love to you, but we need to talk."

She nodded. Was she agreeing with the need to talk or their lust to fuck? Hopefully both.

As much as he wanted to walk down with her, self-preservation forced him to let her go first. Sitting back down, he took a few more sips of his wine, then he too walked downstairs.

He had a momentary fear she wouldn't be waiting for him, but there she was sitting at their table. Relief brought a rush of oxygen back into his constricted lungs.

As before, they were alone in their private corner, so he

spoke freely. "I realize my asking you to stay for another week surprised you. It surprised me. I've never expected to want a woman the way I do you. I took the liberty of reserving an available balcony cabin for you. As I said, you're my guest."

He could almost watch her mind work as she sat a few moments thinking about his offer. Eventually, she said, "As I mentioned before the salad arrived, I have an extra week of vacation."

Biting her lower lip, she stared out to sea. He sat patiently, allowing her time to gather her thoughts—and watched her twist her earring.

With a slight shake of her head, she said, "I don't know what value it is for me to stay if we don't have a future? You're right, I don't belong on a cruise ship—sex-themed or normal. My home is New York with wonderful friends and a wealth of professional opportunities should I decide to look for another job. Your cruise ship can't offer me anything close to what I have. Or really, any job at all."

As he listened to how living on his ship wasn't right for her, he felt the need to get up and pace around the deck in frustration. Instead, he forced himself to remain seated. He now wasn't so sure what her decision would be. Initially, he thought she would say yes, but maybe she wouldn't.

"That being said, I've never known sex could be so fantastic. Nor have I felt so safe with a man and…and I don't want to walk away from a once-in-a-life-time experience," she added after a beat of silence. "So, yes I'll stay. I can use the time to figure out my next career steps."

With those simple words, gratitude flooded his tense body. He hadn't realized he held his breath as she spoke. *Thank you.*

Nor did he want to admit to himself how important her

answer was. Trying to hide his relief, he said, "I wasn't ready to say goodbye." Maybe he'd never be, but that wasn't an option.

"Me neither. Besides, who could resist dinners like the one I just had?" she said, to him with a sensual smile and eyes filled with longing for what could never be.

Staring down at the table for a moment, he too experienced a deep regret for the loss his future held. A bleak hollowness opened inside his chest, like the earth's crust cracking apart with a tremendous earthquake.

Then her voice brought him back to the present.

"You did a marvelous job planning our dinner. What have you planned for this evening?"

SHE COULD TELL BY HIS SLIGHT FROWN THAT HE WAS UNSURE what to tell her. *Well, it must be something kinky or he would have told me immediately.*

Eventually, he said, "I'd like to take you to the passenger show in the Dolphin Salon."

She stiffened at his words. "I don't want to see the shows. I don't want to see passengers being whipped or sexually humiliated. Of course, there's probably a lot more to BDSM, but with my limited knowledge, this is all I know."

Suddenly all the joy of the evening evaporated—the intimacy and sexual excitement that filled her vanished.

"Even if that is what they want?"

She could see by how formal he'd become that he too had lost the magic. His face no longer smiled at her with its open, relaxed warmth. Instead, she looked into unreadable eyes.

Undaunted by his response, she said, "They can do whatever turns them on. I just don't have to watch."

"OK, that's fair. Will you humor me and watch one show only? It'll last for just fifteen minutes, or less."

"What makes it so important going?"

"Because this cruise is for you to try new things, experience new feelings, and escape, even for a few minutes, the controlled and proper life you've been living. And if you're interested in understanding your sexuality, then stepping out of your comfort zone is essential. I'm not expecting you to do what you see on stage; however, you might find it exciting to watch. And it's good to understand our limits. While I find the shows arousing, that kink isn't my style."

Silence. *Well, that's good to know.*

With that thought, her tension evaporated.

"OK, I'll watch one show and then we leave. Promise?"

"Promise. Thank you. And I want you to know BDSM is about keeping the submissive person feeling safe, sane, and knowing everything is consensual. Anything else is abuse—not BDSM." After a short pause, he added, "I'd like you to wear something for me. It's a small, remote-controlled vibrator that goes in your pussy against your G-spot and rests outside on your clitoris. It's meant to be worn walking around, so you'll find it comfortable."

"How do you know I'll find it comfortable?"

"We sell lots of them. If they were uncomfortable, no one would buy them." Quickly adding, he said, "And no, I've never used one before."

Silence again.

"Will you wear it?"

"Show it to me. I'll decide after I see it."

Reaching into his pocket, he pulled out a small bag and gave it to her. Kimberlee took out a petite purple, oddly shaped vibrator that fit in the palm of her hand. Made of soft silicone, it looked comfortable. Anyway, she would only have to wear it for fifteen minutes. "All right. I'll go to my cabin to try it out."

"If you walk through the club, there's a restroom outside the door. Of course, I'd like to fit it in you, but most likely, you'd say 'no' so I won't ask."

Nodding, she got up and walked to the lady's room, returning a few minutes later.

It felt funny inside her, awkward, and slightly uncomfortable, but nothing hurt. Knowing he had the remote created anticipation in her aroused body.

"I don't feel anything. Have you turned it on?" she asked, worried it wasn't strong enough. Surprisingly, she looked forward to trying out this new toy. Already her body began tightening and tingling in expectation of the divine sensations to come when he started it.

"No, I'm waiting until we sit down in the Salon. Why don't you leave and I'll be right behind you?"

SHE SILENTLY LEFT THEIR TABLE AND WALKED UP ONE FLIGHT of stairs to deck six. Each movement rubbed the vibrator against her sensitive parts. She could only imagine what it would feel like when he triggered the remote in his pocket.

CHAPTER EIGHTEEN

*S*he entered the Salon, which was two-thirds full with people clustered around the small stage. Going directly to their dark corner in the back, she sat. Within a minute, he was beside her.

"Looks like the BDSM scenes are a big draw," Kimberlee said, uncertainty in her voice.

Even people who kept their bedroom activities private could enjoy watching what other couples did. Maybe voyeurism gave them ideas for livening up their own sex lives or provided an extra shot of excitement.

This was one more new experience for her—even if it wasn't one she'd have tried for herself. *At least, not for others to watch.* She'd already been freaked by the idea of her friends catching her in the act with Johan viewing the strip show in the theater.

Oh, he's shifted to Johan in my thoughts. I wonder what that says.

Even from their corner, they had a great view of the stage. But then Kimberlee wasn't here for the show, she just wanted to be with him. After their delicious and romantic dinner, she would have rather been in their private grotto for their own sex show between the two of them.

He hadn't steered her wrong yet, so she trusted him even when this performance wasn't her first or hundredth choice. Mentally preparing herself for what was to come, she withdrew into the quiet world of her meditation breath.

Silently sitting side by side, she noted how he respected her need for space and sent him a wordless thank you.

Now she could focus on what she was feeling—a mixture of emotions that bounced between anticipation and apprehension. Yes, being honest with herself, she was looking forward to seeing her first live sex show and learning more about BDSM. At the same time, she acknowledged a creeping unease about watching something out of her safety zone, which included behaviors condemned by the majority of people.

Of course, everything she'd done on this ship was stamped with social disapproval. Yet she still joyfully participated. *I'm bouncing back and forth like a yoyo between the way I was raised and who I am now. I either need to stop being with Johan or jump all the way in—not this half-in and half-out shit.*

Minutes slowly ticked by in the restrained stillness between them. With her anxiety mounting, she unconsciously began twisting her earring, then in the next minute rubbing her hands together—clutching them as her insides clenched in nervousness.

I'm being ridiculous.

As she turned toward the Captain to tell him she wanted to go, he lightly put his hand on her fingers. "Give it a chance," he said. "Watch one scene, then if you don't enjoy it, we leave."

She nodded, secure in knowing she could escape anytime.

Kimberlee didn't have long to wait for the show to begin. Within minutes, a couple walked out on the low stage. The twenty-something, auburn-haired woman wore red, four-inch stiletto heels, black stockings held by a red silk garter belt, a wide red leather collar around her neck, and a thick, red silk ribbon binding her wrists. Nothing else. The man dressed in a pinstripe suit with the crotch cut out and his hard-on shouting for attention.

At first, she studied the two people, intrigued by their comfortable display of nudity and sexual arousal. Then her traditional upbringing kicked in making her uneasy watching something that should have remained private.

She couldn't relate to *Fifty Shades of Grey*, so what was she doing here?

Still some kind of fascination locked her in place. She stayed, eyes glued to the stage. She'd just watch one, then go.

The two people stood staring into each other's eyes. Without help from her Dom, the sub began lowering herself to the wooden floor, making her mouth level with his jutting cock.

Just as the sub's bound hands were reaching for his dick, Kimberlee's vibrator began to softly buzz. At first, she heard the muted sound but felt nothing. Then her body perked up to the new sensation. Her pulse pounded and tingling began deep in her channel.

Her mind jumped back and forth between stage and pussy.

As the sub began licking the Dom's balls and stroking his cock with her bound hands, the vibrator slipped up a notch with greater intensity. Suddenly, Kimberlee's nipples ached, her panties became damp, and her body demanded his skillful caresses. Ripples of ecstasy traveled through her from both the vibrator and the mesmerizing show.

She had never watched people having sex, not even online. *This truly is erotic.*

She also found herself enjoying the sensation of letting the Captain maintain his control of her vibrator.

Very quickly, the pinstriped man's breathing deepened. His full-throated moans filled the theater. His hands dug into the woman's hair, gripping her head forcing her to swallow the entire length. Deeper and deeper he thrust. Faster and faster he shoved himself down her throat.

Just then, the vibrator kicked up another notch, making Kimberlee aware of her pelvic muscles contracting and the beginning of a climax.

As her orgasm began overwhelming her, the vibrator shut off, but too late to stop her coming. Quickly, the Captain leaned over kissing her, swallowing her cries of pleasure.

Laughing softly, he whispered in her ear, "I'm sorry. I didn't know you were so close to coming. I should have shut it off sooner. Obviously, you enjoy watching this scene."

Still chuckling, he kissed her ear and neck. By this time, she just laid her head against the back wall and let him nibble her senseless. All the while, she observed the show through partially open eyes.

Within minutes, the Dom gave one last forceful thrust, unloading down his sub's throat. Throwing back his head, he opened his mouth, releasing a reverberating roar. Kimberlee watched, enthralled, as the sub's throat contracted with giant swallows, while her body remained an obedient vessel. Kimberlee could almost hear the audience sigh in appreciation of a performance well done...just before they applauded.

That was everyone who applauded except for her and the Captain. On the one hand, his eyes looked solely at the woman next to him. On the other hand, she remained in shock from what occurred on stage, as well as how much she enjoyed watching it.

Maybe I do have a bit of a voyeur in me.

While she could never do something like this in public, she was intrigued with the entire scene. So much for her to learn about sex and so little time to learn it.

With the stage empty, the next scene was ready to begin. Everyone remained seated.

Kimberlee thought about leaving, but curiosity won out. She stayed nestled in the Captain's embrace, waiting for the next performance. The horse already left the barn, so no need to shut it now.

This time the ship's maintenance crew carried out a contraption that looked like it was used for torture during the inquisition. Made of steel, it had four, one-foot-long leather pads—two at each end—and an elevated padded bar in the center. Each of the four pads had two sets of steel cuffs to strap down the arms and legs. The distance between the two sets of pads was the perfect width for a person to stand between the sub's spread legs.

Leaning over to the Captain, she asked, "What in the world is that?"

"It's called a punishing bench."

Before she could ask him how he knew, he said, "I've been on this ship for two years and have seen everything. Almost everything, that is. No bestiality or extreme pain."

Immediately, the next couple walked out naked onto the stage…definitely middle-aged. The man, slightly overweight, carried a small black bag. The woman, whose body showed the marks and sagging of multiple pregnancies, carried herself proudly, her hands empty.

She stared, fascinated at a lady who wasn't ashamed of her overweight, non-culturally-approved figure. While

Kimberlee kept her New York self swaddled in Spanx, morti-fied by her ugly, chunky build. She hated looking at herself in the mirror even clothed, but never, ever naked.

No audience member booed or yelled nasty comments… It was as if the viewers accepted the woman just as she was.

What she couldn't wrap her mind around was how natural nudity and sexuality were for some people.

Captivated by the lady's self-confidence, she almost missed the brass clamps attached to each nipple. The clips were, in turn, connected by a brass chain that hung down to her waist.

Captain Johan leaned over to Kimberlee saying, "Those are adjustable nipple clamps with rubber-coated tips. The chain adds extra pull—should extra pressure be needed."

Her face must have conveyed the panic, because he immediately added, "Don't worry. I'm not suggesting you do this… Unless, of course, you want to. Many women and men find these clamps heighten arousal."

"Do you like them?"

"I've never tried them, so I don't know. As you've discovered, my nipples are sensitive, so I'm not sure how these would feel."

Briefly nodding, she whispered back, "If you expect me to use them, you'll have to try them first."

"You've got a deal. I'll pick a pair up. We can use them tomorrow night," he said with a sensual, seductive sparkle in his eyes, shamelessly gazing at her body as if she were already wearing them.

Seeing his look, the breath caught in her throat, whether with fear or expectation she didn't know. Then her nipples tightened as if they wanted him to attach the clips, igniting contractions in her already wet pussy.

Catching movement on the stage from the corner of her

eye, she swiveled around to observe the unfolding performance. She watched, eyes widening in shock, as the man helped the woman onto the bench. With the sub's back facing the audience, she knelt on the two back pads, then bent over the towering waist-bar, placing her forearms on the front cushioned rests.

The raised waist-bar forced the sub's ass in the air into an extreme doggy position. *Just like I must have looked on the side of the bed. Oh my God! How could anyone do this in front of an audience?*

Kimberlee's mouth fell open in stunned silence. The fifteen-inch distance between the two leg pads and her uplifted ass, forced the sub's Brazilian-waxed pussy open to the audience. Nothing remained left to the imagination.

In the next moment, the Dom locked the straps around the sub's wrists and forearms. Then he moved to her calves and ankles. When he finished strapping her down, she was securely bound and had no way of escape until he released her.

By now, Kimberlee remained frozen like a flower trapped in amber. She wanted to watch and she wanted to run. Watching won out. She stayed glued to her seat, riveted on the naked couple.

Out of the bag, the Dom produced a bamboo paddle with five air-flow holes down the center. Standing off to the side, he allowed people a clear view of what he did. First, he slowly and gently caressed his sub's elevated, bared ass with the paddle. Then he moved to rubbing the edge of the BamPaddle between her open, exposed honey-lips. Even bound and bent over the two-inch wide center poll, she still arched her back, moving her hips back and forth asking for more attention—which he gave her.

After a few more intimate rubs, he lowered the paddle

down to his side. Kimberlee sat with the rest of the audience, in breathless anticipation wondering when the paddle would move again. Finally, the Dom brought his arm up and back making a wide arch as he brought the paddle down on her vulnerable behind. The smack reverberated through the theater, followed immediately by her moan. While that first wallop produced a satisfying crack, it wasn't hard enough to leave a mark, just a slight pinkish glow.

His next swing landed harder producing a red imprint on her defenseless cheeks. The following smack turned her ass a brighter red. This time, she wailed her pleasure-pain, hanging her head in total submission.

Kimberlee remained so focused on the spanking scene she didn't notice her vibrator had come back on. Of course, it was on the lowest level, so she wouldn't immediately climax. Instead, her body remained in a heightened state of arousal between watching the activity on the stage and the gentle purr between her wet thighs.

Once the sub's flesh radiated a scarlet brilliance, the Dom placed the paddle back into his bag. He walked back to his groaning sub, softly caressing her burning bottom. Showing both her and the audience his loving care for his partner.

Not realizing she was holding her breath, Kimberlee waited to see what the Dom would do next. He didn't keep her waiting.

Kneeling down at the foot of the bench, he directly faced the sub's soaked, opened-wide pussy. Reaching up, he spread open her ass cheeks revealing her back hole for all the world to see. Leaning forward, he placed a kiss on it, then sucked and licked her puckered sphincter.

Kimberlee released her breath in a great whoosh. This sex play she understood. Something she loved doing to the Captain. And if she was honest with herself, she had loved his finger up her ass. While she didn't have the courage to ask him to do it again, she knew he understood her needs. Needs that he'd awakened and nurtured. Needs that left her starving for more.

Needs that might never be fulfilled once she stepped off his ship.

Aroused by the activity on the stage, the low vibrational stimulation, and her desperate desire for the Captain, she squirmed on the love seat. But nothing released her escalating craving.

Of course, it didn't help that she remained fixated on the couple performing. Gone was her embarrassment of what they were doing. Her judgments of what constituted proper sex shredded. A lifetime of inhibitions demolished in a moment.

The Dom stood in one smooth motion. Uninhibited by his nakedness and arousal, he sauntered back to his tote bag, pulling out two items. Before determining what he held in his hand, Kimberlee realized he was squeezing a dab of K-Y jelly onto a vibrating iridescent pink butt plug with graduated beads. After rubbing the goop around the toy, he stuck his finger between her cherry-glowing behind, smearing his greased finger on and in her back passage.

With the sub well lubricated, he began gradually inserting the toy up her ass. Her deep-throated moans filled the theater.

For Kimberlee, it was as if the Captain was pushing the plug up her butt. Desire burned as fiercely inside her as if she was actually on stage in place of the sub. Now, she began understanding how people could perform in public.

With one final push, the vibrator lodged firmly up to the safety handle. The Dom pushed a button and the toy began pulsating. The theater filled with the sub's sobs…groans from audience members…and moans from an unashamed Kimberlee.

Standing between his sub's forced-opened thighs, the Dom grasped his engorged cock. With one thrust, he pushed his plum-colored, swollen penis head into her glistening cleft. With the next push of his hips, his entire shaft slid all the way in.

Pausing for a moment, he reached around to squeeze and rub her clitoris. Tightly strapped down, all she could do was kneel, sobbing.

Throwing his head back in a deep growl, the Dom hammered his hips. Shortly, his sub's body convulsed with muscle-clenching ecstasy. With one last shove, an orgasm tore through him filling the room with his bellow of triumph.

By now, Kimberlee's vibrator increased a few more notches. Sweat slicked her forehead.

With no defenses left, she could only rest her head against the back wall, gripping the edge of the love seat so she didn't slide off into a howling puddle on the floor. She would have agreed instantly to anything that Johan wanted—including going on that stage.

Just so he never stopped the toy…until she came a hundred more times.

DURING THE TWO SCENES, THE CAPTAIN FOUND HIMSELF TORN between watching the stage and watching the passionate woman sitting next to him. Sometime during the BDSM action, he noticed she began relaxing and became caught up in the performance. It turned him on watching her squirm about on her seat. Exactly what he had hoped would happen.

Seeing her become aroused sent ripples of desire shooting into his already engorged dick. Swallowing a grunt, he tried covertly rearranging his privates, but nothing seemed to release the escalating discomfort. Only being inside of her would relieve his swelling ache.

He wasn't sure how she'd react to watching kinky sex. Of course, he'd hoped she wouldn't be repulsed. But he was afraid to assume she'd find the on-stage activities arousing.

Now as the second act came to its climax, he observed how caught up she was in the show. Funny, he'd never been fixated on restraining or disciplining. But seeing the way she became inflamed watching the performers, he knew he wanted to arouse her that same way.

Should he rent a punishing bench for their grotto?

He knew she wouldn't allow their sex play to remain one-sided. Just as she expected him to use the nipple clamps if she was going to wear them, so too would she expect him to be a sub to her Domme.

How did he feel about that? At this point, he'd gladly do whatever she wanted.

Tonight, he needn't think about those role reversals. Right now, he had to focus on getting back to their grotto. He'd worry about everything else tomorrow.

Pulling her against him, he turned off the vibrator, burying his face against her neck. He loved how she smelled —all woman.

"Kimberlee, let's go. We need to get to our grotto."

No response. She just snuggled closer to him. "Mmm, not going anywhere."

"Yes, you are. Come on now. Up you go."

No response.

Standing up, he reached down gently pulling her up. Not offering any help, she became deadweight in his arms, collapsing against him. *At least, she's standing. That's a start.*

"Just put one foot in front of the other."

Somehow, his voice registered to her because she began shuffling along with him. Sitting in the back allowed them to reach the exit in about the same time it took the maintenance men to remove the punishing bench. The next show began as they reached the elevator.

He bit back a groan as the ship slightly rolled with a swell, forcing her to lean into him for balance—pressing her hip into his raging hard-on. All the Captain could do was clench his jaw, hoping to get into their love-cabin before he lost all dignity and shot his wad into a pair of black dress pants.

Just as they got to the grotto, Kimberlee flopped on top of the covers. He didn't have the energy to undress her or himself. Instead, he collapsed beside her, still dressed. Sometime during the night, they ended up stripped and under the covers. Nestled in each other's arms.

CHAPTER NINETEEN
CRUISE DAY 6

*A*t nine in the morning, sitting al fresco off the Rose Buffet, the four friends enjoyed their first cappuccino, topped with extra-thick foam. The ship wasn't dropping anchor until ten in the Grand Caymans, so they'd indulged in extra sleep. And now they appreciated a leisurely breakfast watching the wake spread out behind the ship as they cruised through the glittering Caribbean.

While the women chatted, Kimberlee's mind drifted off to the early morning, where she'd remained snuggled in bed with Johan. Her nose had burrowed into the crook between his neck and shoulders, with his arms wrapped around her. Having awoken each morning alone, she was surprised finding him still with her. Had he overslept, missing his command on the bridge? Or had something in their relationship shifted, making him want to stay? Her pulse jumped at that last thought.

"Kimberlee, come back to us," Lori said. "Where did you go?"

"Oh, sorry about that. I was just thinking about how the Captain slept in this morning. And what a luxury it was waking up with him. Then I panicked thinking he missed getting to the bridge on time. So I woke him up, only to learn that he didn't have to be there until eight and had set his alarm for seven o'clock. Thankfully, I only woke him thirty minutes early."

"Well, now you're back with us. And we're waiting with bated breath to hear all about last night," Bonnie said. "Don't keep us in suspense."

With that Kimberlee launched into a detailed description of their delicious dinner, which he had the chef prepare specifically for her. She could see by how they leaned forward, hanging on to her detailed account and with a look of wonder in their faces that they too would have loved having such a treat.

"I'll ask him if the galley will make the same menu for you tonight. You'll love it. I almost would like to have it again myself. I'll text him… No, I can't do that because my phone's shut off to prevent the roaming charges. I'll leave him a note before we disembark to see if we can get that yummy meal for us."

Now she needed to broach the subject of staying on the ship for one more week. She knew her friends would support her, but loss of them still tightened her chest with regret. And with a dose of self-honesty, she also had a dose of fear being on her own with him. She wanted the support and guidance of her New York sisters.

Looking down at the empty cappuccino cup, she nibbled on her lip, deciding how to begin.

"OK, out with it," Lori said. "We're not waiting all day to hear about what you have to say."

The other two women nodded.

Kimberlee shifted in her chair. Then exhaling she said, "He asked me to stay one more week."

No one looked surprised. Bonnie took another bite of her raspberry jam-covered English muffin, while Paulette had another sip of cappuccino. Lori nodded as if she was expecting this announcement. They didn't say a word, waiting for her to continue.

"I said yes."

"If you hadn't, we'd have tied you up in your cabin, so you couldn't leave with us," Paulette replied immediately.

A relieved Kimberlee smiled at her companions. Maybe she'd made the right decision after all. "I knew you'd understand, but I was still worried about abandoning you."

And afraid of being alone without you.

"Oh, for heaven's sake," Paulette said, reaching across the table patting her hand. "You aren't deserting us. We're your best friends and want you to be happy."

"And the Captain definitely makes you happy," Bonnie added.

"But we have no future. I can't live on a sex ship. I can't live in a tiny cabin. I can't give up my career. *I can't!*" she said waving her hands in the air.

Lori rolled her eyes. "Don't be so dramatic. Has he asked you to marry him?"

"Of course not. Don't be silly. We just met."

"Exactly," said Paulette. "Then don't jump into talking about a long-term relationship."

Taking another sip of cappuccino, Bonnie added, "Enjoy your time with him, without expectations or sweating the small shit."

"That's easy for you ladies to say. I'm not as experienced as you are."

"Experience has nothing to do with it," Lori replied. "Just keep your mind focused on the here and now. Don't leap to the future, thinking about what-ifs. You know life always holds surprises, which we could never have predicted."

"So now, what did the two of you do last night?" Paulette added.

This was exactly what Kimberlee needed—a change of topic. And one that she was waiting to tell them about. She knew they had seen all the various sex shows, which made her comfortable talking to them about a punishing bench, nipple clamps, spanking paddles, and butt plugs.

By the time they finished a big breakfast, she had an earful of what occurred at the other passenger shows. Some were even more extreme than what she'd seen. And most were more than what she would be willing to do, even in private.

At the same time, she was hungry for all the information she could get about sex. The more the better for her.

When they finished discussing the finer attributes of the different butt plugs, the ship had already dropped anchors off George Town. Needing to be at the dock thirty minutes prior to their eleven-thirty tour, they flew back to their cabins to get ready for their next tropical adventure—a private, two-and-a-half-hour Jet Ski tour with stops at Stingray City and Starfish Beach.

Each woman would have her own wave runner.

Never having ridden a personal watercraft, Kimberlee would once again be the neophyte with this excursion. But that no longer caused a problem for her. She'd become comfortable with who she was—and who she was becoming. Except, she still wished she had a body that could wear a sexy bikini.

GEORGE TOWN LACKED PIERS FOR DOCKING CRUISE SHIPS, requiring them to be anchored out at sea. The MS *Aphrodite*'s crew used the red-orange lifeboats to tender passengers to and from the shore when they couldn't dock.

By the time Kimberlee and her friends boarded their tender, the crew helped them on immediately, because most passengers had left on the earlier ones. Each woman had their own window seat, giving them the best views for their trip across the sun-glittering water.

Sitting in the boat with open windows, allowing the cooling Caribbean breeze to blow around them, added to the adventure of the day. No one talked. They were fixated on the waves the small vessel bounced through and watched the shore as it drew closer. Their five-minute ride ended much too quickly. Before they knew it, the crew offered helping hands.

On the landing, their guide stood waiting for them. Their first order of business required filling out the standard legal forms. Then came the safety and operational demos. Finally, with the coast guard approved life jackets on, they practiced driving around a calm harbor.

Kimberlee quickly got the knack of zipping about on her dark gray and white Jet Ski—a lot simpler than driving the Case tractor on her uncle's farm. Throwing back her head, she laughed. Joy bubbled through her like champagne. Oh, how she loved the independence of moving across the water on her own…exhilarated in the power of the machine between her thighs as her heart pounded from the adrenaline pumping through her. She relished the speed and freedom that came from riding the waves.

I could get used to this. The sea belongs to me. I'm totally on my own. And I'm in control.

They only had a twenty-five-minute ride to Stingray City

—a sandbar filled with dozens of southern stingrays. Their guide helped them off their wave runners, where they were immediately surrounded by the velvety soft fish. Once the women became comfortable stroking the stingrays, the guide hand-fed the sea creatures squid.

Now more stingrays came speeding over for the treats.

Having grown up around animals, Kimberlee loved feeding the stingrays. Her big-city friends watched and enjoyed the feel of them brushing against their legs but wouldn't handle raw squid or offer the gastronomic delight to the four-foot-wide, two hundred pound underwater creatures.

In the midst of a dozen stingrays caressing her skin, her mind leaped to how their silky softness felt so like the Captain's penis. With just that one thought, her abdominal muscles clutched with desire, leaving her weak-kneed and breathless.

She had to stop. That was easier thought than done.

I wonder if he's going to buy those nipple clamps?

And so, her mind flipped back and forth between her wonderful adventure with nature and the one she'd had with her Captain the night before.

Back on their Jet Skis, the women rode to Starfish Beach. This time, instead of a shallow sandbar, they had four feet of water beneath them. After putting on masks and snorkels, they floated on top while looking down at the plethora of large orange cushion starfish.

They knew from Lori's talk they were in a marine replenishment zone, so they didn't pick up the sea stars. Their guide did, but he kept the one he held underwater. He showed them how the eyes were at the end of each of the five arms. And he talked about how they ate, reproduced, and protected themselves. He told them sea stars weren't fish but were still sea mammals.

While this part of the women's excursion wasn't as thrilling as swimming with stingrays, they loved seeing and learning about these remarkable creatures.

As Kimberlee snorkeled, she enjoyed looking, not only at the underwater life, but also how the sandy floor reflected the shifting clouds and sunlight. She even saw a crab scampering from one sand hole to another.

So much amazing life exists under the surface of the sea. So much that I don't know. Even with one more week on this ship, I still won't have the time I need to learn about our underwater world...and definitely not enough time with Johan.

Standing up in the shallow water, she stared out across the dazzling blue ocean with drooping shoulders and a heavy heart. Funny how this gorgeous tropical world spoke to her—as if this was where she belonged. But of course, that was silly. Her life was now in New York with her dear friends, clients, and a wonderful career, which she'd worked hard to build.

The laughter of her companions brought her back to the delight of their excursion and how much she loved being with them.

Ending their short stop at Starfish Beach, everyone zoomed back on their wave runner to their original meeting place. Then once on the ship, they indulged in hotdogs and fries from the pool grill, before showering off the salt and sea.

SHORE-DAY PLEASURES FOR PASSENGERS MEANT SAFETY DRILL work for the crew.

Because the ship was anchored, they had plenty of space

to release the lifeboats. Therefore, the Captain used this time for the thirty-minute abandon-ship practice.

To ensure this exercise remained safe for all crew—and passengers should they need to abandon ship—he had lifeboats and launch equipment regularly inspected and maintained.

Making a public announcement from the bridge, he told all people on board about the safety drill. He sounded the abandon-ship alarm followed by his announcement to abandon ship. Then he repeated immediately the standard drill phrase: "For exercise only. For exercise only. For exercise only."

Even though he knew this was just practice, in the back of his mind existed a hidden kernel that someday he might have to use it. Living on the sea and dependent on the whims of nature, life remained unpredictable. Every sea captain understood the risks inherent in their profession.

Everything went smoothly. Three lifeboats bobbed at a distance from the ship for a few minutes, then returned. Crew members disembarked, and the boats were raised.

Now, with a few hours for himself, he spent time on his veranda trying to sort out his feelings about Kimberlee and what he wanted. He let the vastness of the sea and brisk tropical breeze clear his mind from the crew drill.

Priding himself on accurately and quickly understanding a situation, he disliked not having a ready answer as to what he wanted from this relationship. He found the ocean easier to read than deciphering his present romantic needs. Besides, he had weather satellites and marine-weather forecasts guiding him about what to expect when sailing. No such predictive information existed for their affair. Here, he navigated blind.

What kept recycling through his mind was the quotation he kept since his early days in the naval academy. André Gide wrote, "One doesn't discover new lands without consenting to lose sight, for a very long time, of the shore."

He'd always had the courage to sail the vast seas, without need to see the coast. But not with Kimberlee. With her, he remained docked in the harbor—unwilling to lose sight of terra firma. In this liaison, his courage had deserted him. He'd become risk-averse.

Whether in two days or one week, she was leaving. Still mourning the loss of his wife and unborn child, one broken heart was enough. He didn't want to love again. Plus, there wasn't room for anyone in his life, but Eira.

Yet... Yet in the last ten years, he'd never felt this alive. Instead of going through the motions of living, he watched the sunrise from the bridge and looked forward to the challenges of the day. Night no longer held a bleak emptiness, but filled him with a pleasure he'd never expected to feel again.

Did he have the courage to unmoor his heart and sail into unfamiliar, unchartered waters?

He didn't know. But he'd have to decide soon before the tide left without him.

As he stood leaning on the railing, Ramil knocked on the veranda door.

Glad for the distraction, he waved through the window for Ramil to join him. "I was getting tired of listening to my thoughts," he said. "Thanks for the distraction."

"I've got some beer in the fridge. Have one with me."

When he walked back into the cabin, Ramil handed him a cold bottle. They comfortably sat, both enjoying the relaxed time and conversation.

After a deep swallow from his beer, the Captain said, "I can see by your serious expression you have something to say."

Meeting the Captain's gaze with a direct, unwavering

look, Ramil replied, "You know me too well. It comes from working together so long. I'll be blunt. It's time you put your wife in a special place for safekeeping. You need to open yourself up to life and love again. I know you don't want to hear this, but saying unwanted things is what a friend's for." He took a pull from his beer. "If you keep yourself closed off to your needs, you'll become useless as a leader. You've often told me being a ship's captain is more than just understanding maritime engineering and the sea. It's also living with, guiding, and developing your crew—especially your officers. You can't do this if you remain closed off and shrinking inside."

A part of Johan wanted to tell Ramil to get the fuck out of his cabin, but he also knew he was a true friend who said what others were afraid to utter. That's why he trusted him, because Ramil didn't kiss his ass, but spoke the truth. And to the all-powerful ship's captain, that took balls.

It was also rare to hear the truth spoken.

Choosing his words carefully, he replied, "I'm realizing, in some ways, Kimberlee's perfect for me, but we have such different lives. I can't see a way for us to be together once she leaves the ship. Our personality, intelligence, and passion match well. I'm not leaving my life here. Short of giving up her life in New York and her fancy firm to live on a sex cruise ship, I see no future. And she's not willing to do that. But even if she was, I'm not willing to release Eira. Maybe I'm keeping her as a life preserver to avoid the pain of loving again."

Taking a sip of beer, Ramil said with a compassionate voice, "After ten years, it's time for you to move on, before your life shrivels into nothingness and you become an empty shell. If you want to remain a vital human being, alive to yourself and the world, you can't do that dead inside."

Captain Johan, sat quietly for a few minutes staring through the veranda's glass door.

Changing the topic, he said, "The note you gave me requested the special dinner for her friends this evening. Chef Klaus is preparing the same meal for tonight."

"Will you be joining them?" Ramil inquired.

The Captain shook his head, then added, "Thanks for picking up the toys for me. I'll go through them while they're having dinner." He then handed Ramil a ship's prepaid internet card as reimbursement for all the purchases.

Knowing Ramil didn't want it, he gave him a steely stare.

"Thanks," Ramil said, reaching for it.

After working together for eight years, their comfortable conversation moved on covering a wide range of topics. Captains rarely developed true friendships on their ships, especially with a room steward. But he and Ramil had created a unique relationship, which spontaneously evolved over time. Without Eira to talk with, Johan needed a person he could trust. Ramil filled that void.

Eventually, Ramil left his friend to write the note telling Kimberlee their custom-prepared dinner was set for 1900 hours. A few minutes later, Johan walked into the hall giving the envelope to Ramil. No words were necessary, Ramil knew to leave it in the women's mailbox attached outside the cabin.

Now the Captain had to decide about the nipple clamps sitting in a bag on the grotto's table. He wanted Kimberlee to wear them, even knowing he'd also have to use them himself. He was neither adverse to nor thrilled about trying the clips, but he wanted to put them on her. So, he'd give them a shot... if he had to.

CHAPTER TWENTY

*E*ntering the Rose Buffet for the custom-prepared, al fresco dinner, Belmiro showed Kimberlee and her friends to their table—the same one where they'd shared breakfast in the morning. Instead of a sunny day, they now enjoyed a balmy evening with a slight breeze.

Kimberlee smiled at him, saying, "Good evening, Belmiro. I see you're in charge of us. How was your day?"

With a smile that didn't reach his eyes, he answered, "We had one of our safety drills. Afterward, I spend the afternoon on the beach with friends. Did you ladies have a good time in port?"

Bonnie answered him. "We explored the area on Jet Skis. We had a fabulous time. This is a magical world with gorgeous beauty."

"And now we're looking forward to our delicious dinner," Lori added, giving him a big smile.

He told them, "You know there's no menu this evening. I hope that's OK."

"Given this amazing feast, we're fine without one," Kimberlee responded, taking her seat at the table.

Even after enjoying the same dinner the previous night, she still anticipated having their special meal a second night. She loved the food's complex, fresh flavors, as well as showing her friends the Captain's extraordinary culinary-planning skills. Rhythmically swinging her crossed leg, she almost bounced in her chair when she described for the umpteenth time their coming banquet.

As they talked about the food, her mind momentarily focused on the growing sense of loss tightening her chest. No matter how much she loved being with her friends, somehow the dinner remained slightly off; she wasn't sharing it with her Captain. With the limited time they had remaining, she desired every moment with him. But she also needed quality time with her New York sisters.

So now, she must be one hundred percent with them.

Forcing her thoughts back to their conversation, she didn't want them to catch her drifting off as they had during breakfast. Plus, she planned to make the most of the small window available to them. In about a day and a half, they would be disembarking. She would not.

Five minutes after sitting down, Belmiro placed the salads on the table. With the first bite, she experienced the same burst of pleasure as she did the previous night.

Everyone agreed with her, as evidenced by their enthusiastic comments. "You're right," Bonnie said. "This is simple and delicious. We should have had him creating our dinners this past week."

Mouths full, Lori and Paulette only mumble their consensus.

During the main course, Paulette interjected a new topic to their discussion saying, "Belmiro could be on stage with the Chippendales men. He's quite delicious...like our dinner."

"I agree," Lori replied. "I love his thick, chestnut-brown hair and mysterious, dark eyes. He's built like the cowboy we saw on stage. Definitely irresistible and quite delicious."

Kimberlee said, "Maybe that's why he keeps an emotional distance. On a sex ship, he's bound to have a slew of propositions. If he wants to keep his job, he needs to keep a professional reserve."

"Good for him, but not for us," Bonnie sigh. "There's an intense energy about him that's quite seductive. I, for one, find his mystique intriguing."

Lori declared to her friends, "I bet he has a hell of a story to tell. It's a shame we'll never know it."

Like most of this trip, everyone concurred.

For the rest of the evening, their conversation drifted between their yummy meal and what they had to do on the final cruise day.

From previous experiences, her friends described the last day, which passengers called end-of-cruise-day blues.

Paulette explained, "The best way to minimize our last-night depression is to do some packing tomorrow morning before we head to the pool. This way we have less to do after dinner and packing won't feel so daunting. For me, I get depressed on the last day of a cruise. It happens every time."

"Besides," Lori added, "we have to make sure we leave clothes out for departure. I, for one, don't want to be like those poor people who packed all their clothes and only had their pajamas to wear off the ship. Even worse for a ship like this, when most people sleep naked, they'll have nothing to wear if they pack everything."

A vision flashed through Kimberlee's mind of a poor passenger bare-assed, trying to get off the ship in a robe. Which they'd be charged for.

"Or like passengers who get stuck wearing slippers because they packed their shoes," added Bonnie.

Of course, this wasn't an issue for Kimberlee. She just needed to move things to another cabin. As of yet, she didn't know where her new quarters would be, but that wasn't important. She could be happy anywhere on this ship. Hopefully, it would be closer to his cabin, so he wouldn't have far to go in the morning.

Then it hit her, one benefit of having her own private space meant not needing to get a grotto. *I so much prefer staying in my room instead of running around the ship every morning half undressed and with smeared makeup.*

While enjoying their refreshing homemade dessert, Paulette asked, "What are your plans tonight, Kimberlee?"

"I don't know. He never said anything. I assumed he'd meet me at the end of dinner." She didn't mention the nipple clips.

Just the thought of wearing those clamps made her body flush hot with excitement, yet become cold with anxiety. But her nipples did perk up with tingling interest. While she didn't like pain, a gentle boost of pleasure had its benefits.

What she knew was he'd never do anything she didn't want. She totally trusted him to respect her wishes, making her feel safe. That was a huge gift, which many women never found. She understood her blessings after volunteering in a women's shelter twice a month. She would never take her safety for granted again.

Leaning back in her chair with a contented sigh, she let herself enjoy the rest of the dinner with her friends. Her tummy felt pleasantly full from their delicious feast...and the rest of her would be satisfied later.

WHILE THE WOMEN DELIGHTED IN THEIR DELECTABLE DINNER, the Captain spent his time preparing the grotto for their evening.

That afternoon, Ramil walked out of the sex store holding a bag full of toys. The Captain couldn't give him specific directions as what to buy because he'd had no reason to study the merchandise. But he did provide a list of general items, trusting Ramil to make the right selections.

Once inside the grotto, Johan opened the bag, placing the props on the small round table. Looking over an eclectic display, he smiled. It seemed Ramil had spent time in that shop for his own purposes and knew what to buy. He had bought adjustable nipple clamps, two soft red silk sashes that were looped on one end, a pink silk flogger, and a narrow, starter vibrating butt plug. Those he'd use. He'd skip the pink mask, because he wanted to watch Kimberlee's eyes as she watched him and as her orgasms built.

He had thought of renting a punishing bench, but again wanted to observe her face. Unfortunately, he couldn't see it in that downward position. For him, the pleasures of sex involved all the senses, not just his cock. Looking around the room to see what he could use as a bondage prop, he decided on a dining chair.

That'll work. Her legs will fit perfectly over the armrests.

Using the chair, he could keep her exposed for him to look at, smell, taste, and play with. Just thinking of what he could do with and to her glorious body gave him an instant boner.

Over the years, he'd talked with experienced BDSM passengers. One consistent piece of advice he'd heard centered on empathy. Doms must remain deeply empathetic and totally in-tune with their partners. At all times, tops needed to feel what the bottoms experienced. At no time could they get lost into their own needs, abandoning focus on their subs.

But now, he still had duties before the evening belonged to him. He needed to get his lust under control until he was back in their grotto.

Relaxed by the muted whoosh of their ship sliding through the dark sea, Kimberlee and her friends reveled in the glow of their comradery and a deliciously satiated hunger. Their dinner ended with a refreshing, sweet ice-wine from Canada. Sipping their crisp dessert drink, they unanimously agreed of all their excellent meals on the voyage, this one had been the best.

As their lovely evening came to an end, Kimberlee's eyes began prickling with unshed tears. Even her anticipation of being within Johan's magical embrace couldn't compensate for her friends leaving. She knew from her meditation and yoga practices that joy and sadness could exist simultaneously—as they were right now inside of her. But that knowledge didn't make the loss of her best friends, just for a week, any easier.

Thinking about her jumble of multiple emotions, her body began tingling with energy that came out of nowhere. Looking up, she watched Johan walk toward their table. *Even when I can't see him, my body knows when he's around.*

Something in her face must have communicated to her dining companions, because they immediately stopped talking and turned around. When they saw who it was, they gave him genuine smiles of gratitude.

She could see by the pleased look on his face that he appreciated their responses. While she couldn't take credit for the meal he'd created, she still sat a little straighter with pride. He was her Captain.

After everyone expressed their gratitude, the Captain offered Kimberlee his hand, helping her out of the chair. He didn't appear to be in the mood for small talk. She could sense his eagerness to leave. But then, she too wanted to be in their grotto.

She watched her friends' eyes light with approval for his attention to her. Yes, she wanted them to respect him, not only because he was the Captain, but also because he was a kind person who treated her with respect. *That is, except for our first night.*

Placing her hand into his, a sense of rightness filled her. *How amazing. One minute his hands give me comfort and the next they make me wild with desire. So many layers for me to consider.*

Saying goodbye, they walked toward the side door.

Whispering to her, he said, "I'm sorry, but in public I can't hold your hand."

"I understand," she replied, immediately dropping their clasp.

Quietly, she walked beside him, missing the comfort of his touch, and the energy flowing naturally between them with just a simple contact. But then, even when not touching, she experienced a subtle current running through her body. It wasn't only sexual, but also a special connection which seemed to bind them.

As they headed to the elevator, he told her, "Everybody's about the ship. You ride it down. I'll take the stairs."

"That's fine. You know I'll beat you," she whispered, smiling.

Just before she stepped into the elevator, he softly said, "I bought the nipple clamps."

CHAPTER TWENTY-ONE

*A*fter his brief comment, a subtle throbbing began between Kimberlee's legs. Suddenly, her nipples began tingling, telling her it was time to try his new purchase.

The quick ride took her down five floors. Only one couple joined her. She gave a silent thank you for him not being with her. She didn't want their evening ruined by worrying people had seen them together.

Moving her head side to side released a smidgen of the tension caused by her nipple clamp thoughts. But nothing seemed to stop the mounting uncertainty about using them. Even living with constant sexual stimulation on this ship, she still faced the unknown with building anxiety.

Once off the elevator, she didn't know which cabin he'd reserved. Walking down a few doors to wait, within moments she saw him striding toward her.

Time for the show to begin.

Entering their room, she froze. There on the table before her was a colorful display of sex paraphernalia. After having seen the BDSM show, she knew what everything was for. Definitely kinky.

"This can't all be for us?" she asked, sounding more like a squeak than her normal confident voice.

"We'll only use what you're willing," he replied with a calming tone.

"After last night, I've a better understanding of what everything's for. Now tell me what you're planning."

His eyes deepened with passion as he told her, "Truthfully, I don't have anything specifically planned. I wanted options, so I got a little extra."

She inspected the items. Was she ready for this giant step? She wasn't sure. But neither was she willing to walk away.

Just as she was considering what to say, he added, "I'd like to watch you undress. Just as you watched me strip."

Softly biting her lower lip, she remained quiet for a moment thinking about what she really wanted. Looking into his eyes she felt, as much as saw, the blatant lust smoldering in their depths. Glancing down at his crotch, she let her eyes devour the massive bulge outlined by his black jeans. This man was her fantasy come to life. She refused to disembark without experiencing all the wonders he offered.

However, she didn't want him to see her body in the bright, harshness of cabin lights. Yes, he'd seen her during their other passionate encounters, but the lighting was dim. Fear nibbled at the edges of her self-confidence—worried when he had a bright light look at her, he'd decided he didn't like what he saw.

That's so scary for me.

Bouncing between her insecurity and being enthralled with him, she shut down her thinking brain, courageously tossing herself into the abyss of passion.

Emboldened by the wine enjoyed at dinner, her liquid courage spurred her to say without another thought, "Sit on the couch."

Now that Kimberlee stood in front of him, she wasn't sure where to begin. But strip she would. Bending, she first took off her sandals, tossing them aside. Standing with bare feet, she reached behind, unzipping her dress. But she paused with the zipper halfway down, watching as his breathing become irregular...and a shudder rippled through his exquisite body.

Never taking her eyes off him, she slowly removed her arms from the dress and let it pool about her feet. Now she remained in front of him clothed only in her black silk bra and panties.

A thrill of excitement surged through her.

Stepping out of the puddle about her feet, she draped the dress across the chair. *What do I take off next?*

Reaching behind her, she unhooked her bra, unhurriedly slipping the straps down her arms, then dropping the silky garment on top of the dress.

Her breasts had never felt so heavy and full.

As she remained boldly in front of him, watching his eyes deepen with passion, a flush of power filled her. She lifted her hands to cup her aching breasts, squeezing her nipples until they hardened into taut peaks. Pinching them, she became lost in the sexual current flashing through every cell of her trembling body. With a soft moan, she closed her eyes, tilting her head back in complete abandonment.

Slowly, she glided her hands down to the flimsy thong still covering her moist core. Lifting her head back up and opening her eyes, she stared straight into his hungry gaze. She slipped her fingers under the elastic, stroking her engorged folds. Then she slipped a finger into her slick canal.

Never taking her eyes off his face, flushed with lust, she withdrew her juice-coated finger, slipping it into her mouth. She sucked off her honey, as she had once licked his cock clean.

Through the short show, she relished her uninhibited sexual freedom. She reveled in the dominance she had over this commanding man. A seismic wave had smashed through her thick layers of respectability.

Finally, she reached down with both hands, slipping off her wet panties. The new Kimberlee stood proudly in front of him in all her naked glory.

JOHAN WATCHED, AMAZED BY HER MAGNIFICENT performance. In place of the fearful passenger he'd met the first night, he craved the confident, fiery woman boldly before him.

Within three strides, he reached her. Whispering in her ear, he said, "Just like you told me. I want you not to move and don't say a fucking word." He followed this command by a probing lick inside her ear, then a nip on her neck. He knew what made her burn for him.

Reaching up, he cupped her breasts, letting their weight rest on his palms. With his thumbnails, he scraped her rigid peaks, savoring how her body quivered.

As much as he wanted to take his time pleasuring her, smelling the musky richness of her arousal left his self-control in tatters. In self-preservation, he decided it was time for them to move on to their first BDSM scene.

"Kimberlee, look at me," he demanded.

Immediately, she did as he requested—gazing into his eyes with her newfound confidence.

"I'm going to move you backward to sit in the chair," he said, guiding her to the seat, still gripping her marvelous tits.

After she sat, he told her, "Hook your legs over the arms of the chair."

He observed only a moment of hesitation. Slowly, she

spread her legs wide for him, draping first one and then the other over the sides of the chair.

In shock, he watched as she reached down, fanning open her pussy lips for him.

For a moment, all he could do was gaze at the fabulous feast she offered. He saw from the bright pink color of her folds and the moist slickness how aroused she'd become.

Using his index finger, he reached down capturing a drop of seeping love-juice. Never taking his eyes from hers, he licked his finger clean, showing her how delicious she was.

And implying that he planned to taste so much more of her.

From the tabletop, he grabbed the two red silk bondage sashes. "Put your hands on your thighs," he ordered.

When she immediately complied, he slipped each wrist through the loop, tightening it with a quick jerk. "Your safe word is 'orchid.'"

She nodded. Then, he took the remaining length of each ribbon, wrapped it around a thigh and resting forearm, locking her in place.

While she never said a word, he listened to the purr arising deep in her throat. *By the end of the evening, you'll be screaming.*

Kneeling between her spread thighs, he deeply inhaled her enticing woman's perfume. He loved how she'd willingly surrendered herself to his lovemaking. In this position her body became totally his to command.

With a low growl of lust, he buried his face in her wet, exposed flesh. For a second, he didn't move, just reveled in the delicious scent and feel of her silken femininity. Then, he went to work licking around her pussy. Soon, he began sucking on her clit, flicking it back and forth with his tongue.

He savored feeling her struggle to move, but knew he'd

bound her making motion impossible.

With his face coated in her juices, he reluctantly pulled back to reach for his next instrument of pleasure—the nipple clamps. Tracking his every movement, her eyes flew open when he stopped eating her.

Yes! I love you watching me.

He attached the clips one by one on to her engorged nipples, tightening the clamps until her head fell back in total surrender. He had found the perfect tension that kept her on the edge of pleasure and pain, making sure he never crossed the line of hurting her.

One soft tug of the chain brought a loud groan. Even with limited mobility, her hips began rotating back and forth

Now it was time for her beautiful asshole. Kneeling back down, he began sucking on her puckered opening, as she had his, until her body shook with uncontrollable need. Then his tongue began forcefully pushing against the puckered back passage. In and out, he tongue-fucked her, stopping only when he felt the tight portal relax.

He slid his index finger into her vagina, stroking her G-spot making sure it became well lubricated. Withdrawing his tongue from her anus, he replaced it with his lubed finger. Giving a slight push, he slid in. Rotating it in circles and thrusting in and out, he listened as her moans transformed into sobs.

He gave her no place to hide, no way to run away. He may have anchored her to the chair, but so too had he bound her psychologically.

By now, his clothes had become their own form of bondage. *I've got to get out of these.*

Pulling out his finger with a few extra twists, he washed his hands and rapidly stripped.

From the table, he next selected the beginner butt plug.

Coating it with lube, he rubbed the toy around her loosening hole—watching how it opened even more for him. Then he asked, "Kimberlee, do you want me to stop or go on? Tell me what you want."

"Oh God, don't stop. Please don't stop."

With those words, he pressed the vibrator into her all the way to the base. Just as it slipped in, he pushed the button, turning on the low vibration.

KIMBERLEE'S INHIBITIONS VANISHED, ALONG WITH HER clothes. Watching his eyes devour her provided a shot of energy, strengthening her blooming self-confidence. By the time she removed the bra, her world had shrunk to an acute craving—to make up for decades of sexual starvation.

It wasn't until he told her to hook her legs over the arms of the chair that a dollop of fear flicked across her overstimulated nerves. Even with a pounding heart, her inherent trust overcame the momentary brush of alarm. With her next breath, she lifted one leg and then the other, draping them over the arms.

Freed from the confines of her comfort zone, she used her fingers spreading open her woman's folds, offering herself completely.

She watched as he reached down to her exposed channel, scooping up her wetness, then licking his coated finger. She knew exactly what he smelled and tasted.

Moments later, she observed him as he tightly bound each arm to a leg with the red silk sashes. Briefly, her muscles tightened in a flight response, but with one deep breath, she relaxed, allowing excitement to flood her unprotected body.

Before she could create a logical thought, he buried his face in her soaked slickness. With a low growl, he closed his lips around her clitoris as he flicked his tongue back and forth. All she could do was submit to the exquisite torture. Trapped in the chair, she tilted back her head, letting ecstasy cascade through her.

Suddenly, her eyes flew open when he withdrew his marvelous mouth.

With her passion-clouded brain, she registered he had reached for the nipple clamps. What would they feel like? Within moments, she knew. The pinching on her sensitive tips shot clenching needs deep into her belly. Soft mewling sounds escaped her lips as sweat dampened her vulnerable body.

Oh yes, I never knew.

That was her last coherent thought when he lightly tugged on the chain.

Once again, he knelt between her splayed thighs. This time he claimed her exposed asshole. Just as she did with his, he consumed her with his tongue. While his mouth devoured her, he thrust a finger into her vagina, caressing her G-spot.

Bound tightly, Kimberlee couldn't flee the astonishing sensations engulfing her. He left her no place to hide. Her body and sexual hunger remained visible and available to his every whim.

Lost in her own ocean of desire, it took her a few seconds to realize his mouth had vanished, replaced by his lub-coated finger. Easily, he slipped it in because her anal opening had relaxed. And then, he began finger-fucking her ass.

She didn't care if her sobs filled the room. *Please don't stop. Don't ever stop.*

A short while later, her excitement did pause when he removed his finger. Struggling to open her glazed-over eyes, she watched as he lubed the butt plug. But she didn't have long to wait. In a moment, he rubbed it around her overly sensitive back passage. She heard his voice, as if from a distance, asking her if she wanted him to stop or continue. All she could do was beg him not to stop.

He didn't.

Pushing the toy all the way up to its base, he pressed the button turning on the vibration. Then, he placed the Svakom Echo against her overly sensitive clitoris.

Pulsating energy exploded from the center of her vagina, roaring upward and out her fingertips and toes—fragmenting her into millions of pieces.

BY THE TIME SHE SPRAWLED LIMPLY IN THE CHAIR, JOHAN'S body screamed for release.

Even possessed by raging sexual demands, his muscles still felt heavy and his mind blurred, like he'd commanded his ship through an all-night, raging storm with hurricane-force winds and enormous swells. He wanted this experience to be extraordinary for her, so he focused his energy on her pleasure.

Now he needed to take care of himself.

He leaned forward, burying his face in her still quivering, wet pussy, inhaling the beauty of her scent. He reached his hand down grasping his cock, needing only a couple of rapid pumps to detonate.

With his eyes involuntarily dropping shut, he rested his cheek against the feminine softness at the apex of her thighs. After taking a few minutes to recover, he removed the butt plug, cleaned her, untied the silk ribbons, and unhooked her legs. Gently lowering her down to the carpet with him, he lovingly cradled her in his arms. Too exhausted to move the few feet to the bed, he fell asleep on the floor, tightly clasping her to his chest.

CHAPTER TWENTY-TWO
CRUISE DAY 7

*F*or the friends, their cruise-blues day began early so they could eat a leisurely breakfast and get started packing before luxuriating on the Lido deck. While her companions carefully filled luggage for when the airline baggage handlers tossed them around, Kimberlee just piled her things into a suitcase. All she had to do was roll it to her new cabin, one deck lower.

Watching them pack, she caught herself sniffling a few times and then in the next moment a buoyancy made her want to sing and dance with joy for the extra time with her Captain. Then the next moment, honesty forced her to acknowledge that this coming week would be her last time with him. This wasn't a long-term relationship. It would be a two-week shipboard romance—heartbreakingly, nothing more.

She liked her emotions understandable, not a mishmash of conflicting feelings swirling around inside, as they were now. It would be nice if sentiments could fit into neat columns just like financial numbers. But no such luck. She remained stuck on an emotional roller coaster.

Finally, when they had packed most of their belongings it was time for relaxing in the sun and cooling off in the pool.

Settled into their loungers, each person had their pool towel clipped on to the back of their chairs with chunky, blue dolphin holders.

Basking in the sun, Kimberlee had to admit that a sea day was a lovely way to say goodbye to her trip. Of course, she was saying farewell to her friends and not the ship. Which brought her to decide what to do about this evening. As much as she wanted to be with Johan, she also wanted this last evening with her dearest friends. Plus, she'd have another week with him, but not with them.

She resolved to use the next time she went inside, to write him a note telling him…telling what? That she wanted to be with them more than with him? Well, she did, but only for this one night. When she thought about it, they were her New York family, and he was…just a shipboard fling.

Thinking about him as only a sexy cruise romance made her insides ache with regret. There was no way, however, for them to have more than one more week together. *Sometimes life just isn't fair.*

With that decision made, she closed her eyes letting the ship's motion lull away most of her lingering regrets. The sounds of people splashing in the pool, conversations drifting on the wind and ice clinking in souvenir glasses, helped take her mind off the loss she struggled with.

Lido-deck contentment soothed her mind and body, allowing her thoughts to drift back to their time together last night—and her first BDSM, well soft BDSM, experience. Her sex-drenched thoughts sped up her heart rate and made her breasts feel weighty and tender. As her mind began reliving the chair scene and all those delicious things he did, she felt her tankini bottom dampen and her body beg for his attention.

Thinking about the past week, she'd lived with constant passion and yearning. Almost everything she thought, said, and did focused on sex and more sex. It was as if her life had been filled with an undercurrent of sexual wanting, buried under lawbooks and financial statements. Out of sight, out of mind, but not out of body.

If she were honest with herself, she couldn't have too much sex. Yes, there might come a time where she'd yell stop, too much, no more—but she hadn't found that limit yet. Maybe she never would.

As adventuresome as she was, she was still unsure of herself. She didn't know all the things she wanted. In fact, he knew her better than she knew herself. Yes, it turned her on stripping for him. Not even being ashamed of her body could destroy that joy. And all those things on the table intrigued her. She wanted to try everything. She wanted to lose herself in nonstop lovemaking. She wanted to sink into a cocoon of sex. Nonstop sex. She wanted Kimberlee to vanish, with only sexual pleasure existing.

Floating in and out of last night's erotic replays, her morning slipped away in a haze of sun, sea, and steamy memories.

By early afternoon, Bonnie declared, "I'm hungry! Let's get our last shipboard lunch."

"You read my mind," Paulette said. "I was just about to see who wanted to have something with me."

Looking around for a Lido deck waiter, they noticed Belmiro serving drinks. Getting his attention, he immediately came over to them. "Good afternoon, ladies. How may I help you?"

Kimberlee watched her friends' faces. She knew exactly what they were thinking. They wanted him for lunch. Sadly, that wasn't to be. Just like last night, his professional demeanor told them he was off-limits.

Instead of savoring him, they settled on easy-to-eat hotdogs and more refreshing piña coladas. Eating on their lounge chairs picnic-style, their conversation focused on the special times they'd shared.

What Kimberlee found interesting was no one discussed men—every other topic, including the sex shows, but not men. She had no idea if her friends had met anyone interesting. Each woman had kept that part of their trip to themselves. Knowing them as well as she did, she'd respected their need for privacy.

Before she knew where time had disappeared, the sun sat low in the west, painting the sky with brilliant reds, pinks, and mauves. Kimberlee, let out a deep sigh. "It's time to get ready for our last dinner—and time for me to write that note to the Captain telling him I won't be seeing him tonight." She couldn't put it off any longer.

EARLY THAT EVENING, CAPTAIN JOHAN READ KIMBERLEE'S note with mixed feelings. Initially, he let out a breath of relief, knowing how much paperwork faced him for docking in Miami, ending the cruise and getting ready for a new group of passengers. But in the following breath, he frowned with irritation that she wanted to be with her friends more than she needed to be with him.

Rationally, he knew they still had another week together. But then what? Maybe he should have cut his losses and let her leave tomorrow. Now it was too late.

If he were honest with himself, as difficult as this time next week would be, he'd still rather be with her. He never knew when another generous, sexy, passionate woman would enter his life. It had been ten years since his wife had died, so it could be years before he found another relationship. *Or maybe never.*

Pushing aside the tumultuous thoughts tumbling around his mind, he forced himself to focus on form filling and his myriad captain's duties. By the time he looked at the clock, it was late, and he needed sleep to prepare for the hectic day ahead.

Sleep didn't come easily. Even with a bureaucracy-numbed mind, he once again thought of Kimberlee. It was going to be an empty night without her snuggled in his arms and her scent surrounding him.

He was going to have a lonely life without her joy-filled laughter and sexy moans. No matter how he analyzed the problem, there was no way a sophisticated New York attorney could make a life on his ship…or a home in his tiny cabin. Or could even want a captain of a sex-themed cruise ship.

With sleep evading him, he stepped out onto his cabin's balcony. He'd always found listening to the ocean brought him back into balance. Having lived on the sea for most of his life, he'd learned to accept what was out of his control—the currents, the whims of the weather, inebriated passengers, and demands from corporate bean counters to keep cutting expenses and increasing revenue.

To this list of uncontrollables, he would have to add Kimberlee. Their lives were too different. They lived in two separate worlds which could never meld.

Back in his cabin, he balled up her note, tossing it into the trash. That helped reduce his frustrations with their clashing lifestyles…a little. Truthfully, he hated his cowardice. Ramil was right. He needed to demolish the protective walls surrounding his heart.

Tomorrow offered a new day—and a new life. He'd accept this gift, even if only for one loved-filled week.

Now, he'd try getting some sleep. The familiar rocking of the ship lulled him into an uneasy slumber, until he surrendered to his longings without the censorship of a rational mind. In his dream world, she made his ship her home. His life became hers.

He loved once again.

By 10:30 P.M., THREE SUITCASES STOOD OUTSIDE THEIR cabin doors for the 11:00 p.m. pick-up. The fourth one remained against a wall, waiting to be rolled down one deck.

Kimberlee's friends could have taken their own luggage off the ship if they needed early debarkation, but no one wanted the hassle of getting everything down the gangway and they were in no rush to reach the airport. So, they left their baggage for a crew member to retrieve and take to the terminal.

Of course, they had all documents, money, and travel clothes in neat groupings for easy access in the morning.

Once the lights were off, Kimberlee lay in bed tossing and turning. Her mind wouldn't stop jumping from wanting her captain, missing her friends, and uncertainty about what her professional future held. Catching herself in the beginning of a groan, she plopped a pillow over her head so she wouldn't wake her cabinmate.

Eventually, she fell into a troubled sleep, awaking before anyone's smartphone alarm went off. Because lying in bed made her more anxious with uncontrollable energy zipping through her body, she decided to get up and begin her sleep-deprived day.

After quietly dressing, she left the cabin to stand on deck and watch the beautiful skyline of Miami float into view as the ship headed into the harbor. She had no need to rush anywhere, because she wouldn't be getting to her new room until all the passengers had departed and housekeeping had cleaned it.

This was the first time she watched the docking process and realized how difficult it was to maneuver their ship into a port with four other ships—extremely large ones—already tied up at the pier. The MS *Aphrodite* had a small space open for her to berth, sandwiched between two mega ships.

Sailing into the harbor, she saw how her Captain turned the ship around in a tight circle, so it faced outward for easy departure. Once in position, she was surprised how he literally moved the ship sideways into the tight opening. She never realized how ships, unlike other vehicles, could move laterally. If only cars could move this way, she'd have no trouble parallel parking.

Standing at the railing watching how Captain Johan moored the ship, she realized he accomplished this process while working with winds and currents. Plus, he had small boats zipping around—as if daring him to hit them, which of course, he didn't.

In that moment, she grasped the Captain wasn't a glorified floating tour bus driver. Even after the bridge tour, in the back of her mind, she still saw him more as a maritime worker than a professional like her and her friends. In truth, he had sophisticated and extensive training, knowledge, and skills equal to investment bankers or lawyers, but in a little-understood and unconventional industry.

Pangs of guilt weighed heavily on her. Closing her eyes, she wished away her preconceived notions about his profession. *What other ways have I underestimated him?*

With this disquieting thought about how she'd under-valued him, she gripped the dew-covered deck railing, letting the morning breeze clear out the unease marring her joy in the morning. Still filled with tiny prickles of regret about her deprecating views, she wiped her damp hands on her pants and headed back to the cabin.

The Fates blessed her with one more week with him. She planned to make the most of their limited time together.

CHAPTER TWENTY-THREE
CRUISE DAY - DISEMBARKATION

*B*y ten o'clock that morning, Kimberlee remained one of a few passengers on the ship for the next cruise. Only two couples stayed for the Eastern Caribbean trip. The five of them now sat in the main dining room waiting to be escorted off the ship, through customs, and then back on again.

Returning after the legal formalities, she checked out her new cabin. It had been cleaned, with her suitcase waiting for her. Having no plans until the muster drill, she unpacked. Putting her things away offered a bittersweet experience. The cabin felt lonely without her friends, but she did have plenty of space for her belongings.

Sitting in her stateroom with nothing specific to do and finally having cell service, she decided to check voice mail and e-mail. As soon as she turned off airplane mode, she noticed a slew of voice, text, and e-mail messages all marked with red urgent signs. Stunned, she just stared at her phone, eyes widening in disbelief.

My God, what has happened?

Saying goodbye to her friends, moving into the new

cabin, and thinking about her future time with her Captain, she'd forgotten about work. Now, she was drowning in electronic shouts for help. Starting with her texts, she learned a major client's merger was in jeopardy. Both voice and e-mail explained how the other company's financial analysts had found, what they thought, was fraud in her client's Malaysian's subsidiary. They now demanded an investigation and more stock for their shareholders. What once looked like a great economic deal for her client was morphing into both a public relations nightmare and a major fiscal loss.

As she sat in her stateroom digesting all this information, realization slammed into her. If she could fix the problem, she'd become a star and have an excellent chance for promotion to partner. Jaw hardening with determination, she resolved to seize this unexpected opportunity to shine. Eyes closed, she took a minute to savor the sweet anticipation of success flooding her body.

She'd been waiting for such a moment when the managing partners recognized her worth and rewarded her for years of outstanding performance. A mix of hope and impatience made her jump up and pace around the limited space. Fanning her flushed face with a hand, she forced down a whoop of excitement, willing herself to focus on what she needed to do next.

First, she had to get back to New York and then immediately to Kuala Lumpur, the capital of Malaysia.

Twenty-five minutes after texting her corporate travel agent, she was booked on a 7:12 p.m. flight to La Guardia that evening and had her reservation to Kuala Lumpur for the next day.

Then, she noticed an overlooked text from her friend in HR. Kanesha sent a cryptic message saying, "Up for partner. FL acquisition collapsing. Need you." With those simple words, she dropped down on the couch. Kanesha had the skinny on the firm's latest info. While the note could get her fired, Kimberlee knew how to keep her mouth shut.

Gulping air, she kept rereading the words. She had no idea who the client was or the in-trouble project. But this was her specialty. Two major clients needed her—which meant her company did too.

With thoughts bouncing around in her brain, one kept recurring —everything was possible. She didn't expect to have it all. She just wanted a small slice of the happiness pie. Maybe she could be partner and have a fulfilling social life. With all she'd learned from the Captain—now, no longer *her* captain—she saw herself differently. A sexual confidence existed in place of her feelings of inadequacy and inferiority.

But first, the clients. And then... *Partnership here I come!*

Frantically repacking, Kimberlee realized she couldn't just vanish from the ship. She needed to tell the Captain she was leaving...but how to do it? If she could, she'd sneak away, but that wasn't her style. Nor was she a coward. Thinking through her options, she decided the best course was talking to him on the phone—certainly not face-to-face. She wasn't that brave.

After calling the operator and asking to speak with Captain Johan, she resumed pacing, trying to determine what to say and how to say it. Before she could get her thoughts organized, the ringing phone shattered the silence.

"Hello," she said.

"Hi, Kimberlee. You called. I hope you're comfortable in your new cabin?"

Not having had time to prepare a planned speech, she just jumped into telling him. "I have to leave. I'm sorry, but I can't stay. I need to catch a plane to New York tonight and then fly to Kuala Lumpur tomorrow. There's a major problem with one of my clients that can destroy them financially and ruin a merger I've been working on for the past six months."

When he didn't say anything, she added, "I'm sorry. I have to go."

The voice that came over the phone chilled her with its controlled anger. "I will take your name off of the passenger's manifest."

And then the line went dead.

She stood for a moment holding the phone to her ear, listening to a dial tone, staring into space. A lone tear slid down her cheek. Without brushing it away, she hung up the receiver and just stood there, not remembering what she needed to do. When she should have been dancing with joy for this incredible opportunity—and most likely her long-desired promotion—her body refused to move. It was as if someone had filled her with lead, bolting her into place. Then her legs began shaking. Slightly swaying, she reached back to the bed behind her, leaning on it for support—then abruptly collapsed on it.

Staring into space at nothing, she took a few moments to force air into her lungs and get energy reflowing. Eventually, with a head shake to clear away the numbness fogging her brain, she forced herself to stand and returned to packing the few remaining items. Soon the room looked as empty as she felt inside.

You've made your choice, Kimberlee-girl. You'll never find another lover like him, but you can still have a successful career and a wonderful life with family and friends. And, maybe, someday you'll find another man you can love.

She wheeled her suitcase to the door, then stopped. Propping the door open a crack with her bag, she decided to call Bonnie, leaving a voice mail about Kanesha's message.

Standing by the slightly open door, she hit speed dial to leave the voice mail. Asking her to pass this on to the others, keeping everything between themselves. Ending the call, she excitedly told her, "I'm up for partner. They need me for a Florida client whose acquisition is falling through. The Captain may be a fabulous lover, but I want my partnership. For God's sake, my career's more important than a sex cruise ship captain. Love you. Got to go."

Grabbing her bag, she stepped out into the hall. And froze. There walking down the corridor, she saw the back of the man who she knew intimately. He must have been standing outside the door when she left her news.

Clutching the doorjamb for support, she wanted to throw up. How could this have happened? What was he doing here?

Horrified, all Kimberlee could do was lean against the frame, her hand covering her mouth. Wanting that to be a different person, but knew it was *him*. Devastation made her muscles go weak. Guilt and shame crashed into her like an avalanche and her world went dark, encased in a cold, psychological ice preventing any physical movement.

I must be in a bad dream. I'll wake up and everything will be right.

It wasn't a dream, but a living nightmare with no escape. And nobody to save her.

Knowing she didn't deserve his forgiveness, she managed to gather her shredded emotions enough to leave the ship, then grabbed a cab for the airport. She resigned herself to a sexually desolate life without the Captain. An existence riddled with guild.

CAPTAIN JOHAN HEADED TO KIMBERLEE'S CABIN TO apologize for hanging up on her. And to wish her luck with her promotion. He wanted her to know how proud he was of her and how he hoped for her success. Even as his heat lay broken.

Walking toward her room, he noticed the door ajar with her suitcase. She was talking to someone. Within a few more steps he heard her say, "I'm up for partner. They need me for a Florida client whose acquisition is falling through. The Captain may be a fabulous lover, but I want my partnership. For God's sake, my career's more important than a sex cruise ship captain."

Without even pausing to hear how the conversation ended, he spun around, heading back to his cabin. Rage flooded his body. With long strides, he reached his room quickly. Catching himself before he slammed the door, he pulled it shut with a loud click. Immediately, he turned to music for solace, filling his room with Grieg's "Piano Concerto in A minor."

Sitting down, he closed his eyes, leaning his head against the wall, allowing the powerful melody to fill him. Maybe he'd cranked the volume a little louder than he realized, because at the end, someone knocked.

Opening the door, he met Ramil standing there with a concerned look on his face. "May I come in?" he asked.

Without answering, Captain Johan stepped back, pulling the door wider, letting his friend enter. Immediately, both men sat—allowing the silence to rest comfortable between them.

Eventually, the Captain's bitter voice filled the quiet. "I'm not good enough for her. She's left the ship to get her partnership and look for another man her equal."

Ramil waited.

He began with her call telling him she was leaving. Then, he described the entire wretched episode, not sparing his own stupidity hanging up on her. Finally, he ended by quoting the overheard phone conversation.

With the anger washed away by the music, raw pain filled him. Slowly, tears spilled down his cheeks unchecked. Ramil got up and handed him a box of tissues, taking one himself. These were navy men who'd lived with death and had held dying friends in their arms. Tears, for them, weren't a mark of weakness, but an expression of their humanity. Warriors who understood loss, regret, and the horrors of war.

Like now, sometimes they found themselves facing battles in the trenches of the heart.

Wiping away the signs of grief, he continued, "When I slammed down the phone, I was hurt and angry that her work was more important than our relationship. Looking at the receiver, I was horrified by what I'd done. I don't treat people that way. I wanted to apologize and to tell her, of course, she should leave. I recognize how important careers are. And I wanted her to be successful. I was going to escort her off the ship and see how we could work this out long-distance."

Ramil asked, "Where do you want to go from here?"

"You know, I'm not sure. I think this has shaken my self-confidence about my ability to judge a person's character. I really missed on this one. I feel betrayed. I risked my career for her."

Ramil gazed down at the carpet, then looked back at the Captain, saying, "I'm a simple room steward, not well educated. I feel guilty telling you to open your heart to her and then this happened. I…"

"No, Ramil, that's not true. Wisdom and education aren't synonymous. I've total confidence in your judgment. Plus, she'd already captured my heart. As my friend, you helped me find the courage to admit it. You made explicit what I'd been afraid to acknowledge. If I'm honest, I'd not have given up one moment. And you're not a simple room steward. You're wise and insightful about people. There's no one on this ship I trust as I do you." He sighed. "As much as I hurt now, something opened inside of me. You're right. I need to begin living again."

"I agree," Ramil said. "This past week, you were happier than I've ever seen you. I could feel a shift. I don't want to see you lose that. She isn't worth it."

"No, she isn't. And now I need to move on with my life. There'll be other women out there. Someday, I'll find the right one."

What the Captain didn't say was how he'd deal with his devastation when she helped the bastards go after his company in their hostile takeover. Once that time came, he'd have to find a way to keep from losing his control.

Now, he must put this mess out of his mind and prepare for the coming cruise, with 400 passengers impatiently waiting to board. He had a ship to command.

CHAPTER TWENTY-FOUR

Kimberlee's flight from Miami to New York left on time. With a packed plane, she put in her earbuds to block out the world. While she liked music, her phone wasn't filled with playlists. She had just a few special selections. Tonight, she put her favorite song on repeat—Alexandra Burke singing Leonard Cohen's "Hallelujah." Throughout the long flight north, she drifted in and out listening to the powerful song—with no hope for being saved. She'd walked away from love.

Exhausted physically, mentally, and emotionally, she came down the escalator to baggage claim with a haunted look. Her eyes gritty, with a dull ache constricting her throat.

There she found Mateo, her long-term driver, waiting for her. Forcing a weak smile, she said, "Hi, Mateo. I'm so glad to see you. It's been a tough twelve hours. I need a friendly face."

"You found one, Kimberlee," he replied. "Let's get your bag and get you home. You've got a long trip tomorrow. And it looks like you could use some sleep."

"Yes," she answered, lacking energy for further speech.

Mateo also drove her three friends. He worked for a small family-owned company which provided great service. Over the years, they'd developed a friendship from the amount of time spent talking while stalled in New York traffic. She always looked forward to his smiling presence, especially now when guilt, loss, and loneliness swamp her normal positive outlook.

Sitting in the back of his car, she gave him a quick version of her trip, trying to put enthusiasm in her voice. But she could tell by his limited questions and unusual quietness, he sensed something was amiss. Rapidly, she ran out of things to tell him, allowing them to ride through the dark night wrapped in silence.

Her thoughts slipped back to being in the Miami airport.

Once she'd arrived at the airport gate, she texted her friends about the Captain overhearing her voice mail to Bonnie. Immediately, they wrote back their shock at what had happened. Each woman tried to comfort her as well as relieve her guilt. But to no avail. Nothing helped eliminate her shame and self-disgust.

True, she hadn't purposefully tried to hurt him, but she still held herself responsible for her actions. Sitting in the backseat of the limo, tears streamed down her face. Multiple times, she asked herself how she could have treated such a wonderful person so cruelly. Yes, it was unintentional, but she remained accountable for her actions... and speech.

It was far worse than the way he'd treated me our first night together. Besides, he'd apologized. How am I ever going to tell him I'm sorry?

Her parents had taught their children they must request forgiveness for causing hurt and in turn, forgive when they were injured. It sounded easy when her parents preached these values. Now, it seemed impossible to do. She didn't have the courage to reach out to him.

And, I don't know how I'll ever be able to forgive myself.

Lost in thought, she realized Mateo had parked the car in front of her building. With no traffic, he had her at the door in forty-five minutes.

Usually, she savored coming home after a trip. The familiarity of her lovingly decorated condo gave her the same comfort her mother's warm chocolate chip cookies with milk once provided. She'd carefully chosen each piece of furniture, with most of her decorations bought on trips as reminders of where she'd been. Everything spoke to her of security and serenity.

No matter how expensive the fanciest hotel beds, they never felt as good as her own. But not tonight. Even exhausted, her familiar, comfy queen bed didn't have that feel-right welcome. Waiting for sleep to claim her, it registered what was missing—no rocking. Her condo didn't lull her to sleep like a ship sailing through the seas. She also lacked the wondrous warmth of strong arms wrapped around her. No delicious masculine scent permeated the sheets.

Everything felt wrong—in a home that once felt perfect.

Eventually, sleep descended, gifting her with a deep healing rest. Not setting an alarm, she woke naturally in the morning. Because she'd cleaned out the refrigerator before the cruise, she only had coffee. After a trip down to her neighborhood deli for a breakfast wrap to-go and a bag of her favorite potato chips, she had a quick meal and a long, hot shower. Now she felt ready to begin unpacking her cruise clothes and repacking for her business trip to Kuala Lumpur.

The tears began again when she opened her suitcase. Taking out each item, she viscerally remembered when and where she wore it. How she stripped for him with the black dress. Or what she wore to the BDSM show and the remote-controlled vibrator. Each article of clothing held a precious memory.

Then she found it—her Magic Wand. A part of her wanted to toss it, but then she'd just have to buy another. She shoved it in the back of her bottom dresser draw. Someday, she'd be ready to use it again.

It wasn't until packing her business clothes that the memories temporarily slipped from consciousness. Yet, like a screensaver, those recollections ran silently in the background. She might not notice them, but in moments of stillness they jumped to the front of her thoughts.

Throughout the long day, she kept herself busy by anchoring her thinking to work rather than the self-blame and loss she struggled to banish…without success.

Bonnie, Lori, and Paulette each called her. The conversations bounced between her upcoming trip, possible promotion, and the fiasco with the Captain. No matter what they said, nothing reduced the self-contempt. She wasn't even sure if time would help heal her.

In a few hours, she faced a twenty-four-hour trip, beginning with a flight to Dubai, followed by a short layover. The first leg of the trip didn't leave until 11:00 p.m., so she used the time at home to talk with the audit partner on the account, get additional information from the client and confirm that they would be ready for her when she arrived in the Kuala Lumpur office.

Constantly, she glanced at her watch, wishing hours would move faster. Yet it crawled by. It seemed time mocked her by moving ever more slowly. As the day creeped along, she found herself scratching mysterious itches on various parts of her arms and legs. Then she'd need something to munch on. In desperation, she grabbed her favorite potato chips, which she had bought that morning. She usually kept them for emergency nibbling when she needed the nurturing crunchy, salty, and fatty taste. Within fifteen minutes, the snack bag lay crumpled in the trash can. But the baffling body irritations remained. She tried half an antihistamine, knowing a whole one would make her sleepy. Eventually, the annoying prickliness reduced to barely noticeable.

If she kept moving or eating, she held thoughts about the Captain at bay. She wasn't ready to think about him. Yet, he lurked below the surface, ready to hijack her thoughts. There was no way to escape him...or avoid her painful feelings about him.

When Kimberlee made her international flight reservations, she used her own money to upgrade from business to first class, making sure she'd get much needed rest on the two planes' comfortable sleeper seats. Thank heaven the airlines gave first-class passengers designer pajamas, which meant she wouldn't have to sleep in her business suit and look bedraggled when she met everyone for the first time. She didn't have the luxury of first stopping at the hotel to freshen up before going to the office.

With her suitcase packed, she had time for dinner but wasn't hungry, having low-grade nausea. Except for diet ginger ale and water, she had no interest in eating anything after her chips. She reasoned that her tummy upset was due to the hundreds of million dollars riding on her work. But part of her knew better.

What she couldn't admit was how ending a simple shipboard fling could dramatically upend her life—and make a mess of her insides. She'd rather not think about the guilt eating away at her.

When I should be celebrating my partnership, I'm a wreck.

WHILE KIMBERLEE SPENT HER TIME IN THE MIAMI AIRPORT anxious to return home, Captain Johan focused on the disembarkation and embarkation process with its never-ending paperwork and provisioning of the ship. Feeding only 700 people for a week required stocking his galleys with a huge amount of food, including loading 840 pounds of butter, 50,000 eggs, 34,000 pounds of fruits and vegetables, and 2,100 pounds of flour, just for a start. He knew from sailing larger ships that quantity would increase over ten times as much. He'd stay with his smaller vessel.

Within hours of people streaming off his ship, he had another 400 passengers pushing to get on. Throughout his stressful day, he often found himself rotating his neck and shoulders to release aching, knotted muscles. Not far below the surface of his cool, professional demeanor, he kept tight control over his ready-to-explode pain, frustration, and defeat.

Being honest with himself, he'd hoped for a future with her. He was tired of being alone and wanted a caring woman in his life. He needed a friend and lover. Even against his better judgment, he chose Kimberlee. He knew a cruise ship captain didn't fit into her life—no matter how good the sex. She had even said on the phone, "The Captain may be a fabulous lover, but he can't compare to partnership. For God's sake, my career's more important than a mere sex cruise ship captain."

But it turned out, he did desire her. And needed her. Even if she considered him beneath her.

She offered so much his life had lacked these last ten years. Really, he had only himself to blame for denying the truth in front of him. As a captain, he could only keep his crew, passengers, and ship safe by realistically acknowl-edging and working with what the weather and seas offered. He should have followed that same policy with her. Instead, he ignored the reality smacking him in the face.

It took her saying he wasn't good enough. Even if he hadn't hung up the phone on her, he knew she'd still have harbored those feelings.

Multiple reactions warred inside him, which he didn't have time to deal with, nor did he want to. One image, however, kept intruding into his thoughts: him slamming down the phone and not giving her a chance to explain. He knew changing her mind to stay wasn't an option. He refused to grovel. He wouldn't strip his feelings bare, begging her to remain.

When he'd grabbed a few minutes to talk with corporate about the hostile takeover, he'd learned his side was still winning. Even having been with Kimberlee for only a week, he knew her brains and toughness would end their successful defense when she joined the opposition team.

What frustrated him was now she'd be working with the opposition to destroy his ship and his brother's company.

From her words, she didn't know who the client was or who the takeover focused on. He didn't want to believe she'd actively strive to hurt him. But he also recognized how much she wanted her fancy partnership. If wrecking his career and his brother's future gave her that, she'd do it.

As the day progressed, he found himself clenching and unclenching his hands. A tightness constricted his chest. Moments before exploding at someone, he'd caught himself, swallowing his words. He hated captains who took their anger out on their officers and crew. They deserved his respect and support, not becoming the scapegoat of his disas-trous love affair. Besides, he'd spent his life keeping his personal and professional worlds separated. He wouldn't break that value now. Even though he'd violated another.

While passengers boarded his ship, he had a short breathing space. Needing an objective opinion, he went looking for Ramil in the officers' quarters. During changeover days, Ramil helped the housekeeping staff disinfect and prepare the rooms for the next onslaught. Now, he'd be catching up with his official duties, cleaning the officers' cabins. Walking into the hall, he found him a few doors away. Because they knew each other well, all he had to do was poke his head into the room and Ramil knew to come talk.

No beers for them this time. He needed to steer his ship out of port and into open seas. Instead, they shared a diet cola. While he couldn't express how appalled he was knowing Kimberlee would destroy their livelihood to get her promotion, he could talk about the personal side of their relationship.

Opening the conversation, he shared his bitterness saying, "She doesn't respect me...a mere sex cruise ship captain. I was easy to discard."

"I know you'll find this strange, but I'm not sure that's true," Ramil answered in a kind voice. "Yes, you heard her say that, but sometimes we say things in high emotion we wouldn't say in calmer times. True, I don't know her the way you do, but from what little I've seen and what you've told me, she doesn't sound like a cruel person. Rather than assuming the worst of her, let's see what time brings. I think—"

"No, I know what I heard," the Captain spat out.

"Yes, you heard her say that, but you and I have said things in the heat of emotion, but didn't mean it later. Give yourself time to see what happens and what she does."

Sitting quietly, the Captain contemplated Ramil's words.

Then he replied, "I guess that's what's bothering me, because she really wasn't a hurtful person. She treated the crew with respect. She always had a smile and a kind word. But I heard her say what she thought of me."

Pausing, he continued, "OK, I'll bow to your wisdom. Even if I don't a hundred percent agree with you. I can't do anything now. I've got a ship to sail out to sea. I'll put this mess on a shelf and focus on the coming trip."

Ramil simply nodded. Then standing, he left the cabin. He needed to get the officer's quarters cleaned before they wanted their rooms.

Johan remained sitting, contemplating their conversation.

Later that evening when he'd completed all first-night cruise duties, Johan sat at his desk, struggling to chart a new course for the future. He faced a lonely life. His nights offered bleakness with a cold, empty bed.

For the first time in ages, he wanted to smash something. He could have used a hurricane right now. But instead he was on a cruise ship sailing the tranquil eastern Caribbean with clear skies ahead.

Should he have trusted his initial instinct and kept his distance from her after they'd first met? Would he have really wanted to walk away from a week of paradise?

The realist in him eventually halted the endless, useless, and defeating cycle of should and should nots. It was time he accepted reality and moved on. No matter how he analyzed the problem, there was no way a hotshot New York attorney could make a life on his ship.

He was who he was—the son of a cod fisherman. While they had a special relationship, the unavoidable truth remained; they came from dramatically different worlds. Chemistry and mind-blowing sex couldn't bridge the giant gulf separating them.

Operating on automatic pilot, he pushed himself up from the desk, walked outside on deck nine overlooking the pool, letting the sea bring some balance back into his tumultuous thoughts. But immediately, he realized his mistake. The first place his gaze landed was on the deck railing where he'd met her a week ago this evening. Only one week, but a lifetime for him.

Closing his eyes, he expelled a deep sigh, as if he could rid himself of the abysmal past few hours. Or maybe, he wanted to wash away the entire last seven days?

Physically turning his back on the banister and those memories, he stared out over the opposite side of his vessel. As always, the roll of the ship, the sound of the swells striking the hull, and the warmth of the night brought back a modicum of equilibrium. His muscles started relaxing, with his breathing becoming less tight. Just as he'd found ways to gain some healing after his beloved wife's death, he'd draw on that same resiliency to move forward after this loss.

As the sea recovers from the fiercest storms, so too would he.

CHAPTER TWENTY-FIVE

Kimberlee loved travel, setting her apart from family and friends. Unlike most people, she even found airports interesting. That was one of the things she'd loved about her job, domestic and international trips. Really, she didn't care where, as long as she could explore new places, meet new people, and try new food.

By the time she walked out of her building that evening, Mateo sat waiting for her in his car. His calm presence brought a modicum of ease on their drive to JFK. Nervously twisting her earring, she kept trying to force her thoughts to the work that awaited, but shame for how their relationship ended nibbled around the edges of her mind. By nature, she wasn't a thoughtless or rude person. Treating another human being unkindly created havoc with her self-respect. She'd have to find a way to send him an apology when she resolved this whole merger mess.

What she'd say to him, she had no idea. Maybe the twenty-four-hour travel each way would give her time to compose a message. Right now, her usually quick mind remained a vacuum when it came to *him*.

But then again, he did hang up on her. He didn't try to understand what she faced or what was important to her. With one click of the phone, he dismissed her from his life. Obviously, she was nothing more than fling to him.

Like all of her journeys, she'd meticulously prepared for this grueling trip. On the first leg, she faced twelve hours to Dubai. After which, she'd travel seven more hours to Kuala Lumpur. Because both flights occurred at night crossing multiple time zones, she'd lose one day on each leg. Thankfully, she'd get a two-and-a-half-hour layover between planes, which meant she didn't look like a klutz running to her next gate, dragging roller bag.

Being cocooned in a first-class compartment, she'd avoid the hassle of dealing with other travelers. The experienced flight crew would intuitively know to leave her alone, focusing on people who felt, as first-class passengers, they deserved extra special attention. She didn't have to worry about bored, cranky kids kicking the back of her chair, chatty seatmates wanting to know her life history, or food carts rumbling up and down the aisles banging into her elbows.

With the help of a sleep aid, she spent most of the first leg resting. Her sleeping mask blocked out light and the earplugs reduced noise, allowing her to catch needed rest. Of course, putting on that eye cover triggered thoughts of another mask she'd never worn—but would have if he'd asked.

After having had a good night's sleep on the initial leg of her flight and no nausea, she could enjoy her first experience in Dubai's Al Maktoum International Airport. A leisurely walk between planes allowed her time to observe the mass of international travelers streaming around her and to take in the design of the fascinating ultra-modern, high-gloss terminals. Reviling in the culturally varied airport, she focused not on shopping but on the joys of new culinary delights.

Being Kimberlee, she checked out all the deliciously fascinating food stalls along the way to her gate. Shame the sellers weren't like Costco, offering free samples. She'd be in heaven. Instead, she had to imagine what the intriguing options tasted like. Regretfully, time and tummy space meant limiting herself to only one meal. She settled on grilled lamb kofta in a pita wrap with hummus and khyar bi laban—the Middle Eastern equivalent of Greek tzatziki—for dipping.

For her, the yummy meal satisfied both physical and emotional needs. Momentarily, the gastronomic indulgences reduced the guilt and misery plaguing her, keeping despair at bay. Food had always been her drug of choice when she needed comfort.

Her second flight to Kuala Lumpur was a short seven hours, but still time enough for her to get an extended nap. Once more, she lost a second day traveling all night.

On both trips when not dozing, she concentrated on the financial crisis her client faced…or, at least tried to focus on it. Her mind, however, kept straying to Captain Johan and her shock when she saw he'd overheard her voice mail. Or her thoughts flipped to her almost-certain promotion when she took over the Florida client and then contemplated how her life would change for the better with this partnership. But who was that client in Florida with acquisition problems? She'd have to check out their Miami customers. Being in the New York office, she knew nothing about the other locations.

A few times on the flights, she caught herself staring off into nowhere with moist eyes, while clutching a crumpled tissue.

During sleep, when her defenses lost their tenacious grip, grief slipped in, showing her how truly vulnerable she was. Then she experienced moments when the motion of her plane felt like the gentle rocking of a ship, causing her anguish to flare as a fire reignited from forgotten embers.

Grateful for her two long segments, she used the time to not only work, sleep, eat a little, but also begin the healing process. Of course, given the consummate professional she was, she'd fake it until she made it.

According to the International Date Line, she arrived two days after leaving New York. A jet-lagged Kimberlee finally landed in Kuala Lumpur at 8:30 a.m. Checking her appearance in a restroom mirror, she nodded in approval how even looking a little travel-worn she still presented an executive appearance. Hopefully, no one would notice her bloodshot eyes with all the makeup she'd applied.

Ever the professional, she trusted her analytical skills would kick in, along with the caffeine she'd be consuming. She could heal a broken heart later—now was the time to apply all her years of education and experience.

AFTER GETTING THROUGH MALAYSIAN PASSPORT CONTROL, airport customs, and the city's massive traffic congestion, Kimberlee walked into the corporate headquarters, greeted the CFO Controller, and assorted accounting professionals who had compiled the data creating the uproar.

She entered a conference room permeated with fear of possible corruption being uncovered. Employees had already organized the data, which they all needed to laboriously analyze over the ensuing hours. Computers and actual financial records filled all the available space—including files being stacked on the floor. Nobody wanted to rely solely on electronic records. They needed hands-on backup evidence.

A sideboard covered with drinks and food provided

needed physical and emotional support for the intense time
ahead. Each person there provided knowledge in specific
areas. Kimberlee pulled everyone's work together into one
financial product. All people were expected to stay until
they had examined every bit of information and had an
answer as to the integrity of the numbers—fraud or no
fraud.

Fifteen hours of slogging through financial data proved
that all internal and publicly provided records were accurate
and free from deception. Too exhausted to celebrate, they
were just grateful the company wouldn't have to go through a
criminal investigation.

Kimberlee documented each step of the analysis process,
e-mailing updates to her firm and client. They could then pass
the results on to the other company. The merger would go
through…and she could finally get to her hotel room.

By two o'clock in the morning, her body ached, her brain
stopped processing and she had trouble keeping her eyes
open. Between travelling halfway around the world, jet lag,
mental exhaustion, a broken heart, shame, and the depletion
of crisis-response adrenalin, she had nothing left to keep
going. She only wanted sleep and oblivion. Her mind and
body needed healing time to forget about and be free of the
horrible mess.

During that intense analysis, she remained focused,
allowing her battered heart breathing space. But she could
sense the pain hovering in the background waiting to pounce.

Once in the hotel room, she slipped on her airline pajamas, which she'd kept with her from the plane, and collapsed
in bed, letting an exhausted slumber claim her. For twelve
hours, she lay in a comatose-like state, oblivious to the world.

Slowly coming to, she initially wondered why the ship
wasn't moving…and where was her Captain? Was he already

on the bridge and she'd slept through his docking? What port were they in?

Then it slammed into her. There wasn't a Captain anymore. She wasn't on his ship, but a hotel room in Kuala Lumpur. Covering her face with her hands, she curled into a ball on her side, giving despair free rein.

The burning agony of loss devoured her. Time had no meaning as she huddled in her hotel bed.

She'd learned from her yoga and mindfulness practice that nothing remains constant. And by letting the pain flow through and out of her, healing would begin. And so it did. Once again, she became aware of her surroundings. Almost ready to join the land of the living.

Ever the analyzer, she forced herself to evaluate what she could have done differently when she jumped ship. And how she could have prevented him from overhearing her voice mail. Yes, she should have been more skillful telling Captain Johan she was leaving. No, she couldn't have stopped him from listening to her comments. Regardless, remaining with him on a cruise ship wasn't an option. She had determined her life's path and stay on it she would.

It wasn't just the status that came with partnership. She also wanted a life with financial security and the ability to help her parents when they retired should they need support. Plus, how could she ever tell her traditional Methodist Iowa family that she was living on a sex ship with a cruise captain after they'd worked so hard putting her through eight years of higher education? Would they even talk to her again? She wouldn't risk finding out.

Even if he would take her back, the possibility of being with him remained firmly closed.

Which brought her back to the second issue. For heaven's sake, she couldn't have known he was outside the door. What could he have possibly been doing there? *I hope he hadn't come to apologize. Oh, how horrible for him to have heard what I said.*

Giving herself more time of tearful self-pity, the pragmatist in her woke up and slowly began evaluating available options. First, she needed coffee and food. Then a shower and preparation for a twenty-four-hour return trip to New York. While waiting for room service, she went through her voice, text, and e-mail messages. Gushing congratulations filled her phone.

Then, an e-mail from her client jumped out with the subject "General Counsel." Breath caught in her throat as she stared transfixed on her phone. Slowly reaching out, she tapped the message. It was short and to the point—they were offering her the position of chief legal officer for the newly merged company. A dream opportunity—up there with being a partner in one of the Big Four public accounting firms.

Maybe even a better job. Because she didn't have to spend her life hustling for work and fighting for billable hours. Rather, she would do the hiring, letting firms compete for her business. As the client, she had the decision-making power. And that was an intoxicating feeling.

In the middle of contemplating her intriguing professional options, room service knocked.

Sitting at the square in-room dining table, she forced herself to sip a cappuccino while nibbling at her nasi lemak, the national dish of Malaysia. True, the coffee provided a caffeine kick, but the delightful coconut rice dish tasted like sawdust rather than the much-needed comfort food she was hoping for…or the celebratory meal she deserved.

When she should have been reveling in a fabulous job offer, her heart ached, and life felt as if it had spun out of control. She wanted to explain away her red, swollen eyes as coming from a bad case of jet lag and not getting enough sleep, but the realist in her knew better. Some losses couldn't be balanced out by gains—no matter how wonderful those successes were.

She had made her decision when she walked off his ship. Now she would find a way to live with it. Hopefully, her appetite would return. Food had always been a source of solace for her. Yet, not now, when she needed it the most.

The rest of the afternoon passed in a blur of excitement and speculation about what the future held. When partnership arrived, she'd always expected it would bring with it a successful social life and eventually the man of her dreams.

On some level, she believed she wasn't deserving of a wonderful personal life, if she lacked professional success. Now with either general counsel or partner, her future should fall into place.

She didn't want to have it all. Just two small victories. That wasn't asking for much.

Yet, no matter how hard she tried, moments of desire for the Captain and resulting devastating loss ambushed her. She'd pushed these unwanted feelings back down, but they never vanished, clinging to her the way a skunk smell stuck to her dog after he got sprayed. It took weeks of bathing him with special soaps, before the rank scent left.

Unlike the dog, only she was conscious of the accompanying odor of sorrow—and she didn't have any over-the-counter solutions.

With a few hours remaining until leaving for the airport, she let a hot shower ease some of her tight muscles and soften her despair, but it couldn't totally revitalize her spirits.

By midnight, Kimberlee found herself back in the airport waiting for her 2:10 a.m. flight. The first class lounge gave her privacy to think about the astonishing direction her life had taken with one simple e-mail. Unfortunately, she couldn't enjoy the wonderful glass of red wine with the delicious tapas the hostess placed in front of her. *Maybe, when I get home, my appetite will return.*

Yes, if she could, she'd have done things differently. But that was in the past. Having burned the Captain-bridge behind her, she could only move forward. Where to, she didn't know.

CHAPTER TWENTY-SIX

*T*wo days after returning home, Kimberlee sat with her friends in a neighborhood Indian restaurant, bringing them up to date. Even with her disorientation, fuzzy mind, and fatigue from jet lag, she still pushed herself to meet her New York family.

"OK, Kimberlee," Bonnie said, "we're waiting with bated breath to hear what's happened. We won't let you leave without telling us everything."

Lori added, "Nothing in our ordinary lives comes close to what's been happening in yours. We want all the juicy details."

Paulette nodded.

It was time to finally explain the events of the last week. She had so much to tell them, but also knew they'd have plenty of questions, even some probing ones she wasn't ready to answer. Or didn't know how to, because she hadn't explored what her emotions actually were.

"Your wish is my command, but only after we've ordered," Kimberlee answered with a tired, but warm smile.

They had their favorite cozy corner table for both privacy and the ability to hear each other in this popular dining venue blasting Bollywood music. The unpleasant jet lag symptoms and an aching heart only slightly diminished the pleasure filling her as she sat with her dearest friends. As in the past, they'd share their favorite dishes of saag paneer, dal makhani, and shrimp vindaloo. For her, food and friends brought balance and comfort into her out-of-kilter life.

Thank heaven I can eat again. Maybe being home was exactly what the doctor recommended.

As soon as they'd ordered, she started with the panicked messages waiting for her when she turned on her cell phone while still on the ship. Because she provided excellent detail, no one interrupted with questions. By the time she finished her story, their meal had arrived, and her friends sat staring at her in stunned silence. Luckily the food appeared steaming hot.

Ever the one with the most empathy, Bonnie asked, "How are you doing? I mean, emotionally. We can see you're surviving physically."

"I would like to say fine, but I'd be lying to you and myself," Kimberlee answered. "The last time I hurt this much was when my grandmother died. I guess I'm going through another loss."

Everyone sat quietly for a moment digesting what she'd said, then finally started eating. Practical Paulette broke the silence, asking, "Have you done a pros and cons list about both positions?"

"Of course, I have. And the pros come out the same for each job. Much more than the cons.

"Where do you go from here?" Lori inquired.

"I've been asking myself that same question. Partner will give me more money. But the general counsel gives me greater control over my life. I like the idea of doing the hiring, rather than being the one on the street hustling for work."

Her friends nodded. They understood the competitive and ruthless world she worked in.

Then Bonnie approached the topic that hovered around the table, but no one mentioned. She asked, "Have you also done an analysis for living on the cruise ship?"

"Of course not," Kimberlee replied irritated. "Don't be silly. That's not an option. Besides, after what I said about him, he'd not want me near his ship."

"I don't think I'm being silly. And, yes, it is an option. Not one that's socially acceptable in our world, but still a valid choice," Bonnie responded without being offended. "Plus, you don't know what the Captain is thinking until he tells you."

Paulette immediately chimed in, "You shouldn't take it off the table. Don't limit your opportunities. You're at a major turning point and should look at all available possibilities before you make a final decision. The road you've selected now will affect the rest of your life."

"I agree," Lori added. "To be honest, I've been exploring cruise ship jobs for you. And I found one that might fit. Of course, you won't make great money, but then you can't put a price on love and gorgeous scenery."

"I'm not in love," Kimberlee shot back. "A week of great sex doesn't mean love."

"Then why do you hurt as if someone has died?" Lori countered.

Biting her lower lip, Kimberlee sat with a rigid stillness looking back at her companions. When no one said a word, she broke the silence. "OK, I'll admit I cared for him, but this is about my career. Not my love life."

"Wrong. It's about your whole life," Paulette replied.

"Few people have the opportunity to make an informed decision about creating the future they truly want. You do. Don't waste this extraordinary chance to design something special and uniquely you."

Before someone could say anything, Kimberlee immediately countered, "He hung up on me. He didn't ask a fucking question. Nada. Just slammed down the phone. That's not the action of a man who cared. Let alone one who loves me."

And then the tears flowed, showing her friends the anguish which she desperately tried to hide from them…and herself.

Before Kimberlee could reach in her purse, Bonnie handed her the needed tissue saying in a soothing voice, "I'll grant you, he didn't act like a man in love, but then sometimes people who feel deeply hurt do things they regret later. Maybe he was coming to apologize when he overheard your voice mail. So, let's leave love out of this equation for a moment."

Using that opening, Paulette said, "In this time of your life, what ultimate career decision you make is irrelevant. What's important is you grab this rare opportunity to explore your options—even the ones that don't immediately seem relevant."

Lori slid an envelope across the table to Kimberlee. "Here's a generic job description for chief purser on cruise ships. Some of the responsibilities you're overqualified for and others you could learn quickly. But, I guarantee, you won't be bored, and you will be overworked with long exhausting hours. Read this at your leisure."

"Remember, you don't have to decide immediately," Bonnie said in a gentle, encouraging voice.

Frowning, Kimberlee sat looking at the package without moving to take it. Then tentatively she reached out, using her index finger to pull it toward her. She grasped it carefully with just her thumb and first finger—almost afraid it might burn her. Cautiously slipping it into her purse, she returned to eating, mumbling an insincere thank you.

THAT UNWANTED ENVELOPE SAT ON A BOOKSHELF OUT OF sight. But the contents lingered in the back of her mind.

So too the Captain hovered in the background of her thoughts. Throughout the day, she wondered what he was doing. What port he was sailing into?

Does he hate me?

Do I love him?

Don't be stupid. He didn't try keeping me on his ship. He let me go without a word.

What she knew in her heart, if he'd asked her to stay, she wouldn't have. In that moment on the ship, she'd focused only on fixing her client's problem, being the hero who saved the day, and moving to Florida for her promotion. Nothing, not even her magnificent Captain, could have kept her from rushing off. And he probably knew that. Releasing a deep sigh filled with regret, she accepted begrudgingly her part in this disastrous mess. It wasn't all his fault. Plus, he didn't ask to overhear her enthusiastic declaration about finding a man her professional equal.

This realization didn't enhance her self-respect. Nor could she hold him responsible for their relationship's demise.

But couldn't he have still asked her to not leave? Could he really have cared so little for her?

True, at one time she'd expected to marry a person in a profession similar to hers. Now, she really wasn't sure what she wanted. Anyway, it didn't matter because her world turned topsy-turvy, relegating a social life low on the priority scale. She had no way or desire to meet new men. She wasn't exactly finished with men, but she'd lost all interest in wasting time on lost causes.

For her, the nights presented the greatest challenge. Not only did jet lag keep her awake, but she also struggled with an aching need coiling deep inside. In jumbled dreams, she relived his touch, the feel of his powerful body on top, under, and besides her. Even one night, her dream became so erotic she woke in the middle of an orgasm as she rubbed her damp pussy on the bed. Other nights, her sensitive breasts throbbed with such intensity she couldn't lie on her stomach. As much as she tried to force him out of her life, he wouldn't go.

Or maybe, she didn't really want him to leave.

He had invaded her molecular system. His presence, charisma, and passionate spirit filled her like oxygen nourishing her body. She'd hoped his unwanted presence would fade over time—ride off into the sunset like an unwanted cowboy. Or in this case, like an unwanted cruise ship captain sailing over the horizon never to return.

ONE WEEK HAD SAILED BY FOR CAPTAIN JOHAN AS HE commanded his ship in the Eastern Caribbean. The trip Kimberlee should have been on.

Now, he cruised through the Southern waters—night after lonely night. Up until the moment he turned off his bedside light, he kept himself busy with making sure passengers received their money's worth of cruise fun, the crew had what they needed to work their exhausting twelve to fifteen hours a day, and the ship remained safe, on time, and on course.

In windows of free time, he'd chat with Ramil. This afternoon as they sat together, he needed to let off steam. "I'm still pissed at myself for hanging up on her." He added, "I prided myself on having courage, but all I see now is my lack of it. I didn't even try to keep her on board. Even knowing she wouldn't have stayed, I still could have shown her how much I cared, how important she was. But no, hurt pride forced me to slam down the receiver in righteous anger, acting as if she was the villain.

"My grandmother taught me, when problems arose, look in the mirror. That's where I'd find my answers. The difficulty being, few people want to take responsibility for their troubles. So much easier to offload the blame. I've spent a life proud of my battle skills, only to discover when it came to my heart, I lived as a coward fleeing from the first sign of rough waters."

When he paused in reflection, Ramil offered him another take. "You're too hard on yourself. First thing, you haven't been in a relationship for ten years. You wouldn't expect to live ashore for a decade, then walk on the bridge taking command with no learning curve. You need to give yourself some slack. Beating up on yourself doesn't help. And it makes you feel worse."

"You're right. The problem comes when my mind replays the phone conversation, which I accidentally overheard. She considered me a lowly sex cruise ship captain. Until then, she never acted like a snob, but obviously she considered me below her. I can't imagine how I could have misjudged her so badly. She never acted like someone who considered herself better than others."

"She treated everyone with respect," Ramil agreed. "Even Belmiro spoke highly of her. And you know he keeps women at arm's length. As I said before, I don't think you misjudged her. Something we don't know about may have happened."

Shaking his head, the Captain replied, "I know what did. On that call she mentioned how she was up for partner. She figured, once she got her fancy title, men would flock to her and she'd find some hotshot investment banker. They can have her. She can find someone else to be her sex toy."

They sat lost in their own thoughts. Interrupting the natural silence, he continued, "I opened my heart to her. I took a chance caring for her. And if I misjudged her so badly, then I'll also do so with other women. I'm better off being celibate and out of relationships."

"Making broad generalizations like that isn't the person I know," Ramil commented.

"Well, maybe in this case it's appropriate. Perhaps, I wasn't meant to find a loving relationship. Obviously, I don't have the profession women look for.

"I had such an incredible relationship with Eira and maybe that kind of love only comes once in a lifetime…if lucky. Some people never get that lucky. Maybe I was being greedy wanting a second chance. I should count my blessings and let this mess go."

As the Captain sat lost in thought, Ramil left the room, closing the door quietly behind him.

Brooding, Johan's rumination turned to focus on another topic—the last communication from corporate about the hostile takeover. He couldn't discuss this with anyone, not even Ramil, who he trusted.

Yes, they were still successfully defending themselves against those corporate pirates. But someone in the law department had heard a rumor how a major M&A partner from New York was arriving in Miami to manage the enemy's acquisition project.

He knew who she'd be.

One part of him wanted to shake sense into Kimberlee or

find a way to stop her altogether. But another side of him understood her decision to take the job. She had a right to further her career. He just wished it wasn't his company she destroyed for her insatiable ambition.

How he hated feeling helpless. Out in the middle of the Caribbean there was nothing he could do. But then, even if he were docked in Miami, he was a sailor, not a lawyer or accountant. All he could do was wait for the whole mess to play itself out.

Too agitated to sit still, he wanted to walk the decks, but that only rubbed salt into his wounded pride and heart. Any place he went, memories hounded him with what had been, but now no more. So many places brought her to life, igniting vivid recollections of their times together, along with a granite-hard, throbbing cock. The feeling of her in his arms, her woman's scent filling his senses, and the sounds of her passionate cries followed him day and night.

Short of jumping overboard, he had nowhere to escape from her. No place to hide from himself.

Hopefully, the days cruising the waters of the Southern Caribbean would allow time and sea to erode his anger and anguish…just as the relentless waves ground down granite cliffs into sand.

Holding on to his fury kept pain at bay. Now, without the protection of outrage, he had no place to hide from the hurtful mess he'd found himself in.

He felt raw.

Like his years of training had taught him, he'd force himself to carry on through the ever-present storms of rejection and grief.

Which was why I kept away from women. They only cause heartache. I've had enough loss and hurt to last a lifetime.

CHAPTER TWENTY-SEVEN

*W*hen Monday finally arrived, Kimberlee returned to work with a newfound confidence. Getting ready in the morning, her eyes sparkled as she hummed Jimmy Buffett's "Margaritaville"—one of those favorite Caribbean songs which seemed to follow her home from the ship. *Even if Johan couldn't be bothered to come after me.*

All morning in the office, she basked in a hero's welcome for the great job solving the fraud issue in Malaysia. The glow of success created a bounce in her step and bubbling laughter. However, she sometimes saw a flash of jealousy in people's eyes, underneath the comradery. Working in a fiercely competitive environment, she'd grown used to the envy, so much so it had become an unremarkable part of the job. But today, the subtle resentments troubled her. This wasn't the way she wanted to spend twelve hours a day.

By early afternoon, her admin announced the scheduled meeting with her senior partners would begin in five minutes. For heaven's sake, she shouldn't have been nervous, but her palms felt damp and her chest constricted. Part of her concern

came from not having decided which of the two jobs to take
—stay with her firm or move to the client. All her lists of
pros and cons couldn't help her decide which one to accept.
Something didn't feel right. Neither opportunity made her
heart sing. But then, she was working for money, not looking
for a job which gave her unlimited turquoise-blue water. And
mind-blowing sex.

She walked into the expensively furnished board room
with two walls of floor-to-ceiling windows. Three of the
senior partners stood waiting for her. Surreptitiously, she
wiped her hands on her skirt just before entering, hoping no
one noticed her damp palms when they shook hands. These
were the same people who thought she didn't have what it
took to make partner. Moist hands would have told them they
were right.

Each man greeted her with a firm handshake and bright
smile—as if she were the most important person in the office.
She studied them carefully, trying to determine what they
were actually thinking and what was really behind their hail-
fellow-well-met welcome. All three were the ultimate in
game playing or they wouldn't have gotten where they were.
Even their eyes gave nothing away. She knew from experience they did nothing spontaneously. Every action, word, and
facial expression arose from well-planned strategies.

Kimberlee needed to discover what their hidden agendas
were.

Inwardly sighing, she settled into a watch-and-wait mode.
Eventually they would let her know what they were thinking.
In fact, she really didn't have long to wait. After their
congratulations and inquiring about the trip, the managing
partner immediately asked, "Well, Kimberlee, have you
accepted the client's offer?"

She wasn't surprised they knew; in fact, she expected

them to. Information like her job proposal never remained a secret for long.

"No, not yet," she said, watching their reactions.

Instantly, she felt them relax and saw their smiles take on a more genuine shine.

Following a few moments of more general conversation about the merger, they broached the topic of partnership. By the time they arrived at that stage in the meeting, she'd relaxed and was almost enjoying the cat-and-mouse game… but for the first time in her career, she didn't feel like the pathetic mouse.

Of course, I'm still that white rat collapsed on the bottom of the cage when it comes to Johan.

Instantly, the managing partner said, "Great! We want to offer you partnership. We have a major client in Miami who needs a project partner experienced in M&A for a deal in trouble. You're that person. Of course, you'll need time to hand off your other clients before you leave. We hope you can do that in a week."

When they made their proposal, it was announced with a large dose of artificial congeniality. Then one of the other men added, "Obviously, we feel you'll do an excellent job," while beaming his most winning smile, which never reached his icy eyes.

She could tell by their body language they expected her to be thrilled with their gift…to someone who'd never be one of the guys. A partner in name only.

Two weeks ago, she'd have been ecstatic. But something had changed in her. Yes, they wanted to keep her as a high-paid work mule, but not as a peer. As much as she'd dreamt of that promotion, and accompanying social life benefits, something felt off.

She knew her value, even if they didn't.

Years of working in this pressure-cooker environment had taught her how to play their game. Flashing them a glowing look of pleasure, she never verbally responded one way or the other—letting them draw whatever conclusions they wanted.

The managing partner said, "The client's folder should be on your desk now. Read through it. The issue is a natural for you. The Miami office is getting everything ready for your arrival. Let them know what you'll need."

One of the other men added, "This is an important client for us. We know you'll save the acquisition. We're counting on you."

After more smiles and meaningless conversations, everyone ended the meeting with jovial handshakes.

She no longer had damp palms. Rather than insecurity and self-doubt eating away at her, she now possessed confidence. Where it came from, she wasn't sure.

From the fancy, plush boardroom, she rushed to the worker bees' dreary, windowless conference room to discuss her present client's merger. Fifteen people sat around a large table. Carefully observing the interaction of her peers, she watched how everyone fought to make their ideas the best. Each person desperate to make sure the partner leading the meeting knew how invaluable they were.

How could she have never noticed the constant show-boating and grandstanding?

Oh God, I hope I wasn't like them.

Was this the way she wanted to live the rest of her life? No way.

A few times during the meeting when her mind numbed-out listening to people chest pounding, her thoughts slipped into analyzing where her recently discovered self-assurance sprang from. How could a week of spectacular sex with

Captain Johan change the way she saw herself? Obviously, it couldn't. It must be having two job offers.

Now's not the time to analyze this. Wait until you get home.

By eight thirty that evening, the mentally and physically deadening meetings finally ended. When she left for home, the morning bounce in her step had shifted to a tired drag. Yes, people still saw her as a hero. Yes, she still had her partnership offer. But no longer was she willing to remain a second-class citizen, begging for acceptance. She had options. Maybe not on a cruise ship, but a great job with a grateful client.

Once in her living room, she'd finally got to read the Miami client's file. *I really need to keep my options open.*

Collapsed on her couch with a glass of white wine, she opened the folder stamped with red CONFIDENTIAL all over the cover. Within the first few lines, her stomach clenched and she wanted to throw up. Grabbing her cell, she texted her friends with a cry for help. Within five minutes, they had a Zoom conference arranged for 10:00 p.m.

Too restless to stay seated, she jumped up and paced around the condo. Each time she passed the bookcase, a miniscule corner of Lori's envelope caught her attention. She had only to reach out and pluck it up. Reading what was inside didn't mean she had to do anything with it. There wasn't a job opening for her anyway. And really, the Captain wouldn't allow her back on his ship. He could have found her phone number in her passenger profile. But he hadn't contacted her or shown any sign that he wanted her return.

Finally, in an act of desperation, with a trembling hand, she grabbed the offending document. She sat for a few minutes gripping the sealed packet—gathering the courage to open it and see what the job specs were for a cruise ship's chief purser. Before accepting the client's offer, she really should look at other opportunities, regardless of how unlikely a fit.

Holding that thought for courage, she opened it cautiously, as if it might explode. By the third reading, she'd realized there were bits and pieces that interested her, with other responsibilities that left her cold, indifferent, or out of her area of expertise. She'd definitely have a steep learning curve because she lacked the experience required for many of the duties.

She'd have no trouble with the accounting and financial aspects of managing the ship's money, including payroll, cash flow, and corporate reporting. But she knew nothing about running the reception desk and passenger information, maintaining the bureaucracy of port-clearance documentation, managing crew and passenger embarkation and debarkation, and assuming the responsibilities of the hotel manager in her/his absence.

Thank heaven it was time for their video call. She didn't want to deal with cruise ship jobs anymore. In fact, she wanted to get as far away from them as possible. But with her new Miami engagement, that wouldn't be possible.

At last, sitting in front of her desktop computer with her headset on, she logged on to her video call. Oh, how much she needed to talk with them and get their advice.

It took a few minutes for the others to join.

Three concerned, loving faces looked back.

Immediately, Bonnie said, "Kimberlee, tell us what's happened." Two other heads nodded.

Without further encouragement, she launched into her meeting with the partners. When she came to the Florida client, she could barely get the words out, finally saying, "It's a mega cruise conglomerate attempting a hostile takeover of a tiny cruise company with just one ship—the MS *Aphrodite*."

"No," Lori shrieked. "You mean our little ship?"

"Yes."

"Well, at least they're so successful someone wants to buy them."

Then Kimberlee explained, "They're going after the parent company, SeaWinds Corporation."

Paulette asked, "Does your partnership depend on taking over the engagement?"

"Yes," a crying Kimberlee wailed.

No one said a word. Their business minds analyzed the implications.

Finally, Lori filled the silence, "In other words, if you take the partnership, you must destroy the Captain's life?"

All Kimberlee could do was stare back at them, defeated. She didn't have the emotional strength to answer. Hearing Lori state the unavoidable, horrible truth left her no way to pretend there was a positive spin on the hideous situation.

She just sat staring at her monitor, tears streaming down her cheeks. Eventually, she whispered, "It wasn't supposed to be like this. I've waited my whole life for my partnership and now…"

"It's poisoned," Bonnie filled in for her. "You know, love, maybe the powers that be don't want you to take it. You've talked about how sometimes life has its own plan for us. Maybe you weren't meant to continue working in a soul-sucking world. In your drive to make partner, you've compromised many of your values. You're an incredibly loving person, who squished her soul to be accepted.

"How many times have we heard you describe the appalling way people were treated—including yourself. Some days, you were devastated by the cruelty and wanton pain you witnessed.

"If you work long enough in a culture like that, it's who you'll ultimately become."

There was nothing Kimberly could say. She already noticed subtle changes in her own thinking and behavior. Truth be told, she'd figured she could live in a dog-eat-dog environment and still remain untouched by it.

Is it possible that Bonnie's right? Oh, please don't let her be. I want that promotion. I've worked so hard for it. I deserve it. The Captain can get another job. I'll never find another partnership.

For some inexplicable reason, Kimberlee began telling them about the Captain's father losing his fishing boat, his livelihood, his life to another greedy takeover. Listening to herself, she realized she couldn't do that to him. She couldn't consciously destroy another human being's life. And not someone she cared so deeply for. Not someone she'd given not only her body, but also her heart.

Paulette's voice quietly filled the space, "You aren't without options. You have the general counsel's job. And as you've said, in some ways it's better than walking the streets hustling for money and billable hours."

Taking a few deep breaths, Kimberlee replied, "I love you all so dearly. I don't know what I'd do without you. I'm sorry. I need to think this through. I need to hide under the covers." With that, she exited their conference.

Remaining seated on her chair, she contemplated the general counsel's position offered by her client. Yes, in some ways it was a dream career move, but imagining herself in it, left her agitated and feeling constricted.

Looking down at her desk, she noticed the chief purser's job description. Grabbing the paper, she began to rip it, when a voice in her head yelled *stop*. No way did she want to keep that page, but she wasn't yet willing to abandon an option—even one not really feasible. After slipping it back into the envelope, she re-hid it behind the books.

Right now, she desperately needed sleep. Tomorrow morning, she had to be in the office early, working on the merger. Experience taught her that the big guys would expect her to gratefully accept their offer, so no one would bother her about what she'd decided.

THE WEEK SLIPPED BY IN A FLURRY OF LEGAL, FINANCIAL, and accounting issues concerning the merging of two public companies. With everyone focused on the all-consuming effort, neither the firm nor the client followed up on their job offers—each assuming she would accept. And that was perfectly fine because she wasn't ready to make a decision.

Although everyone on the client's team was slogging through complex details all weekend, she was able to sneak in a Saturday night relaxing dinner with her friends. They met at a local Spanish restaurant for tapas, paella, and a large pitcher of sangria. Halfway through the meal, Lori inquired, "Well, did you look at the job description I gave you?"

"Yes." Nothing more.

"OK, what did you think," Bonnie asked?

"I can't live on a sex ship."

"I didn't ask you that," Bonnie immediately replied. "What did you think of the chief purser's responsibilities?"

"Why don't you guys get the fuck off my back?"

Paulette reacted instantly. "If this were me, you wouldn't let me be a coward, burying my head in the sand. You'd hound me until I found the courage to look the situation squarely in the face. You'd remind me about the importance of self-honesty."

No one said a word. They sat sipping their sangria, waiting for her reply. She knew how well they understood her, and it was now up to her to come clean. Taking a sip of wine and a forkful of paella, she stalled trying to gather her thoughts. Clearing her throat and struggling to find the right words, she sighed. "Truthfully, I don't know what to think. And frankly, I'm afraid."

Silence.

"I've realized I don't want a begrudgingly offered partnership...even if *his company* wasn't involved. And the legal counsel's job, while a great opportunity, doesn't turn me on as much as I thought it would."

"You mean, not like the Captain does," Lori replied.

"That's not fair. You didn't need to bring him up. Besides, he doesn't want me because he couldn't have been bothered contacting me. Not shit from him." Kimberlee wanted to jump up from the table and flee. Her stomach clenched and her mind froze in panic. She had nowhere to hide, even from herself. *Maybe they're right. I need to face this head on.*

Taking a couple of deep breaths to steady herself and clear her thoughts, she haltingly said, "OK, I did find some of the chief purser's responsibilities doable, but there were many others where I lack the necessary experience. Plus, I can't tell my parents I'm living on a sex ship... I just can't." She looked around the table, her eyes pleading for them to understand her bind.

"Kimberlee, I'm playing devil's advocate now," Paulette said. "We'd still love you if you lived on a sex ship. In fact, your parents would also continue loving you. Yes, some of your acquaintances would shun you, but you don't need them.

Besides, you don't have to tell anyone the type of ship you're on."

Bonnie quietly added, "Don't make this an either/or choice. You can have a wonderful career and a fabulous love; they aren't mutually exclusive. It will, however, require you to think and live out of a socially acceptable box. It will mean taking a gigantic risk, but a calculated one."

With that last comment, Lori slid another envelope to Kimberlee, telling her, "The MS *Aphrodite* has just posted a new job opening for chief purser."

"Is this some kind of joke?" Kimberlee asked. "I mean, things like this don't happen in real life."

"Of course, they do. It just happened," Bonnie said.

And then Lori dropped her bomb, announcing, "I also sent your resume to the listing website."

Frozen in shock, Kimberlee stared with an open mouth. Slowly looking at each friend, they just gazed back. Bonnie, who sat next to her, reached out, taking the envelope and putting it into Kimberlee's purse. Just in time because she grabbed her handbag, jumped up from the table and bolted from the restaurant.

CHAPTER TWENTY-EIGHT

*C*aptain Johan counted the passage of time by post-Kimberlee empty nights. It was day twelve since she'd fled his ship—discarding him. He couldn't compete with her high-powered New York City job. Plus, it still enraged him how she had such low respect for him and his profession. Really, though, he had only himself to blame. He knew better than getting involved with a passenger. It hadn't occurred before and would never happen again.

Hovering in the back of his mind, however, remained the knowledge that he hadn't tried to keep her. But even if he had, she'd have still walked off without a backward glance. She expected to find someone her professional equal when she made partner. That person wouldn't be him.

He'd thought during these past ten years, time had helped him recover from the devastating loss of Eira and their unborn child. But he realized that wasn't the case. Not if this mess with Kimberlee could hurt so horribly.

It was as if his broken heart was only partially healed and she ripped off the scab.

When he'd lost the two most important people in his life,

he'd learned how love caused agony. No love, no pain. Closing himself off to caring, protected him from being torn apart…again. And so, he let her walk away.

He was so tired of hurting. Afraid he'd never heal from losing them. He'd be willing to give up all relationships to avoid feeling like this. Hell, he'd be willing to spend the rest of his life jacking off. A small price to pay to avoid suffering.

He couldn't blame her for his lack of guts when faced with rejection. He had options when she told him she was leaving, and he chose to shut down and lock her out of his life.

Now his ship plied the waters of the southern islands. He'd always enjoyed these less congested ports. Maybe with more time, his scab could regrow, protecting his reopened wound.

The evening of the fifth day, after departing St. Bart's, found him in his cabin listening to Grieg's "Holberg Suite." Sitting at his computer, he opened an e-mail from human resources. They'd sent him applications for his vacant chief purser's job. Quickly glancing through them, he stopped, staring in disbelief at what appeared on the screen.

This has to be some kind of sick joke.

In front of him shone a job application from Kimberlee Tuckmann who lived in New York City. There could only be one of her. She was supposed to have been in Miami, destroying his company. Instead, here she was applying for the chief purser's opening on his ship.

What in the hell is she thinking?

His breathing froze, chilled by shock. Unconsciously exhaling the trapped air, he automatically sucked in much needed oxygen. Closing his eyes and then reopening them, her employment form remained staring back at him. It wasn't a mirage.

Without reading the entire application, he rapidly typed a message to HR telling them he didn't want this person. Just as he moved the mouse to hit send, something stopped his hand.

In his mind, he listed a litany of reasons he should e-mail the not-wanted note—including, he couldn't have her reporting to him. Except in this industry, many shipboard relationships and marriages followed more relaxed guidelines.

So, he deleted the message. This whole thing didn't make sense. What in the fuck was she up to?

More importantly, what did he want? He couldn't possibly want her back on his ship. Or did he?

After a moment's hesitation, he called Ramil. When his friend picked up, Johan said, "Sorry to bother you. Please stop by. Just walk in." Then hung up.

Waiting for him, Johan clicked the tab on the top of the screen that stated "Resumé." Here she was in all her professional glory. He knew she had an impressive background, but never gave it thought. Now reading her CV, he realized just how imposing her credentials were—of course not for this job nor his ship.

But still, pride for what she'd accomplished blazed bright. He respected how she succeeded in the grueling academic and professional world she lived in. He'd just wished loyalty and dependability were part of her strengths.

As he came to the end of her application, Ramil walked in. Immediately, the Captain told him, "You know we have a job opening for chief purser. Here's an application I want you to see."

He moved his chair so Ramil could read what was on the monitor. Looking back at the Captain, his eyes wide open and his mouth formed a silent O.

"I don't understand," he said. "Is Kimberlee applying for the job?"

"That's what it looks like."

"But you haven't talked to her…have you?"

"No."

"But, I don't…" Not finishing his sentence, Ramil dropped into the nearest chair.

"I don't understand either." Pausing, Johan continued, "But, I'm ashamed to admit, even if it's only a slim chance to have her back on my ship, I'd not abandon this opportunity.

"I'd begun accepting a loveless life—free of storms and pain. And then her damn application appeared. I must be a glutton for punishment."

Ramil immediately replied, "No, you've refound your courage. All the years I've known you, you've never shrunk from hard choices. You've never allowed fear to dictate your actions."

"Well, I did when I hung up on her."

"But you went back to apologize."

"Stupid me. If I hadn't, I'd never know how poorly she thinks of me."

"Then why want her back?"

"Again, stupid me. In these past ten years, she's the first woman who made me feel alive. Even with all the pain, I don't want to walk away from what could be. I'm not sure if I'd call it courage or lunacy."

"Right now it doesn't matter. Let's return to her application. Is she qualified?"

"She's overqualified for the fiscal responsibilities and sorely lacks experience for most everything else. This just doesn't make sense to me. Unless she'd been fired. But that isn't logical either. She has the brains and talent employers pay big bucks for. Something must have happened. I can't imagine what."

Ramil got up, fetching two beers from the fridge. Opening them, he handed one to the Captain. "We need something stronger, but we must keep our wits about us."

"Thanks," he said, reaching for the bottle. "Any words of wisdom?"

"No."

"I just wish I'd taken time to learn more about her. She probably knew my job better than I did hers. I can't blame her for not being committed, when I didn't care enough to discover the details of her life."

"You're being too hard on yourself. This was only supposed to be a week-long shipboard affair. Personal specifics weren't necessary. Stop beating yourself up. All you can do now is wait and see what happens. Of course, you could tell HR you don't want her."

"I thought of that, but decided not to. As you've said, time will give us the answers. I just need to let this travesty play itself out. Thanks for listening."

Their conversation moved on to ship business. When they finished their beers, Ramil left allowing the Captain to ponder the bizarre twist life had taken.

Sailors existed with uncertainty, a natural by-product of life on their liquid blue planet. Rarely were things predictable, except for the lack of predictability. By some quirk of genetics, he became energized when challenged by the unforeseeable. He never felt bored on his ship. That resumé of hers piqued his curiosity.

To be honest, a small spark of foolish, unrealistic hope flared to life that maybe, just maybe, a future might exist for them. He just wasn't sure how.

Sending that job application required amazing guts. She definitely got his attention…and respect.

Like previous nights, this evening's worst time occurred when he lay in an empty bed tormented by the memories of what he'd lost. Unable to sleep, he once again found himself standing on the balcony outside his cabin letting the sea, the breeze, and the night sky fill the aching hollowness Kimberlee's leaving had created.

He also opened himself up to past losses. Slowly, he let his mind touch on Eira and their lost child. With Eira, he could find a balancing of her life and death. But not with their unborn baby. Rarely would he allow himself to think about this tragedy. The devastating pain tore him apart. Grief for the loss of an unknown being gave him no way to mourn. He had no pictures, no memories, no familiar touch from the spirit realm. He remained trapped in a void of hell, with no closure. A never-ending bereavement, without a way to heal.

While he would talk with Ramil about his wife, their dead child remained off-limits, which he kept locked away—even from himself. But for some reason this evening, the whisper from the sea unlocked a door to this pain. He allowed himself to feel the deep love for that treasured being he'd never met. The night brought an opening, releasing his anguish into the universe.

He allowed the wind to sweep through him, carrying his torment into the healing heavens. It wasn't exactly a farewell, but rather a natural letting go.

Drained of all feeling, he leaned against the railing staring into the inky distance until exhaustion forced him back to bed, allowing sleep to claim him, along with the ever-present Kimberlee-passion-filled dreams. As with many of the past mornings, he awoke with the dampness of his wet dream sticking to him.

Over the days commanding his ship, he focused on his maritime and passenger responsibilities with a lightness, which hadn't existed before. Plus, he no longer obsessed on what Kimberlee was up to, knowing he'd eventually learn her plans. He'd developed patience living on the oceans and hunting behind enemy lines.

He could be patient where she was concerned.

FIVE DAYS AFTER THE FATEFUL MEAL WITH HER FRIENDS, Kimberlee sat on the couch eating comfort food out of a Chinese takeout container. With slippered feet propped up on the coffee table, chopsticks in hand, she nurtured herself with spicy, crispy orange chicken and broccoli over fried rice.

After their disastrous meal, she'd received text messages from her friends, but never responded. In fact, she was too angry to read even one communication. Right now, she needed space. Hurt and betrayal made reaching out impossible for the moment.

Now, she had neither her dearest companions nor her magical Captain lover. Her empty life remained filled with only work. Nothing sparkled or glittered anymore. The world around her held an ash gray film, void of the joy needed to nourish her spirit. *When all this merger chaos is over, I should go home to see my family.*

Thankfully, the simple paintings she'd collected on her overseas travels still filled her with memories of where she'd been and the adventure of buying them. Looking at them hanging on the walls around her small condo, she slipped into reliving the places where she was when she'd purchased each one. Unfortunately, she'd never gotten the chance to explore Kuala Lumpur on her own, so no souvenir from that trip.

In the middle of her musings and an emotional first-aid meal, the cell phone rang. It came from an 800 area code. Initially, she wasn't going to answer, but then she had nothing better to do and wanted to stop feeling sorry for herself.

Picking up the phone, she answered, "Hello?"

"Hello. May I please speak to Kimberlee Tuckmann?"

"This is Kimberlee. How may I help you?'

"Hi, Kimberlee. My name is Adele Ringsdorf. I'm head of HR with SeaWinds Corporation, owner of the MS *Aphrodite* cruise ship. You applied for the chief purser's job. And I'm intrigued about how someone with your amazing background, but with no cruise experience would be interested in this position. You do realize this is a sex-themed cruise ship?"

Choking on a piece of broccoli, she coughed a few seconds, trying to catch her breath and clear her throat, as well as frantically thinking of something to say. Her first reaction was to tell Adele she wasn't interested and immediately hang up. Instead she said, "I'm sorry for coughing in your ear. I had just eaten some spicy Chinese food."

"Oh, I'm so sorry for interrupting your dinner. Would you like me to call you back?"

"No, that's OK." *Let's get this over with so you can go away.*

Then she quickly added, "I really didn't expect anyone to call me." *That's the truth.* "I know I'm overqualified for the financial side of the job. And lack the required experience for all the other responsibilities." *That's putting it mildly.*

Continuing, she said, "I do realize it's a sex-themed ship. I was on it a few weeks ago with friends." *Really, ex-friends.* "To be honest, I...I...I filled out the application on a whim. I'm in the middle of a career change and decided to keep my options open." *Oh God, how do I get out of this? I'll kill them.*

"To be honest, Kimberlee, I was hoping you'd say that. We're looking for a person who understands business, finance, and managing a large number of people. I see from your resume you've managed groups of up to two hundred forty five people. Plus, you've worked closely with customers. As you know from your experience, the technical side of most service jobs is not rocket science, but the human side is by far the more challenging. Nasty passengers and overworked, exhausted crew require a person with a special set of skills. And based on your resume, I think you have the necessary qualifications."

Of course, she did.

Her dad forever lectured her to keep her options open. She could always say no. Shit, she had nothing to lose. She might as well see where this led.

"I do enjoy the people side of my work, probably as much or more than the technical."

And so, the conversation flowed for twenty minutes as they chatted about job responsibilities, people management, life on a cruise ship—specifically working on a sex-themed one.

Just before hanging up, Adele asked, "Kimberlee, are you aware that your firm is working for a Miami cruise company engaged in a hostile takeover of SeaWinds?"

Oh fuck, what do I say? "Yes. I just learned about it after I sent in the application." *Well, that's not a total lie.* She'd learned about it after her friends had sent it in.

"As long as I don't discuss this engagement with you, I'm not violating confidentiality."

"And if you should sign on, would you be able to help us?"

"No. Not officially as your legal counsel." *But I might be able to make some suggestions on the side, which will cut them off at the knees.*

By the time they'd hung up, Kimberlee's dinner had become cold and she'd agreed to a job interview in eighteen days. *Fuck! What did I just do? Oh God, no. My parents will disown me.*

Hell, he might not let me back on his ship. Then what do I do?

CHAPTER TWENTY-NINE

The next day at work, Kimberlee found her mind drifting off, lost in a void. Sometimes, she'd aimlessly reach for items she had no need for. She struggled moving, as if walking through an ocean current trying to drag her out to sea. Underneath it all, she had a constant feeling of nausea.

A late Friday night found her exhausted and discouraged. In the past, when still working this late, she'd have been energized by the challenges of merging two major corporations, but not now. All she wanted was to be home cocooning.

Looking around the conference room, she relaxed slightly when no one seemed to judge her for unenthusiastic and sluggish behavior. She must have been putting on a great show of normality regardless of how disoriented and dispirited she felt inside. Nor did anyone comment on her bloodshot eyes, which came from having spent a sleepless night crying over a life that was falling apart. But then, her eyes didn't look different from many of the other people sitting around the table: everybody struggled with exhaustion and overwork.

As the night marched on with people slogging through

massive data, her mind flitted off to a ship navigating the gorgeous Caribbean. She figured Captain Johan would be in the southern waters, with the western itinerary next week— the one they were on together. They never did get their eastern cruise. *His next Eastern trip would be in a week—the week before my I've-got-to-be-out-of-my-mind job interview.*

Looking down at her blue-lined notepad, she saw during her doodling she'd written "Make cruise reservation." *Where in the hell did that come from?* But she knew. It came from a deep-down hunger to see her Captain again. And it arose from a need to flee the mess she'd found herself in—two firm job offers, neither of which really spoke to her. And now one potential offer on a sex ship. Of course, she could settle for one of the two traditional positions, but life was too short working at a job which she only tolerated. She wanted something she loved that nourished her.

Finally, at home by twelve fifty in the morning, she toppled exhausted into bed. At seven thirty Saturday morning, her cell alarm went off. Time to be heading back to the office, even when her eyes had difficulty staying open, her body barely moved and her mind felt like a tub of cotton candy.

Thank heaven, they got Sunday off. She needed to do laundry and catch up on sleep. She also desperately sought some quiet time to think about what she wanted to do with her life.

BY EARLY SUNDAY AFTERNOON, SHE GAVE UP THE STRUGGLE of going it alone. She needed to talk to someone who knew her and would, hopefully, give her objective advice. With trepidation, she picked up the phone, speed-dialing her parents.

On the second ring, her dad answered.

Kimberlee had just said hello then burst out sobbing—a sure sign she needed help. She heard her father tell her mother to pick up the other phone. In a few seconds, she had both parents on the phone but remained too upset to talk coherently. Through her well of despair, her father's voice brought some sanity.

"Are you OK?" he asked. "Have you been injured? Are you pregnant?"

When she managed to let them know she was physically OK and she wasn't expecting their first grandchild, her father then said, "OK, Kimberlee-girl, start at the beginning and tell us what's happened."

Having her defenses down and needing comforting, she took a deep breath and launched into her frustrations about work and how her friends suggested she join them for a cruise...on a sex-themed ship. No one dropped the phone receiver in a faint when they heard the word sex. Nor did either parent begin yelling. They just waited on the other end of the line, giving her the space to continue at her own pace.

With returning emotional equilibrium, she described how she'd met the Captain the first night. Of course, she left out the intimate details of that evening. However, her voice, hesitations, and stuttering, she gave herself away.

Through simple words of encouragement, her parents kept her talking about the trip and her relationship with the ship's commander. Without discussing their physical relationship, she told her story. As her breathing became relaxed and her muscles released their tension, private snippets slipped into her monologue. And then she mentioned how this was a BDSM ship, causing her to sputter and choke into silence.

Figuring she needed to explain that term, she launched into an embarrassingly high-level description.

Immediately, her father interrupted, "You don't have to explain. We know what BDSM is."

"You can't. You're my parents," she exclaimed.

"How do you think you and your brother got here? You didn't fall off a turnip truck. And we did read *Fifty Shades*."

Kimberlee sat frozen with the phone plastered against her ear, mouth hanging open. Before she could utter a word, her mother said, "Your father and I have a wonderful relationship…and that's also sexual. Being parents doesn't mean we've stopped living and learning. Now that we're empty nesters, we've had the opportunities to focus on each other."

After a moment's pause, her mother continued, "We raised you and your brother to live ethical lives, such as being honest, compassionate, and showing respect to all people—and that also included sexuality. We've made sure never to express judgments about what's right or wrong between two consenting adults, except for maintaining your physical and emotional safety. Each of you must create your own life as to what works for you in intimate relationships. We've trusted you would make personal choices based on the values we raised you with. That being said, I just want to know if he treated you with care and respect?"

"Yes, Mama, he did. But I didn't treat him with respect." And with that, she launched into how she had told him over the phone about leaving and then the voice mail he'd overheard. Once again, her parents listened quietly, letting her evolve the story as needed. By the time she described her future interview with SeaWinds Corporation, she sagged against the couch letting her head fall back with relief. She'd told them everything. Now she needed to know what they felt.

Within a few moments, her father said, "First thing, we want you to be happy and if that's on a cruise ship, then we'll support you. But most of all, we want you to take your time choosing what your next job will be. And we want you to do what is right for you, not what others think you should do. And certainly, not what you think we would want."

Quickly, her mother added, "Didn't you mention you still had a week of vacation coming?"

Kimberlee nodded, then realized they couldn't see her, so she answered, "Yes. I've still got a week."

"Well then, take that week for the Eastern Caribbean. You can use the time to evaluate what living on the ship would be like. You can talk with the crew about their job and experiences, plus you'll then have a better idea of questions to ask during your interview."

"But what if he doesn't want me?" she asked in a fear-filled whisper.

"Then you'll know, and you won't need to go on that interview," her father replied with love. "Kimberlee-girl, sometimes uncertainty can be worse than facing the truth. As a spunky three-year-old, you'd run out greeting the world with open arms. You felt safe, because you knew we were there, ready to pick you up. If he rejects you, skip the interview and come home for some TLC. Then we can discuss what your options are. Remember, you aren't alone."

"Kimberlee," her mother said, "first thing, you must know we aren't surprised about your intrigue with life on a cruise ship. You've always been a slightly unusual child. Even as a toddler, you were different from other children, with their picky eating habits. You wanted to try new foods. By the time you were in kindergarten, you'd choose a burrito over a ham sandwich, or a Chinese restaurant instead of Denny's.

"Then when it came to dolls, your friends wanted the

American Girl Dolls with all the clothes and furniture. But not you. Somewhere, you saw a Madame Alexander International doll and that's all you wanted. The more colorful and unusual the costumes, the happier you were. Even in elementary school, you focused outside of Iowa."

"I still love those dolls. You'll need to keep them longer for me."

"They're here whenever you want them."

"You know, Kimberlee-girl," her father said, "we knew early on you weren't going to be content spending your life in the cornfields of Iowa. In sixth grade, you discovered *National Geographic* and became obsessed with pictures from foreign countries. Your room still has pictures from those magazines on the walls."

"We're traditional and simple people, who God blessed with a dynamic, adventurous daughter. We're happy where we've lived for all of our lives. But we also understood that wasn't you. When you moved to New York, we knew it wasn't just because it's a big city. You thrived on ethnic restaurants, foreign films, and traveling around the world. None of these things we could give you. You had to do it on your own."

"You're right, Dad, New York is perfect for me. I love my life here…and don't want to leave, but who knows."

Her father said, "We wanted to send you to an Ivy League college back East, but couldn't afford it. And we made too much money for you to get a scholarship. That has always been a—"

"No, Dad," Kimberlee cut in. "I got an excellent education at Iowa. I can take on any of those idiots from the fancy schools.

"To be honest, one of the reasons I wanted to work in a big firm was to make the money to help when you retired and if you needed assistance with my brother's education. You've sacrificed so much for me and I wanted to show my appreciation."

For a moment, she heard nothing, then a quiet sniffle. Finally, her mother began talking with a shaky voice, "Even before we got married, we began two financial accounts. One for our retirement and one for our children's education. We've been blessed that both investments have done well. Yes, we were careful with our money because we wanted both of you to have an opportunity-filled childhood and excellent education. But now you don't need to worry about us, we have a solid retirement nest egg.

"It's you who is important. We knew your career met your intellectual demands but didn't answer your emotional needs. And there was no way we could help because we didn't know what options were available. All we could do was trust your innate wisdom and the values we raised you with. We've prayed you'd find your path.

"And if that's on a cruise ship—sex or otherwise—we support you."

Now it was her time to keep from sobbing on the phone. Before she could answer, her father said, "You must live your life for yourself, not for us. We've been blessed with an easy road from the beginning. That's not the way your life's unfolding.

"Some nights, we hurt for you. We know you haven't shared a lot with us, but even with the little, we could feel your frustration and discouragement. We may have been more aware of your turmoil than you were. It's always easier to see things when you're on the outside looking in."

"We'll always love you," her mother said. "And we're here for you, whatever decision you make. We just want you to be happy. You've always had a great instinct for choosing what's right. Trust yourself."

Even with more to say, all the important things had been discussed. She'd promised to keep them informed about her trip, interview, and of course, the Captain. With kisses and telephone hugs, they said goodbye.

Trust yourself. If only it could be that easy, she mused while ending the call.

Now she needed a good, healing cry.

CHAPTER THIRTY

*K*imberlee's last night in New York City, found her having an emotional farewell dinner with her friends. Sitting at their neighborhood's Lebanese restaurant down the street from the Pilates and yoga studio, they had much catching up given all that happened since their last meal together. And, they needed to say their goodbyes, as she planned to fly to Miami tomorrow night.

On Sunday, after talking with her parents, she immediately sent off an apology text to her New York sisters. She explained how both her mother and father supported her, not only about taking the chief purser's interview but also working on the MS *Aphrodite* if that was what she wanted... and if they offered the job. She ended her message typing an all caps THANK YOU followed by a line of hearts and kisses.

With tapping send, all the built-up tension drained from her body, leaving her exhausted from the turmoil and grateful for people who supported her. Even after her healing cry, a few tears of happiness slid down her cheeks as she sat curled up on the couch, emotionally and mentally bruised from the weeks of uncertainty and chaos.

Even with the euphoria of relief, her mind began naturally listing the things she needed to accomplish before her coming week of vacation in the Caribbean.

Thank you for your support, Mother. I needed that little push.

And what she should put in place if she decided to stay on board. Well, if the Captain wanted her to remain on his ship.

Yes, she had gigantic unknowns surrounding her future, but they couldn't overwhelm the sense of liberation creating a lightness in her spirit. She didn't know what her next job would be, but whatever it was, she had the skills and tools to succeed.

She also had no idea if the Captain would welcome her back, but here too she'd find the strength to move on if he didn't want her. Of course, she'd skip her job interview.

Sitting on the sofa contemplating her topsy-turvy life, Kimberlee felt hopelessness transform into a tiny spark of anticipation. Her future remained full of question marks, but her innate self-confidence filled her with growing hope. *After all, Hope's my middle name.* Plus, her Iowa and New York families would support her with whatever direction she took.

She wasn't alone in this fluid, shifting world of hers.

After sending her "I'm sorry" text, she immediately booked a cabin on *his* ship for the Saturday departure to the Eastern Caribbean. Then she bought a flight to Miami for Friday night. Her friends had drummed into her head, you always go to the embarkation city the night before in case something delayed her plane or an accident backed up the freeway. She wasn't going to miss this departure.

Now it was Thursday night. She and her friends shared both a joyful reunion, tempered with the underlying knowledge she might be leaving them permanently. Knowing each other so well, they didn't discuss their meal—automatically ordering their usual build-your-own combination platter of hummus, stuffed grape leaves, spanakopita, baba ghannouj, tabbouleh salad, and feta cheese with olives.

Between tears and laughter, they chatted about what had transpired in their lives over the past two weeks. Kimberlee leaned forward, listening to what had occurred in their diverse worlds. She'd sorely missed both her time with them and the quick messages they'd exchanged describing their activities in between their weekly gatherings. A sense of contentment spread a healing warmth through her body. If she was going to leave, at least they'd healed their relationship, allowing her to depart on a positive note.

The women demanded all the details about her telephone interview with SeaWinds, which she gave them. Then they listened intently to her conversation with her mother and father. They showed no surprise at how supportive and under-standing her parents were. She could see in their eyes a shade of sadness that they wouldn't have received the same open-minded and caring response from their families. Sending a silent, loving thank you to them for their gift of unconditional acceptance, her heart expanded with gratitude for the people who raised her.

Putting her fork down, Bonnie announced, "Kimberlee, I've been thinking about something you've said." All heads turned to look at her. "You've mentioned how once you made partner, your social life would improve and you'd find your true love, who's also your professional equal."

Kimberlee looked at her, giving a slight nod.

Bonnie continued, "I think that's an unrealistic expecta-tion. Do you really think men will find you more attractive with 'Partner' after your name?"

She thought a moment before answering. "Well…some

will be intimidated by that. So…no, it might not improve my social life. But couldn't it make a difference for some?"

Paulette answered. "You know, for me, the higher up the ladder I went, the less comfortable men were with me. I suspect you'd find the same issue. Strong, successful women threaten most men. Unless you find a self-assured male, successful in his career, that is."

"I suppose you're thinking of the Captain," she asked?
"Yes."

Lori jumped into the discussion. "I think men in professions similar to yours will be the most threatened and see you as competition. A person, like the Captain, who has a totally different occupation and well-developed inner strength will appreciate your extraordinary abilities."

Listening to them, Kimberlee knew they were right. She wished it wasn't so, but that was reality. And she did pride herself on analyzing situations with honesty and logic. Having nothing else to add, she shifted the discussion to the chief purser's job.

"I know I'm overqualified," Kimberlee stated. "Looking online, I've learned all cruise ships want someone with an accounting background who is well organized, manages budgets, payrolls, profits from shops and the casino, understands exchange rates, credit accounts, and immigration issues. I lack most of those skills, even though I can quickly learn them. However, they certainly aren't going to pay for a CPA with a law degree and an MBA."

"Of course, they aren't," Paulette said. "That's why you're perfect for the job. You'll be giving them so much more for their pittance of a salary. But then again, you won't pay New York rent, transportation, and food prices. Plus, you won't have to buy expensive dress-for-success suits; you'll be wearing one of those sexy, white officer uniforms. And we want pictures…lots of them."

Bonnie jumped in saying, "They should be grateful you'd even think of taking the job. They don't get people like you applying for an accounting job on a floating resort with such poor pay."

"I keep telling myself that, but deep down I worry they'll find someone with better qualifications. But should they accept me, the Captain may not take me back."

"Of course they'll want you, love," Bonnie said, giving Kimberlee a hug. "People with your incredible professional experience don't usually take a quarter-million-dollar pay cut to sail the Caribbean. As for the Captain, if he's stupid enough to sail away without you, then he wasn't right for you and you're better without him."

The other two women agreed that a stupid captain wasn't worth a broken heart.

"Always remember," Lori added, "you have a family with us and we're here for you."

Staring down at her empty plate, Kimberlee's throat tightened with unshed tears for the possible separation from her dearest friends. How she was going to miss them … The deep bond forged over the years, candid conversations, shared meals, and special exercise time together. Still, they'd promised to visit her on the ship. *Providing he wants me to stay.*

When their check arrived, she reached for her credit card, but Bonnie stopped her with a shake of the head saying, "This dinner's on us."

Now, she could no longer hold back the flood of tears. She'd almost willingly take one of the other jobs just to stay with them. And maybe she still might have to.

After dinner, they all stood outside the restaurant. Kimberlee didn't care about the tears ruining her carefully applied makeup, and the way everyone cried. They remained oblivious of the passing strangers staring at them. Each gave Kimberly a fierce goodbye hug before she walked away. Every couple of yards, she'd turn around, wave, and blow them a kiss.

CHAPTER THIRTY-ONE

*T*he Monday before the farewell dinner with her friends and the day after the call to her parents, she showed up at work as if nothing had changed. Putting on a great show of normalcy, she juggled working on the merger, organizing her other clients' material for someone else to manage while she was on her so-called vacation, and speculated about her upcoming interview.

The hardest part of her day came when she told the partner she was taking her remaining two weeks of vacation. She explained how she needed time to sort out her future. She answered each of his arguments with calmness and resolve. Even when he raised his voice, she held her ground. By the end of their conversation, she knew should the Captain not want her back, neither did they. *So be it. I can go with the client if no one else wants me.*

Kimberlee had always known what she wanted when growing up, throughout college, and with her present job. Until now. Today, she existed without the comfort of a personal or professional vision. The future remained a void for her—an unfathomable chasm of uncertainty.

Life had blindsided her by leading her to believe one thing and now it forced the exact opposite on her. From the world she had grown up in, she'd experienced and expected consistency, predictability, and controllability. No longer. Instead, she now struggled with a present besieged by inconsistency, a lack of predictability, and loss of control. Nothing prepared her for the emotional chaos and indecision overwhelming her like a tsunami engulfing an island.

Even with all the internal mayhem on the inside, she appeared the masterful professional on the outside. Only her Iowa and New York City families would have recognized the buried inner turmoil. At least once a day, she'd make a run to the little deli in the building to grab a bag of chips or almond caramel corn. Munching on something relieved tension when internal pressure became overwhelming. Right now, she couldn't worry about a few extra pounds.

By Friday evening, she had work matters well organized. Now, she could focus on getting to the airport. Her suitcase sat next to the apartment's front door waiting for her to grab it on the way downstairs. She had just opened the door when she stopped to look around her lovely, loving home. *Will I be leaving all of this?*

Scanning the living room, she noticed simple little treasures, like her grandmother's handmade bright pink, purple, and blue throw pillows or the Buddha from Bangkok sitting meditatively on the top of the bookcase. Then her gaze landed on a tulip-designed, handmade Turkish tile she'd bought in Istanbul, now resting on the end table. Without a second thought, she walked over, grabbed it, and nestled it in her suitcase between clothes. What she'd do with it, she had no idea, but something told her to take it—so she would.

After locking the condo, she found Mateo waiting for her

at the curb. Once in his car, they had a short ride to the airport, because rush hour traffic had reduced considerably.

Finally on the plane, she nestled in the EXIT window seat but found sleep impossible. She tried meditation, which relaxed her a little, but an agitated mind kept returning to fears of rejection. Repeatedly, she released her thoughts about the Captain not wanting her, only to find they kept returning to haunt her like a toothache that wouldn't go away. Then she'd replay Bonnie's comments concerning her unrealistic expectations about partnership. How had she held such a stupid view? *I wonder where it came from?*

Giving up forcing herself to relax, she decided to focus on her coming interview, just in case the Captain didn't toss her off his ship. The ever-meticulous Lori had given her a slim binder of cruise ship information about immigration laws, financial reporting, and a pile of other relevant material.

Thank you, thank you, Lori.

Once again, her achievement-driven training came to the rescue. Reading stopped the unproductive mind chatter, allowing her to lose herself in the intellectual fascination of cruise ship documents. Before realizing it, the flight attendant announced they were landing in Miami.

EARLY SATURDAY MORNING, CAPTAIN JOHAN DOCKED THE MS *Aphrodite* in Port Miami. After completing the immigration and other documentation requirements, he seized the slim window of free time to scan the electronic passenger manifest for the coming cruise. Immediately clicking on the T's, he found what he'd feared to hope for—Tuckmann was listed. She'd booked passage on his ship.

She was sailing with him!

Letting out a deep breath, he leaned back in his chair, closing his eyes in relief. Now he just had to keep from fucking it up.

He had hope, which was more than he had this morning. But hope for what? He knew she had her interview in nine days. But that didn't mean she would take the job when they offered it. And they would. He'd seen to that.

Once he'd gotten over his shock of seeing her resumé fill his computer screen, he'd talked with HR. From her initial phone conversation with Kimberlee, Adele was impressed with her even if she didn't possess the perfect skillset. At the end of their discussion, he'd told Adele that if she considered Kimberlee right for the job, make the offer.

Never did he expect to see her before the interview. He had to give it to her, she was one hell of a gutsy woman. A warrior in her own right. She'd walk on his ship not knowing what her reception would be. Of course, she could decide the last minute not to board. Time would tell.

Throughout the day he checked his monitor watching as security scanned passengers aboard. At one, her name appeared as being on his ship. While he was filled with gratitude, his guts knotted with uncertainty.

What could he say to her? He owed her an apology. Plus, sometime early in their meeting, he should tell her he'd overheard her conversation, unintentionally, that was. Did he need an apology? Maybe. Maybe not. But he did want to know if she still considered his profession beneath her.

Three weeks had sailed by since their disastrous phone call. So much had changed for him, and obviously for her. They needed to talk about how their relationship ended. And where they wanted it to go.

Would we have anything in common? Would the sex still be good?

So many questions he needed answered before he could map a future.

He'd been thinking about Ramil's wise counsel. Yes, Eira would have told him to move on with his life. She'd have wanted him to find love. Not to live an empty, desolate existence. But would Ms. Tuckmann be that person?

With her, he found himself sailing blindly into unexplored waters—and hated it. He seemed to be doing that a lot with this woman…both the unmapped journey and the lack of visibility of what lay ahead. This time, he was going to be the intrepid explorer sailing into the unknown. Better for him to live with disappointment and battered self-worth than remain trapped in the harbor afraid of losing sight of land.

Then there was the issue of sex. How long could he keep his hands off her? Let alone hold off burying his face in her pussy? Would she want him as much as he craved her?

Of course, he worried about her willingness to live on a sex cruise ship, with minimal privacy and cramped quarters.

So many unanswered issues, but now, he needed to let them go until boarding was completed and they were sailing in open waters.

As the day progressed, he could finally shift his focus from the demands of arrival to those for departure. At last, with a few minutes of freedom, he sat in his cabin reviewing options for when they could meet. He found only one possibility open to him—later that night. He must remain on the bridge until the pilot disembarked and the ship sailed out to sea. That meant the earliest they could talk was after seven in the evening. But his vessel would still be in the throes of the celebratory sail-away party. Not a good time for conversation.

How ironic the best possibility for their first face-to-face talk would be the same time as their initial encounter. While the delay frustrated him, it also allowed him the opportunity to plan what he wanted to say. Except he still had no idea what that would be.

CHAPTER THIRTY-TWO

*S*hip check-in went smoothly, with Kimberlee boarding by one o'clock Saturday afternoon. Curb to ship took only forty minutes because everyone passed their health screening tests.

Cabins weren't ready for another hour, so she couldn't go to her room. Instead of facing the loud, food-grabbing people in the buffet or by the pool grill, she sat in a corner of the Dolphin Reception until the cruise director announced staterooms were available.

The hour wait dragged by. Deep down, she'd hoped the Captain would have found her. Of course, he'd have to roam the ship looking for her, which wasn't likely. But then, if he really, really wanted her, he would have discovered where she had parked herself. Was this a sign that he no longer cared? And if he didn't, should she jump ship now?

Oh, she detested the indecisive person she'd become. She didn't know what job to take and now she didn't know if she should remain on the ship. This wasn't who she was, but it seemed this was the woman she'd become…for the moment.

Constantly glancing at her smartwatch only made time

grind to a crawl. Trying to stop focusing on the clock, she forced herself to read her e-mails and tried to enjoy her first piña colada of a supposed vacation. Nothing seemed to help. She caught herself wringing her hands, then fiddling with her earrings—sure signs of how anxious she felt.

Eventually, the cruise director's welcoming voice came over the speakers, announcing cabins were available for occupancy. Once in her stateroom, she unpacked, but even then, a part of her mind kept waiting for a knock on the door or the phone to ring. Instead, everything remained quiet…except for the excited voices of new passengers filling the hallway.

As she watched the mandatory muster drill video in the room, her heart ached and unshed tears filled her eyes as she listened to the Captain's familiar, velvety voice over the TV. He talked to passengers about the importance of safety, the need to keep using the hand sanitizers stationed through the ship, washing hands with soap for twenty seconds regularly, and how they were supposed to have smooth cruising weather.

He's so close, yet so far away. How am I ever going to bridge this humongous gap between us? I can't do it alone.

Sitting in her lonely cabin, time crept on, filling her with ever-mounting fear and desperation. Without hearing from him, her limited confidence began wavering, leaving her jittery with a growing sense of panic. Pacing the stateroom didn't help reduce the internal tension. Standing on her balcony watching the gorgeous sea slip by only reminded her of that first night when she stood by the railing above the Lido deck. Nor did standing outside help eliminate the disconcerting flushes of heat rushing through her as foreboding mounted. Even if her stomach would let her, munchies wouldn't reduce the dread hovering in the background.

Kimberlee skipped the boisterous, on-deck sail-away party, remaining locked in her cabin during dinner. She wasn't hungry, plus she didn't feel like dealing with people celebrating their first cruise night. She knew from her own experience there existed something thrilling about cruise day that left people filled with a fizzy excitement—like the champagne everyone drank throughout the night.

It began looking to her that a toast to a new future wouldn't be happening on this cruise.

By nine o'clock, the cabin walls began collapsing in on her, making her breathe in short, shallow gasps. She needed to get out of the room—now. She wanted fresh air to clear the panic from her mind so she could begin considering her future. With a cloud-covered night, she decided to hide in the soothing darkness by the side of the railing on deck nine...the opposite side from where she met the Captain that first time.

Hopefully, she wouldn't be tormented by a drunk passenger.

Feeling the breeze from the moving vessel, the silky warmth of the humidity and the lights from the ship reflecting on the wake as the hull moved through the sea offered a healing balm to her frazzled nerves.

In time, the cooling air reduced the heat radiating from her face. The whooshing sound of the ship gliding through the waves provided a backdrop to the mantra of "I've built a life once; I can do it again." If she said it enough times, maybe she'd begin believing it.

Leaning on the deck railing, Kimberlee let the ship's movement rock her, releasing the humiliation for being on this ship, her anger at herself for caring about a man who didn't care about her, disgust for not deciding on which job to take and guilt for letting down her parents, even though they said how proud they were of her.

What the moving ship couldn't do was wash away the craving for his touch and his smell. With her head bent, she let the tears silently flow for…

His scent? I must be imagining it. I must be going mad. Even the air is beginning to smell like him.

And then a pair of hauntingly familiar arms reached around on either side of her, with strong masculine hands resting on the railing.

Oh God, he's come.

Without a second thought, she leaned back into his powerful body, savoring the sensuous feel of his warm breath on her neck, as his lips kissed her sensitive skin under her jaw. Then he whispered in her ear, "I was stupid letting you leave my ship without trying to talk with you. Yes, you needed to grab your chance for partner. And I needed to give you the space to reach for the stars, even if it tore me apart inside. I have one more month on this ship before my three-month leave and then I would have come to New York, trying to find a way to make our different lives work. Sea captains have built successful marriages with their wives who have remained on land."

Spinning around, she squeaked, "Marriage. Did you say marriage?"

Then like the perpetual watering pot she'd become, Kimberlee buried her tear-streaked face on his shoulder, finally allowing the weeks of loss, fear, and emptiness to pour out in muffled sobs.

"How could you want me after the way I treated you?" she stammered between bursts of weeping. "I saw your back walking down the hall. I'd realized you heard my awful comments."

Lifting her head, she looked him directly in the eyes. "I'm

so very sorry. I'm not usually a cruel person. And I don't think your career is any less important than mine.

"I was offered the partnership, but they tied it to taking the job in Miami, in charge of the hostile takeover of your company. Yes, there was a moment of wanting that partnership at any cost, but selling my soul was too high a price. Even if you didn't want me back, I still couldn't do that to you.

"Somehow, I got the bizarre idea my failed social life would automatically improve with a promotion. I'd meet the man of my dreams walking out of the boardroom and into my life. Instead, the man who makes my heart sing, commands a ship. I'm not usually so stupid. I do have another job offer waiting, but that's only my default option if you wouldn't let me back on your ship.

"I hope you can forgive me?"

Crushing her tightly against his chest, he whispered, "Neither of us handled this mess well. I'm sorry for how I acted. Hanging up on you was a dumb thing to do. I was afraid of my feelings for you."

Tilting her head to look up at him, she blurted out, "I didn't think men said sorry."

"This man does." With smiling eyes, he added, "I rarely fuck up this badly, but when I do, I'm not afraid to apologize for my stupidity. My ego isn't that fragile. But then hanging up on you wasn't my proudest moment.

"These last ten years, I've kept myself closed off and my heart protected. I'd decided to live an emotionally empty life rather than feel again the pain, which tore me apart when Eira and our unborn child died. Yes, that made me a coward.

"After meeting you, loving you, I couldn't go back to my hollow existence. But…but by the time I found my misplaced courage, you were gone. And I'd made a mess of everything.

It wasn't until Adele in HR told me you were interested in the job that I gained an inkling of hope I may not have lost you."

Oh, Kimberly did have more tears left. Held in his protective embrace, she allowed the hurt to flow through her into the healing, welcoming night.

Reaching into his pants pocket, he pulled out a tissue, lovingly wiping her tear-stained face—ignoring his own damp cheeks. Bending his head, he kissed the tip of her nose, enfolding her back into his encircling warmth.

With her face nestled against him, she said in a muffled voice, "I have a confession to make. I was a coward telling you over the phone. That was so wrong of me. As much as I wanted my partnership, I also knew if you asked me to stay, I might have and I didn't want to face such a gut-wrenching choice. Plus, if I saw you, I might not have had the strength to walk off this ship. It was easier for me to run away. No, not my proudest moment either. I'm sorry."

He held her tightly, kissing her hair, then her face while murmuring his love. Kimberlee never expected to feel his magnificent arms around her again. In this moment, perfect contentment healed and nourished her.

Clasping her protectively, he began talking. "I'm ever the practical person, so we need to discuss living arrangements. My captain's cabin is fine for one person, but will be cramped for two. Giving this a lot of thought, I realized chief pursers have a decent sized room. You won't find it convenient to keep your things in one space while living in another. But that will give you a place to store everything. Also, every three months you'll have to pack up when our contract ends. Which, I know from experience, is a pain in the ass."

"Like you, I've also been thinking about how to make life work sharing a small cabin. Yes, moving between two cabins will be a hassle, but a minor one. Something I can live with. It's a small price to pay for us being together.

"On our three months off, can we visit my parents and friends?"

"I would like that. I've never been to Iowa or New York. And I'd like to meet your family."

"Thank you."

Taking a deep breath, she continued. "But I do have a favor to ask. I have sixteen special international dolls, eight inches tall. Until my mother reminded me, I'd forgotten about them, but they represent who I was and still am. Can we find a home for them in your cabin? If not, I'll keep them in the chief purser's room. For some reason, I want them to become a part of my life, as I travel with you. It's a way of bringing the two parts of my world together."

Looking down at her with joy, his eyes told her how pleased he felt she wanted to make her home with him. "I know exactly where we can put them. I have a small credenza off to the side, which I pile my to-do papers and books. They would fit perfectly there and I can find another place for that overflow pile.

"I want you to make my cabin your home."

"When I talk to my parents, I'll ask them to send them to me, but I don't know how to get mail on a moving ship."

"I'll give you the address."

Looking at him with a serious expression, she said, "Well then, we have one more important topic to discuss. You still have a promise you haven't kept."

"What's that?" He watched at her with a worried frown marring his once joy-filled face.

Snuggling up closer to him, making two bodies one, she said, "You haven't worn the nipple clamps."

The Captain threw back his head with a shout of laughter.

Then he buried his face in her neck, still chuckling. "Oh, Kimberlee my love, please never lose your magnificent joy for living…and sex. You're such a gift. I don't know how I was so blessed to have you in my life."

For a few moments, they stood cocooned in their own intimate world, letting the roll of the ship rock away their hurts, while the tropical breeze filled them with the promise of a future lived together sailing through the magical Caribbean Sea.

Feeling his voice vibrate in his chest, as much as hearing what he said, she mentally and emotionally absorbed his whispered words, "Regardless of how our lives turn out, I'm willing to give us a chance for happiness. Living on this ship with me won't be easy or the exciting New York life you're used to. It will be cramped, with limited privacy and our time controlled by the demands of passengers, crew, ship, and sea. But I promise you my loyalty and unconditional love."

Lifting her head, she lovingly licked away each glistening tear gliding down his sun-bronzed cheeks, relishing the salty taste that was uniquely his. And knowing that she had a life-time of savoring all of him—every salty taste.

Kimberlee and her Captain invite you to join them on their next MS *Aphrodite* Series cruise. In *Room Service for Emma*, they'll help Emma and Belmiro find the love missing in their lives. Please sail with them in the lovely Southern Caribbean.

A LOVING THANK YOU

I published my first book, a work of nonfiction, with a traditional publishing house. For Kimberlee and her Captain's story, I wanted to give them (and me) the freedom to tell their story the way we wanted. I desired, however, that our book maintain the high standards found in the publishing industry. For this, I worked with amazing professionals who possess outstanding graphic design and editorial skills. I also turned to romance reviewer podcasts and educational writing sites for a greater understanding of this dynamic genre.

You see, even a lifetime of reading romances couldn't prepare me for the astonishing writing journey I found myself on. *Her Captain and Commander* is truly the product of a large, highly skilled, and diverse community whose members embrace the joys and adventures found in romance novels.

Jaycee, of Sweet 'N Spicy Designs, created the most delicious cover, as well as the external and internal designs of the book. On many a discouraging moment, her cover kept me believing in my story—and kept me writing. She also developed my website, pearlberri.com.

Carmen and Christine of Bootcamp Edits patiently

educated me about the mysteries and rules of novel writing. They had a tough job given how unprepared I was for this voyage.

Kat, of K.A.T. Editing & Writing, maintained her serenity and humor during the developmental editing process. She naturally integrated the role of editor and coach, guiding me through the murky world of tropes and character development.

Megan, of Megan Records Editorial, copyedited an 80,000-word manuscript, identifying both writing and story problems. With her incredible skills, she pointed out issues and obstacles I could have never recognized on my own.

Johanie, of Tessera Editorial, provided eagle-eyed proof-reading. She tied up loose ends that I didn't even know existed.

Smart Podcast/Trashy Books and The Wicked Wall-flowers Club provided wonderful insights into the world of romance novels. Listening to their fabulous interviewers and reviewers became an integral part of my writing life.

The powerful DIY MFA website offers some of the best online author training and workshops. Gabriela also has a book that offers in-depth material for writers looking for comprehensive educational support.

And finally, to the readers, for taking this love-filled journey with me.

Thank you, everyone!

ABOUT THE AUTHOR

Pearl lives in the American Southwest, surrounded by the gorgeous high desert. A world, on the surface, quite different from the stunning Caribbean she writes about. But, in reality, both settings offer amazing vistas of life on earth.

From an early age, Pearl fell in love with romance novels, keeping her home stuffed with books so she'd never be without. She lived with an underlying worry that she'd finish a book without having another immediately available to begin. When Amazon opened, she bought so many books that by Christmas the fledgling company sent her special tumblers as a thank you for her voluminous purchases. Pearl started her reading journey with historical romances, then ventured into all the romance genres, thrilled by the skill and creativity of extraordinary authors. Something about these fabulous stories spoke to her need for joyful endings, where people find their happily ever after.

Cruising became another passion in Pearl's life. For her, nothing provided more healing and delight than spending time afloat our liquid blue planet. She loves sea days as much as port times. Happiness is being on a ship watching the endless ocean flowing by and feeling the cabin rock her to sleep. Sailing became an additional opportunity for her to explore new worlds, enjoy new cultures, and savor new foods. Like Kimberlee, Pearl gets to know new people and new places through their eyes and their foods. While most folks hate wasting time in airports, she sees these cavernous spaces as a unique way to watch human life unfold in all its marvelous distinctiveness.

Pearl has a master's in speech pathology and doctoral work in educational psychology. With this background, she's taught learning-challenged children, worked in management consulting, and started her own company assisting managers lead corporate change. Throughout the years, writing romances remained a dream, which has now become a reality.

For the past forty years, Pearl has practiced mindfulness meditation. And for the past twenty years, she's taught meditation to both beginner and experienced meditators. Her life and meditation have become intimately entwined.

Please let Pearl know how you liked *Her Captain and Commander*. And be assured, book two, *Room Service for Emma*, is on its way in the growing M.S. Aphrodite Series.

Find her online at www.pearlberri.com